I0693234

True Horizon

by

Laurie Winter

Warriors of the Heart Series

True Horizon

Cover Art by *Tina Lynn Stout*

The Wild Rose Press, Inc.
PO Box 708
Adams Basin, NY 14410-0708
Visit us at www.thewildrosepress.com

Publishing History
First Sweetheart Rose Edition, 2017
Print ISBN 978-1-5092-1791-5
Digital ISBN 978-1-5092-1792-2

Warriors of the Heart Series
Published in the United States of America

"Do you know how to ride? Horses, that is."

"That's a negative, ma'am."

"Well, I guess it's time you learn." She rubbed her hands together. "The ranch is fun to explore on horseback."

"As grateful as I am that you sprung me from jail, I'm not interested in death by horse. Is there anything else I can do? Wash your car? Paint your nails? I'm building your wedding gazebo, don't forget." His internal temperature rose along with his panic. The thought of riding one of those huge beasts made his nausea revisit with full force.

"You were in the Army, right?" she asked.

Afraid of where this line of questioning was headed, he nodded.

"You jumped out of planes? Fast roped out of helicopters? Was shot at?"

"Affirmative."

"But you're afraid of riding a sweet, tame horse?" A smirk formed on her face.

"I didn't say I was afraid." Too late, he realized his assertion of fearlessness was tantamount to surrender. How would he get out of this situation with his male pride still intact? *News flash, soldier—you're not.* Grace was on the offensive and showed no signs of surrender.

"Great! I'll go change and meet you in the stables." She smiled and took off toward the house, her spry legs moving quickly across the lawn.

He forced his gaze away and slowly walked to the stables. "I survived multiple tours in a war zone only to be ensnared by a bewitching siren and lured to my death on horseback," he muttered to himself.

Kudos for Laurie Winter

"I enjoyed this book so much, and I knew it would be a hit with Laurie Winter's talents and charms."

~RomanticReviews.blog

~*~

"Laurie Winter captures her audience's heart and attention right from the very moment they flip the first page."

~UnderneathTheCoversBlog.com

~*~

"This was a great story with great characters. I really enjoyed this book and look forward to more from this author."

~Mara W. (Netgalley)

~*~

"I just loved Julie and Reagan's story. This is a great read, and you won't want to put it down. Cannot wait to read more from Laurie."

~Sarah C. (Netgalley)

~*~

2015 Pages from the Heart Contest
2nd Place—Hero of Our Heart Award
Honorable Mention

~*~

Dedications

To Paul, Kailey, Jenna, Brandon, and Nicolle,
whose support and encouragement
provide me with endless inspiration
~*~
A special dedication to Luis Carlos Montalván,
former Captain in the US Army,
and his PTSD support dog, Tuesday
~*~

Several years ago, while doing research for *True Horizon*, I had the honor of attending a presentation by former Army Captain Montalván and Tuesday. His presentation, along with his book—*Until Tuesday*—brought to life the daily struggles and heartaches that many of our service members experience after coming home from war. Former Captain Montalván worked tirelessly to bring the issue of PTSD to our attention and understanding. Despite the fact he was afflicted with chronic pain, he and Tuesday traveled around the country giving lectures to the public.

In December of 2016, Luis Carlos Montalván lost his battle with PTSD. While many, including myself, grieve his loss, his life's work continues.

Chapter One

Besides the crashing waves or the occasional honk of a horn, the night had turned blissfully silent. Just in time, too, because after being stuck in that hot and musty motel room for the past three hours, Heath Carter needed a release.

Fourth of July used to be his favorite holiday. Back in high school, he'd been that annoying kid who'd shot off tons of fireworks and freaked out the neighbors' dogs. But lately, any loud explosion had the ability to bring him to his knees. So now that the fireworks had fizzled out for the night, he could find an escape in the bottom of a cold beer.

Heath stepped out of his motel room and took in a deep breath. The fresh air still held strands of the humid heat that earlier in the day had blanketed Galveston. But the breeze was now coming off the Gulf of Mexico, carrying the water's crisp chill. He didn't bother to lock the door behind him. Nothing inside worth stealing, except for the small wad of cash, which he'd safely stashed. The unlit motel parking lot sat quiet as he cut across toward the street.

Walking down the sidewalk, he approached a large, rambling building bustling with activity. The wooden sign attached over the door read, *Breakers*. Its faded blue and yellow lettering proclaimed it to be the last local hangout. Inside, the smell of beer mixed with salty

1

sea air reminded him of the places where he and John, his late brother-in-arms, hung out in North Carolina.

Breakers appeared to be a typical beachside bar, full of local flavor. Colorful flags hung from the ceiling and the walls looked like a scrapbook, cluttered with pictures of Galveston and its fun-loving citizens. He sat on a stool at the far end of the worn bar, away from the crowd, and asked the bartender for a beer. A large group of loud twenty-somethings gathered at the other end. From the sound, they were likely capping off a day of partying. Heath watched them with mild interest then turned his attention back to the cold bottle wrapped in his hand.

In three long swigs, he drained the bottle and motioned the bartender for another. Out of the corner of his eye, he noticed a young man with pink board shorts and a white sleeveless shirt approach. The dude's skin was flushed red, a mixture of drunkenness and sunburn. With a lopsided grin and bloodshot eyes, he didn't appear threatening, just annoying.

"What's your deal, man?" He pointed a wavering finger at Heath's chest. His slurred words tinted with a southern twang. "You look like you just washed up on shore after a shipwreck." The man laughed at his own joke with a few of his friends joining in.

"I did." Heath ran his finger over a deep gash in the wood of the bar top. A sliver pricked and dug into his skin. "The ship of the dead."

The man grunted an unintelligible reply and stumbled over to rejoin his group. "The freak over there needs to chill," he said. "Like havin' arms full of tattoos makes you a tough guy or something. Bro, I've seen homeless people with better grooming. What a loser."

Heath tightened his hand around the neck of the beer bottle. Over the past year, he'd grown used to that type of reaction over his looks, but he'd be lying if he said hearing it didn't bother him. People were narrow-minded and ignorant. They only saw what they wanted to—never stepping out of their own sheltered world. Forcing calm, he glanced at the TV screen that hung crookedly above the bar. With the distraction, his brief flash of anger dissipated.

On a neighboring stool, a heavy-set man seated himself and barked out a demand for a whiskey on ice. From the irritated look on his face, he seemed as inclined to make conversation as Heath.

After several minutes of peace, the rowdy group regained Heath's attention.

This time, their jokes were directed at two men wearing Army ball caps, who sat in a booth across the room. The loudmouth in the pink board shorts pointed toward the men. "The only people who join the Army are losers who can't make it in the real world."

A red haze permeated Heath's vision. *Leave—walk out the door—go.* He stood and dropped a ten-dollar bill on the damp, sticky bar. Instead of following his head, he walked over to the man still on his tirade and tapped him on the shoulder. "Excuse me." Heath's feigned politeness vanished.

The man turned with a cocky smirk on his pretty-boy face.

Heath's fist connected with his jaw. Soft flesh yielded under hard knuckles. The next thing Heath knew, he was lying on the ground, both hands squeezing the man's throat. The face beneath him blurred into a wavy mirage. John's face. The sound of

3

shouting snapped Heath back to reality. John wasn't here. John was dead.

A stranger's bug-eyed face came into focus.

Heath jumped off the man, still sprawled out on the floor. His breath heaved through his constricted throat. Stumbling, he tried to stand. His vision scanned the growing crowd.

The bartender, a middle-aged man who was as wide as he was tall, started around the counter.

Without hesitation, Heath turned and strode toward the door, walking into the darkness of the night.

****

Four hours of restless sleep felt like a luxury. Heath packed his olive duffle bag, which took all of sixty seconds. He grabbed a few pairs of jeans, several old shirts, a letter from his grandparents' lawyer, and the cash he'd hidden. He counted out the remains of his last paycheck. Why couldn't his cash multiply like the fat cockroaches that hid in every corner? Should be enough money to last him until he found another job. Too bad he didn't know when or where that would be.

He studied the grease stuck under his fingernails, a memento from his last job working on an oil rig in the Gulf of Mexico. At the time, working in the middle of the ocean sounded like a perfect escape. But after three months, when his contract was over, he jumped on a chopper to shore and never looked back. That was his life since separating from the Army, darting through short-term jobs with nothing holding his interest for very long.

With bag in hand, he exited the motel room he'd called home for the past few nights. Leaving his room key on the unoccupied front office counter, he strode to his motorcycle and put all his earthly belongings securely inside the saddlebags. He straddled the bike and started it. The deep-throated engine roared to life. The bike vibrated under him. His black Harley Davidson meant freedom. The world wanted to confine him, hold him down, and label him as damaged. As long as he kept moving, no one would ever have that power.

After riding for hours, he reached Austin. Unsure if he should head north toward Dallas or continue his trek west, he mentally gave control to the bike. She always knew the right direction and now pulled toward the exit leading north. He followed her lead, eager to explore the Texas prairie landscape he'd read so much about.

The sun glared intensely overhead like an unblinking eye. Even his dark sunglasses couldn't block the strong glare reflecting off the pavement. The next exit was for a town called Liberty Ridge. His growing hunger ordered him to stop for chow.

He parked his motorcycle in the lot by a small café that sat on the town's Main Street. Red-and-white striped awnings covered the tall windows of The Daybreak Café. He walked inside, and then took a seat on a stool at the counter. The smell of coffee and grilled meat sent his stomach growling. A waitress, who looked old enough to be his grandmother, came over and handed him a menu.

She gave him a welcoming smile. "Anything to drink, honey?"

"Coffee, please." Heath was surprised by her friendly manner despite his disheveled appearance. She must need a new prescription for those thick glasses perched on her nose. Either that or she had a thing for scraggly men.

"You got it." She winked before heading through the double doors of the kitchen.

He didn't bother to pick up the menu since he always ate the same large meal. Many days, he might only get to eat once, so he'd learned to make his food choice count. While waiting for the waitress to return, he glanced around the mostly empty café.

A couple of old timers sat at the other end of the counter, talking about rainfall and cattle prices.

Three women occupied the corner booth. Plates, cups, paperwork, pictures, and fabric swatches littered their table. His gaze rested on one of the young women. Something about her held his attention. Her dark hair rested over her shoulder in a long braid—one he'd love to use his fingers to untangle. Glowing in the sunlight streaming through the window, her copper skin and her high cheekbones hinted at Native American ancestry. She was beautiful.

The waitress returned with a tall glass of tea. As she set it on the counter before him, the ice cubes clinked inside. "Do you know Grace?" She pointed to the dark-haired girl.

"No." His response sounded overly harsh. Heath dropped his gaze to the counter. Over the past year, he'd forgotten how to interact normally with people. He needed to get out of here.

Mabel, that was what her name badge said, only smiled and tapped her pen on the order pad. "How 'bout I get you something to eat? You look six courses short of a seven-course meal."

A hint of a smile formed on his lips, and a short chuckle escaped. A long time had passed since anyone had made him laugh.

****

Grace Murray had been too deep in conversation about bridesmaids' dress fittings and ornate floral arrangements to pay much attention to the strange man at the counter. But she glanced up when Mabel, with a deep-throated chuckle, placed three heaping plates of food before him. Only one look and she couldn't tear away her attention. She was sure she'd never seen him in town before, because she would definitely have remembered him. His brown hair hung long, tied behind at the base of his neck. His beard was equally scruffy, and the clothes he wore were old and faded. Each arm bore a patchwork of colorful tattoos. Sweet mercy—despite his crazy appearance, she actually found him kind of attractive. Simply because of the timeless appeal of a bad boy.

He looked over to catch her gaze before returning his to his food.

The light color of his eyes surprised her, compared to his dark brows and lashes. And the lost expression in those eyes—he reminded her of one of her dad's calves who'd gotten cut off from the herd. She could sympathize, since she had experienced the same disconnected feeling the first few years after leaving home.

"I think we've checked everything off your list." Jenny Murray started organizing the papers that littered the table. "So enough wedding talk. How's business going, Grace?"

Grace took a sip of her drink and focused her attention on her future bridesmaids. "Good, I can't complain. Right now, I have more work than I can handle."

Jenny handed over the fabric swatches.

Grace ran the smooth satin through her fingers before putting them into her bag. "Yesterday, I got a call from a Major Peters from the Army. He offered me a chance to bid on a cyber security contract for a new weapons system they're developing."

"That sounds like a great opportunity," said Molly, who swung her glossy brunette ponytail over her shoulder. "You gonna bid?

"Government contracts are like milk and honey to a business," Jenny said.

"I already told Major Peters to take my name off his list. I'm not interested in helping secure a system that's only purpose is to kill." She didn't see herself as one of those anti-war hippies, but she didn't want to profit from the military.

Molly stole the last French fry off Grace's plate and popped it in her mouth. "Whatever you think is best. Do you have time to come over to the police station and take a look at our server security? Our computer tech just up and quit last week."

"Sure," Grace said. "I'll stop by tomorrow afternoon."

"I'm so happy to have you home." Molly squeezed Grace's hand.

Yes, even if only for two months until the wedding. She'd lived in Dallas for so long, away from her family and close friends, that she'd forgotten how much she enjoyed her small hometown. Once again having the opportunity to enjoy a quiet lunch with her best friend and her sister-in-law. And to be surrounded by familiar places and people.

Jenny turned her head and pointed to the drifter. "Do you see that guy sitting over there? What do you think his story is?"

Grace returned her gaze to the man, whose focus stayed fixed on his lunch. His face was only shown in profile, but enough to capture her imagination. The beat of her heart quickened with a nervous thrill.

"I think he took a wrong turn while traveling through Montana," Jenny said with a glint in her eyes. "He looks like one of those wild guys living in the backcountry, hanging out with grizzly bears."

"Maybe he hit his head while hiking and lost his memory," Molly whispered. "He's been wandering around the country ever since. I should run a missing persons query and see if his picture pops up."

The two women looked at Grace.

They tilted their heads in unison, appearing like a pair of curious puppy dogs. "I think he looks that way because he's hiding from the world," Grace whispered. Her heart squeezed with sympathy. What could have happened to this man, who seemed very handsome under the long hair and beard, that could have made him so antisocial? "I don't mean that he's hiding as a criminal, Molly." She didn't want her police officer friend to assume the guy was on the wrong side of the law. "I would say he wants to keep people at a distance. I think he has a troubled soul."

Wide eyed, Molly and Jenny looked at each other and then back at her.

"If I didn't know you were already engaged, I'd think you were captivated with our mysterious visitor." Jenny gave a wink.

"Grace always did have a soft spot for anyone in

need." Molly tapped a finger on the plastic table. "When we were young, her dad's barn was always full of injured animals she doctored. Something tells me that guy would be a lot harder to fix than a bird with a broken wing."

"I'm not captivated, just curious." Grace figured Molly knew her far too well to fall for that line. Tempted as she was to approach him and learn his story, she had to stay focused on why she was here in the first place—her wedding. "Don't worry, I'll leave the rehabilitation of people to Officer Hernandez here."

"Ha," Molly said with a snort. "I don't fix 'em. I just lock 'em up."

The man at the counter stood to leave.

Grace watched as he placed a few bills next to his empty plate and headed for the door.

As he opened it, the attached bell gave a ring, and he shot a sudden glance in her direction.

With their brief eye contact, her world shifted. Seconds later, he stepped outside, and the door closed behind him. The spell was broken. Grace opened her purse and pulled out her phone, noticing several missed calls, two from her mother. "I got to go. Thanks, both of you. I'd go crazy if I had to deal with my mom *and* the wedding stuff all by myself." She stood and lifted her leather tote. "Jenny, let me know when you've scheduled the twins' flower girl dress fitting. I'd like to be there."

Jenny pulled her into a hug. "You bet. I'm so happy for you, Grace. You will make such a beautiful bride. I hope Tyler knows how lucky he is."

"Thanks for treating us to lunch. Love ya." Grace gave her brother's wife a kiss on the cheek. She hugged

Molly and looked around to make sure she'd packed all the wedding paraphernalia. Throwing her tote over her shoulder, she grabbed her purse, waved goodbye, and headed out the door.

Stepping outside, Grace sucked in a breath, the intense heat breaking her skin into an instant sweat. She walked along the sidewalk, staying in the shadow of the brick buildings that composed downtown Liberty Ridge. As she past the last building, the shade ended, and she stood under the glaring sun. Blinking to adjust her vision, she headed toward her car, but changed her mind and instead walked toward the Hickory River Bridge. The old, covered wooden bridge was the town landmark. It connected the town's two sides, otherwise cut in half by the Hickory River.

Grace stepped onto the low bridge, stopping when she reached the center. Glancing below into the swirling water, she saw a wavy and disjointed reflection. She remembered all the times she had come here as a teenager and seen a younger version of that reflection. Over the years, this river had absorbed many of her tears.

A sudden low rumble stole her attention. She twisted to see a black motorcycle turning onto the road. The scruffy stranger from the restaurant was several blocks away, heading straight toward her. Her pulse quickened as he got closer to the bridge. She wanted to run in the other direction. Instead, her stubborn feet refused to move, as if nailed in place. Her body clearly wasn't following her brain's orders. Her fluttering stomach now called all the shots.

Chapter Two

When Heath stepped out onto the sidewalk, he'd breathed a sigh of relief. Inside the cafe, the walls had begun to close in, and the women's conversation had only made him more eager to leave. He'd heard it all. At first, their speculation about him had been amusing. But, then the woman with the dark braid, Grace was her name, had hit straight on the truth. He'd felt as exposed as a bug pinned to a board.

Straddling his Harley, he sat for a moment and took in his surroundings. Liberty Ridge was exactly what he'd grown to expect of a small, rural Texas town—one long main street with time-aged buildings running along either side. American flags hung off light poles and a wide banner stretched across the street, advertising the annual Founders' Day Celebration in two weeks.

After levering up the kickstand, he started the bike and drove it to the edge of the parking lot, until its front tire connected with the street. His gaze followed the rows of storefronts until they gave way to an old, covered bridge. Where to go now? The question hung in the hot air. He could cross the bridge and take the back country roads—his destination to be discovered along the way. Or, he could return to the interstate and continue to Dallas.

Weighing his options, he sat there, until he noticed

her step out of the shadows and onto the bridge. As she walked, her long braid swayed with her hips, moving in a unified dance only he appreciated.

She suddenly stopped and peered into the river.

He took her presence on the bridge as a sign, leading him to roads and places unknown. Heath revved the engine and drove his motorcycle slowly down the road until the rumble of wooden planks hit his ears.

An old VW Beetle approached from the opposite direction. The beater's front fender hung on by a few rusted bolts and a large dent decorated the hood.

He looked at Grace, who stood as still as a statue, watching him advance.

In a flash, she pivoted, putting her body in the trajectory of the rickety car.

The startled driver swerved, but he was too late and struck her in the leg.

Seconds passed in slow motion. Every sense in his body heightened in swift reaction to the impending emergency. He watched her body be pushed toward the waist-high rail, flip over, and fall headfirst into the river.

The car came to a screeching halt, and its body shook with the sudden stop.

Heath hit the throttle and crossed the bridge, coming to the grassy embankment that sloped into the river. With the steady concentration that came with years of military training, he killed the engine before jumping off his bike and letting it fall. The river running faster than he'd expected. He could see no sign of anyone in the water.

Sliding down the riverbank, Heath came to rest on the gravel lining the water's edge. He quickly slipped off his boots and socks while sending a quick prayer for the well-being of his bike. When he stepped into the water, cool mud squished in between his toes. His sole focus shifted to locating Grace. Judging from the current flow, he believed she would have been towed under the bridge and farther downstream.

"Call 911," Heath yelled to the young driver, who had finally exited his car.

The kid stood on the bridge and looked over the rail, his mouth gaping. "I already did." His voice wavered. "Do you see her?"

"No. I'll swim with the current and search for her." He now stood waist deep in the water. The chill shocked him. But without hesitation, he dove in and started swimming.

As he passed under the bridge, he saw a blue object bobbing about thirty feet ahead. Adrenaline surged, and he moved swiftly through the water. He was finally within arm's reach when her body sank out of view. Diving, he opened his eyes but couldn't see his hand in front of his face. In a last-ditch effort, he flung his arms around until—*thump*. He finally connected with something hard. Heath clamped onto Grace's arm, pulled her first toward him, and then back above the water's surface. He gasped and his lungs filled with air, burning with each inhale.

Grace wasn't breathing, so he raced to shore, and then pulled her onto the rough pebbles that lined the bank. Panic swelled at the sight of her limp body, threatening his self-control. In an effort to calm himself, he pushed aside his emotions. His medical training kicked in, and muscle memory took control. He performed CPR until she turned her head and coughed out a stream of water. Some of the adrenaline left his body, and he began to shake in gratitude that she was alive.

Once she'd regained her breath, she stared upward with unfocused eyes. Her coughing started again, and she moaned.

The strong pulse in her carotid artery reassured him she was no longer in danger. He set his hand on her head and stroked her hair. "You had a little tumble in the river," he murmured. "You will be okay."

Her hand, speckled with dirt, came up to cover her mouth. Then, she reached to take hold of his arm, grasping his hand. "Don't leave me."

Her voice sounded quiet but firm. As she pulled their joined hands to rest on her chest, Grace's grasp was unyielding. Her eyes fluttered like the delicate wings of a butterfly. A fierce protectiveness filled him. This beautiful woman would stay under his guard for as long as he was needed.

"Please don't leave me," she said once more before she closed her eyes and stilled.

Her skin warmed in his hand. She breathed softly, looking angelically peaceful. Sirens sounded in the distance, shaking him out of his daze. Soon, two EMS personnel came running toward him.

"She's breathing," Heath said as they approached. Water droplets fell from his beard and hair. "She might have hit her head during the fall."

"We'll take it from here." A young, stocky paramedic knelt beside Grace to take her pulse and looked at Heath. "Please step back."

Heath tried to remove his hand, but her hold stayed tight. "I can't. I'm not leaving her side until she's safe at the hospital."

****

A distant beeping broke through to her groggy mind. When Grace moved her head, a sharp pain shot up the back of her neck and settled behind her eyes. As long as she stayed still, she was, for the most part, comfortable and warm. Waves of memory washed over her, rising before dissipating.

She remembered stepping onto the Hickory River Bridge, and then stopped to look at the river. A sound, like rattling metal, increased, and she'd turned to see an old car. She felt no pain when it hit her, pushing her toward the railing.

Then nothing but darkness and icy cold—a sensation that chilled her to her core. Strong arms wrapped around her and pulled her close. When she opened her eyes, the bright sun temporarily blinded her. A deep voice whispered in her ear, saying everything would be okay. His rough hand stroked her hair and brushed it off her face. When she'd reached for him and found his hand, she was unwilling to let him go. Her body felt as weightless as a helium balloon, floating in the air with only a single tether. If he released her, she would simply drift away.

As Grace slowly came into the present, she opened her eyes. The bright fluorescent lights burned. She squinted and tried to make sense of the dark figures standing around her. "Where am I?" she croaked.

"Hey, Butterfly. You're at the hospital."

Her dad's soft voice was gentle and soothing. "Daddy?" She refocused her eyes to see her mom and dad standing close to her bed. Her mother's smooth-as-ivory hand took hold of Grace's.

"I'm so glad you're all right." Joslyn Murray dabbed her eyes with a tissue and sat on the bed, next to her daughter. "Travis Grabel just feels terrible about the accident. He must not have been paying attention to where he was going. That boy shouldn't be allowed to drive."

Joslyn accented her words with a honeyed Southern drawl. One Grace had been trying unsuccessfully to emulate for years. "The accident was my fault," Grace said. "My mind was wandering, and I turned right into his car." Her throat felt as dry as straw. Sitting, she felt a flare of pain behind her eyes. She took a sip of water from the plastic cup by her bed. "Yuck. I still have that nasty river taste in my mouth."

"You swallowed quite a bit of water." Her dad took the cup.

"Daddy, I hope you didn't call Tyler. He was supposed to be in meetings all day, finalizing a big acquisition deal. I don't want to bother him with my stupidity." As desperately as Grace wanted her fiancé by her side, she knew he was a busy man with important obligations.

Her mother huffed. "Bother him? Don't be silly. I contacted him right after Molly called about your accident. Tyler was in a meeting, but he said he could leave in a few hours. He should be here by the end of the day. A man should never be too busy to take care of the woman he loves."

Her dad's large hand enclosed her own. A tear glimmered in the eye of the normally stoic man, which made her heart overflow with gratitude and love.

"We're so lucky that you're here with us. The young man who fished you out of the river is in the lobby, waiting to see you. He wouldn't leave until he knew you were gonna be okay. Can I send him in?"

Picturing her savior, she felt her stomach tighten into a knot of nerves, but she nodded. "I'd like to thank him personally."

"I'll be right back." Bruce leaned over to kiss her on the forehead before walking out.

"Where's my bag?" Panicking, she scanned the room, and then glanced at her mother. "And my purse and shoes? Please don't tell me they're lost in the river."

"I'm sorry, but you didn't have them when you were pulled out. I'm afraid they're lost." Joslyn patted Grace's shoulder. "What a shame."

"Ugh," Grace moaned. "I had my huge wedding organizer in that bag. And my shoes cost a small fortune. I'm sure my dress is probably ruined too."

"All those things can be replaced, but you can't." Joslyn's eyes widened. "Did you backup your wedding lists on the computer?"

"Luckily…yes."

The door to her room opened, and her dad entered, followed by the stranger who'd saved her life.

"Joslyn, let's give them some privacy." Bruce held open the door.

"We'll go to the cafeteria and grab a coffee." Her mother walked toward the door but before she left, she stopped and turned to face the stranger. "Thank you so much for saving our daughter."

Grace could see both her parents were holding back tears as they exited the hospital room.

He remained by the door, dressed in scrubs.

She watched him stand there, arms folded, the

muscles in his arms twitching, causing his tattoos to ripple. "I'm glad they found you something dry to wear." She spoke first to break the silence.

The man took a step forward. "Some kind nurse took pity on me." He continued walking toward her.

His stride was long, and his posture formal and straight. "I never got your name." She motioned to the empty chair next to her bed. He sat and placed a bag, which most likely held his wet clothes, onto the floor.

"Heath Carter, ma'am."

"Grace Murray." With soreness burning in her shoulder, she reached over to shake his hand. "It's nice to officially meet you. Thank you for jumping in after me. You saved my life." Her soft voice conveyed her gratitude. His hand trembled slightly at her touch. When she looked into his eyes, she saw emotions swimming just below the surface. Fear? Compassion? Vulnerability? No denying the connection she felt with this man, even if he was a stranger.

"Glad I was there to help. How do you feel?"

"Besides the bump on my head and a sore throat, I'm all right. Most likely, I'll survive."

"That's good." He rested his forearms on the tops of his thighs and leaned forward.

Heath was so close that she felt a vibrant energy pass between them. "You know, my little spill off the bridge won't surprise anyone who knows me," she said with a laugh. "My mother named me Grace, thinking I would become a beauty queen like she was. Little did she know, my name would end up as a contradiction of my entire life. I'm the least graceful person you'll ever meet."

With a smile brightening his face, Heath looked

years younger. She guessed he was maybe in his early thirties. Heath sat at her bedside, in borrowed doctor's scrubs. His brown hair and beard were still damp, and the tattoos on his arms only added to his odd appearance. He looked like a jungle doctor just returned from some wild expedition. The many contradictions Heath presented intrigued her, which increased her desire to learn more.

"Personally." He straightened in his chair and raised one hand, his index finger swirled in the air. "I thought you performed a very graceful twirl and dive. That little kick at the end was a nice touch. I'd give it a score of nine points out of ten."

Grace tried laughing but coughed instead. "You're very generous, thanks." He kept a good sense of humor hidden behind his usually serious expression.

As Heath stood, a smile flashed on his face, but just as quickly, it vanished. "I should let you rest. Nice meeting you, Grace. Take care and keep both feet on dry land."

"How can I contact you?" She couldn't let him walk out the door, knowing she'd never see him again. "Would you leave your address or phone number?" She would need to find a way to repay him. *But how do I properly thank someone for saving my life?*

"I currently don't have a home address. I don't have a cell phone. Sorry." He stuffed his hands into the low pockets of his blue shirt.

"Oh." She forced a bright smile to hide her disappointment. "Well then, I guess this is goodbye. Thanks again for risking your own safety. I owe you my life."

A grimace crossed his face. He bent his head,

allowing his hair to fall forward and hide his expression. "Goodbye, Grace." With those parting words, he left the hospital room.

Part of her was relieved he was gone, because something in his eyes called to her. He unsettled her and rattled her inner peace. In two months, she would marry Tyler, the man of her dreams. Heath exiting her life was for the best.

But something whispered in the back of her mind, a devil on her shoulder, who hoped today wasn't the first and last time she saw Heath Carter.

Chapter Three

Heath could have stayed and talked with her all day, which was why he had to leave. Too much time with the lovely Grace was not a good thing. The large engagement ring on her left hand couldn't have made it any clearer, flashing like a warning light—keep away, danger ahead.

Bruce Murray stood waiting at the end of the hospital corridor. Grace's father was a solidly built man, who looked like he'd spent his life working with his hands. Heath could tell a lot about a man by his hands, and Bruce's were large and calloused.

"Heath." Bruce closed the distance. "Let me give you a ride to the bridge and your motorcycle. It's the least I can do."

Gratitude was written all over his sun-worn face. "That would be helpful, sir. I'd appreciate it." A short ride was the only thank you Heath would accept. And even that made him uncomfortable.

The two men walked out of the hospital in silence.

Bruce led him to an old truck parked at the back of the lot, far away from the other cars.

"Don't want anyone puttin' a dent in her," Bruce said with a laugh.

"No, sir." Heath ran his hand across the hood. "You need to cherish a classic beauty like her."

Bruce opened the driver's side door. "No locking

doors here. Liberty Ridge is a safe town. We watch out for each other."

As they drove, the truck's radio crackled out a classic country song. Modest houses and well-maintained yards rolled past Heath's window. The Texas town was the idealized picture of all-American wholesomeness, which left him with a pang of longing.

"You just passin' through?" Bruce asked. "I don't remember seeing you around town before."

He straightened in his seat and turned his gaze from the rolling prairie landscape outside to the man sitting to his left. "I've been traveling around Texas. Just stopped here today for lunch."

"Used to dream about hittin' the open road, traveling round the country…back in my younger days. Never got a chance, though. Right out of high school, my dad had me working on the ranch full-time." He drummed his fingers on the steering wheel. "Then, I got married to Joslyn and had a family. Time slips away fast."

"You still a rancher?" Heath peered at the man sitting in the driver's seat. *Dumb question.* Bruce was the embodiment of a man who made his living off the land.

"True Horizon Ranch has been in my family for seven generations. We raise Texas Longhorn cattle. They're real beauties and very gentle. Every spring, Gracie would spend her days out in the field, playing with the calves." Bruce smiled and pointed at a faded picture taped to the dashboard. "This here's the entrance to the ranch. That picture must have been taken nearly twenty years ago, but it's still my favorite."

Heath looked at the soft colors of the faded picture. An iron sign arched over the driveway with scrolling letters—*True Horizon Ranch, Established 1845*. Underneath stood three people: a younger Joslyn Murray, a pre-teen boy with sandy blond hair, and a little dark-haired girl who looked out of place with the other two. Heath wondered if Grace had been adopted. Her striking coloring was in contrast with the rest of her family.

In the picture, Joslyn had a tight hold on her daughter, as if struggling to keep her still long enough to get the shot. He could imagine a young Grace, being reprimanded by her elegant mother for running in the muddy fields and ruining her new dress.

"Where do you call home?" Bruce cranked down the window a few more inches.

The truck had been built before air conditioning became standard. Warm air blew in, doing little to cool him.

"Well, sir." Heath paused, giving that question consideration, not sure how much he wanted to share. "I grew up in Florida, and then lived on and off for years in North Carolina. Now…I live wherever I can find a decent job."

Bruce slowed as they approached the bridge.

Down the embankment lay Heath's bike, resting on its side. The front end was dipped in shallow water. His stomach dropped at the sight. Once they'd stopped, Heath jumped out and strode downward. After pulling the bike out of the river, he gave it a onceover.

"You think it'll still run?" Bruce stood by his truck, leaning his elbow on the hood.

Heath shrugged, not confident in his luck. He

needed to get out of town as soon as possible. He'd become too comfortable talking with Bruce and that couldn't continue. Again, he mentally reviewed his mission objectives. Stay unattached to everyone and everything. Move through life like a ghost, not touching or being touched by anything around him.

He took a close look at his wet motorcycle. If water had seeped into the engine, he wouldn't ride out anytime soon. With teeth clenched, he turned the key, which somehow hadn't fallen out of his pants pocket during his swim, and pressed the starter button. The motorcycle gave a sound that could only be described as cruel laughter, and then it sputtered and died.

"She's not behaving for ya?" Bruce asked in his deep drawl. "Maybe needs some time to dry out."

Heath looked across the bridge toward downtown. He might be stuck here for a few days, at least until he got his bike up and running. "Is there a motel in town?"

"Well." Bruce scratched at his scruffy, graying beard. "Ol' Rusty runs a motor lodge just down the road, 'bout a mile. I wouldn't recommend it, though. The last storm did some damage to the roof. Plus…I don't think that cheapskate's purchased new bedding since the Reagan administration."

Heath's stomach twisted in a sickening knot. Right now, he should be riding the open road, not contemplating whether to sleep outside or in a dilapidated motel.

"We have an empty bunkhouse." Bruce pulled out a red checkered handkerchief from his pocket and wiped the back of his neck. "Used to have our ranch hands live on the property, but now they all have their own homes in town. The little house is clean and all yours, no charge. For as long as you need it."

Choking back emotion, Heath cleared his throat, recalling the same generous spirit he'd once enjoyed with his Army brothers. "That's nice of you, sir, but I don't want to impose." He glared at his traitorous motorcycle and gave it a hard kick. "I'll figure out something. I'm used to flying by the seat of my pants."

"Nonsense. If my daughter and wife find out I left you on the side of the road with a broken bike, they'll skin me alive." Bruce took hold of the right handlebar. He pulled the bike toward the truck. "Let's get this thing in the back, and I'll drive you to the ranch. You can fix your bike there, and then get on the road."

Heath recognized the firm look of determination on Bruce's face and didn't seem left with much choice. Bruce would not leave without him. "Thank you, sir. That's a kind offer."

"Great."

Bruce's large hand slapped Heath's back, causing him to stumble forward. The man was as strong as an ox.

"And no more 'sir.' Just call me Bruce."

"Old habits die hard." Heath cleared his throat, pushing away the words he wanted to say, but he couldn't. Tears burned in his eyes.

Bruce only nodded.

Between the two of them, they lifted the motorcycle so it lay secure in the bed of the truck. Heath wiped the sweat off his brow with the back of his hand. No matter how hard Heath worked to hide his past life, it always came creeping back. People like Bruce and Grace Murray frightened him. They had the ability to peel off the protective layers and see the man inside. The man he couldn't outrun.

****

"I'm so glad to be out of the hospital." Grace tipped back her head to rest on the passenger seat of her mother's car. Thankfully, when she'd awakened that morning, the world had finally stopped whirling around her. Although, this car ride was reinstating her nausea. "Sleeping through the night with nurses coming in every couple of hours is impossible. I'm so tired."

"Maybe next time, you'll be more careful and keep your head out of the clouds." Joslyn turned the A/C from cold to polar bear blast. "I wish Tyler could have stayed longer."

Disappointment lingered in her heart. "I know, but he did spend the night with me in the hospital. He had to return to Dallas for a meeting. Something about a lawyer and a land contract. Sounded important."

"I hoped he would have stayed for dinner." Joslyn turned the steering wheel and directed the car onto the long gravel driveway and under the iron arch of True Horizon Ranch.

As they drove down the driveway, Grace lowered the car window and deeply breathed in the fresh air of her favorite place in the world. Acres of grassland enveloped the earth for as far as she could see. For eighteen years, this ranch had been her home. Land where she had run wild and free, a dirty but happy little girl. Those hills and fields, spotted with her beloved Longhorns, had been her playground.

Her mother had insisted Grace leave home for college, in hopes if she left the ranch for a few years, she'd finally mature into a lady. To her mother's delight, she'd blossomed while living away. Big city life had transformed her from an awkward, homely caterpillar into a butterfly.

They parked in front of the attached garage. As she opened the trunk to get her bags, Grace noticed a motorcycle sitting in front of the old bunkhouse. "Do we have company?" She shifted the weight of the bag in her hand.

Her mother sighed and waved her hand toward the bunkhouse. "Your father brought Heath Carter here yesterday. His motorcycle wouldn't start so he invited Heath to stay until it was fixed. I told him I wasn't comfortable with a stranger living so close. Of course, your dad didn't listen to a word I said."

"Heath is staying here?" she croaked. The idea of having him here made her gut churn with nerves. Was the feeling caused by the memory of his rough hands on her skin, or the heat in his hazel eyes when they'd locked onto hers? Grace shook those thoughts out of her head. She'd be married soon, on this very ranch, to a man she loved. The only reason she'd come home at all was to prepare for their wedding.

Tyler was perfect. He was everything she wanted. Nothing, not even her unexplainable and unfamiliar attraction to Heath Carter, would interfere with her dream wedding.

Grace followed in her mother's wake as she walked up the front steps and onto the wraparound porch.

"Dad invited Heath over for dinner. Alex, Jenny, and the twins are coming, too. If you're tired, I suggest you go upstairs and take a nap. I'll need some help in the kitchen later this afternoon." Joslyn opened the creaky screen door and stepped inside the house.

Instead of going in as well, Grace turned to look at the motorcycle sitting across the yard. Tools and parts were strewn about the ground. Her body flushed with heat at the memory of Heath straddling that very bike, riding toward her.

Suddenly, the front door to the bunkhouse opened, and Heath came outside. He wiped his hands on a ragged towel.

Despite being separated by a distance of approximately two hundred feet, Grace could see him approach his bike with long strides, his attention totally focused on the gleaming, black machine on the ground. He wore jeans, seeming to mock the heat. When he caught her gaze, she felt a shiver pass over her body.

His hand extended in a leisurely wave.

She responded with one of her own before fleeing into the safety of her parents' house. Up in her old bedroom, she flopped onto her twin bed, which groaned at the weight of the woman she'd become. Her bedroom still was one of a little girl, with dolls and stuffed animals decorating every corner. Countless trophies for various Western riding competitions stood proud on the tall bookcase. They gave testament to the fact that once upon a time, she had been a country girl. Such a girl, who loved the fresh air and horses, really had existed.

She placed her head on the pillow and closed her eyes but struggled to fall asleep in the too-quiet house. The silence stood out in sharp contrast to the constant noise of her apartment in downtown Dallas. Instead of honks and sirens, she now heard the buzz of insects outside and the occasional creak of the house. She'd only been home a few days, but her body and mind had quickly calmed in the peace and quiet of the country.

"Ugh, I can't fall asleep." She groaned and hit the pillow, an easy target for her irritation. Heath was coming tonight for dinner. He would be sitting in her parents' house, at their table, and eating with her family. Would he clean-up and shave, or keep his appearance dangerously masculine, featuring lots of facial hair and exposed tattoos? She doubted she'd get any rest with that image running through her head.

Chapter Four

"Grace." Joslyn snapped her fingers and pointed to the stove. "The gravy is boiling over."

Grace looked at the pot she'd been entrusted with and saw bubbling, thick liquid had broken over the top, preparing an escape onto the clean stovetop. "Got it." She picked up a wooden spoon and frantically began stirring. "The gravy looks done. Should I take it off?"

"Keep going for another minute." Her mother looked into the pot, and then went back to the vegetables she'd abandoned.

The steady beat of the knife started again. Grace worked in silence until one minute passed then she turned off the stove burner and set the pot on the granite counter to cool. "Do you need me for anything else?" She whispered a prayer to be released from kitchen duty. Not only to get out from under her mother's watchful eye, but her stray thoughts about Heath were making her very jumpy. If she didn't watch it, she'd ruin their dinner.

Being in the kitchen with her mother reminded Grace of the many times she'd been a disappointment. As she recounted the years spent attempting to please, only to realize she'd never be the daughter her mother had envisioned, the heavy weight of failure settled on her shoulders. Recently, their relationship was slowly improving, mostly because Grace was no longer

31

running around the ranch like a wild child. She'd swapped ripped jeans and dirty T-shirts for designer outfits and expensive shoes. Living and working in Dallas had been the catalyst for many changes, and her relationship with Tyler was proof.

"Why don't you set the table?" Her mother waved her away from the stove. "We need eight place settings. And don't forget the salad forks."

As Grace entered the large pantry off the kitchen, a knock sounded at the front door.

"Hello, hello, hello." Her dad's voice boomed from the entryway. "Come in, Heath. Glad you agreed to join us."

Her stomach fluttered with nerves as footsteps sounded. Thankfully, they moved toward the family room. Grace counted out eight plates, which were decorated with delicately painted country roses, and then carried them to the dining room. Through the open door, she watched Heath stand beside her dad, listening as Dad told a long-winded story. She grinned at Heath. His posture was straight, feet wide set, and his folded hands rested against his lower back. If he was to survive her family, he'd need to loosen up.

Her dad looked like he'd just gotten in from the fields, standing tall with his fingers hooked in the straps of his overalls. As she set the table, she overheard their conversation. Cattle prices were stagnant, and property taxes were too high.

Heath remained quiet, nodding every once in awhile.

Her mother entered the family room and approached Heath. "Welcome. Can I get you something to drink?"

"Would you like a beer?" Bruce asked.

"Yes, thank you." Heath settled on the oversized leather sofa. His gaze darted around the room.

Maybe searching for an escape. He reminded Grace of a cornered animal.

Joslyn exited the family room and caught Grace peeking through the door of the dining room. Her mother shot her *the look*, along with a swift nod, motioning toward their guest.

Darn, I've been busted. With her hiding spot discovered, she wiped her sweating palms on her skirt and left the safety of the dining room.

Heath stood as she entered. "Hi." A small smile pulled at the corners of his mouth, which showed underneath his beard.

"Hello, it's good to see you again…under drier circumstances." She smiled, taking in his appearance. Although he still sported a bushy beard, she could tell he had showered and run a comb through his hair, tying it back with a leather strap. His clothes looked crisp and clean, with his shirt sleeves rolled up just enough to show off the tattoos covering his forearms. *The guy cleaned up pretty well.* Grace sat in the rocking chair across from the sofa. A good spot for studying their dinner guest.

Joslyn came in holding two beer bottles, both dripping with condensation. She placed them on the coasters set on the coffee table and looked at her husband. "I hope you plan on changing out of those dirty overalls before dinner, Bruce Murray."

"Sure, sure. Let me finish this." He lifted his beer bottle. "Don't worry. By the time dinner's ready, I'll be as shiny as a pig on Sunday."

Her mother's laughter followed her out of the room.

Heath coughed with muffled laughter before taking a drink.

Now, his smile brightened his entire face. Too bad he hid his good looks underneath all that hair. With a cut and shave, she was sure he'd look like a totally different man.

"How's the bike comin' along?" Bruce took a long drink before setting the bottle back onto the coaster.

"The parts I need should be in tomorrow. The guy from the auto store said he'd drop them off."

"Yeah, that sounds like Jerry. He's a good man. Honest, too."

"Have you decided where you're going once your bike is fixed?" Grace asked.

"No, ma'am." Heath turned in his seat to face her. "I was heading to Dallas, but I've changed my mind about staying in a big city."

She pondered the fact he had no set plan for his journey. Her thoughts were interrupted by the opening of the front door and the arrival of two blonde girls running into the family room.

"Papa!" they both yelled in unison and jumped onto Bruce's wide lap.

Heath scooted over to make room for the squirming little girls.

"How are my favorite twins?" Bruce gave them each a kiss on the cheek.

"We're great," Kara said while her sister, Lizzy, nodded.

As Alex and Jenny came into the room, Grace stood to give her brother and sister-in-law a hug. "Hey, girls," Grace said to the twins. "Granny's in the kitchen. Go see if she needs help." The girls, who never missed an opportunity for fun with Granny, jumped off the sofa and made a beeline for the kitchen.

Alex sat and crossed his ankle over his knee. "You're asking for trouble, Grace. Mom hates being called Granny, and the last thing she wants is a pair of six-year-old tornados helping her prepare dinner."

"I know." Grace rubbed her hands together. "That's why it's so much fun."

A surprised cry came from the rear of the house. Everyone in the family room laughed.

"Heath, this is my son Alex and his lovely wife, Jenny." The lines around Bruce's mouth deepened with his smile. "Those two dolls now in the kitchen helping with dinner are their daughters, Kara and Lizzy. And this young man here is Heath Carter."

Alex reached over to shake Heath's hand. "Pleasure to meet you, Heath."

Alex and Jenny cuddled up on the small loveseat placed under a large picture window.

Through the window, Grace could see her favorite mare grazing in the field by the stable. The sun's strong rays bounced off the stable's tin roof. Another beautiful summer day in God's country.

Bruce stood. "Guess I should go change." The stairs creaked as he made his way to the second floor.

"So, Heath." Alex leaned forward and rested his forearms on his lap. "I heard you and my sister took a little swim in the Hickory River yesterday." He turned to Grace and winked.

Oh no. Grace shot her older brother a look that could have halted a stampeding bull. But of course on

Alex, her efforts were useless.

"Thanks for jumping in after her." He kept charging on with his story. "Funny thing, though, that's not the first time she's been saved from drowning."

"Alex." The heat of embarrassment colored Grace's cheeks. "Don't go there."

He avoided Grace's stare. "In high school, she got a cramp while swimming in the community pool. She needed the lifeguard to save her. No doubt, she planned the stunt to get the attention of her crush, Tyler Ross. That time, he tossed her a ring buoy. Ten years later, she managed to get an engagement ring from the guy."

"My leg really did cramp that day." Grace's cheeks grew even warmer. Why did her big brother love to tease?

"See those pictures on the mantel?" Alex pointed at the row of framed pictures. "The one on the far left is Grace, freshman year. Tyler was my best friend, and she used to follow him around like a puppy dog, but he had little interest in that version of my sister."

If she would have had a cow pie handy, she would have launched it at Alex's head. Now that would have shut him up. She knew from experience. *Good grief.* Grace had been home for a few days and already slipped back into the role of country girl. But to be honest, the thought of a good ol' cow pie fight did make her giddy.

"Stop teasing your sister, Alex, or you'll sleep on the couch tonight." Jenny gave her husband a pinch on the arm.

Heath studied her high school picture, while Grace fought the urge to grab it, and then run and hide. The combination of braces and glasses, along with blotchy

36

skin and a bad hair style, made her look like someone's cruel joke. For years, she'd begged her mother to replace that picture, but her dad insisted it stay.

Heath caught her gaze. "You were beautiful. Don't ever feel otherwise."

"Where were you when I was sixteen?" Grace murmured.

Alex, mouth hung slack, was struck silent, and looked from Heath to Grace, and then back to Heath.

Soon, her mother appeared in the room, followed by Kara and Lizzy, who were cool, calm, and under control. "Supper is ready. Y'all, go wash your hands and get ready to eat."

Bruce came downstairs, dressed in clean clothes, and walked with Heath to the dining room. Jenny went with her daughters to the bathroom.

Grabbing Grace's arm, Alex pulled her back. "What's up with him?" He pointed to Heath. "He's a little odd, huh?"

"No, he's not odd. He has more going on than meets the eye." She was so curious about his story. Where did he come from? What had brought him to Liberty Ridge? Why had he jumped into a cold river, and subsequently damaged his bike, to rescue a stranger?"

"Pops took him into town today." Alex tipped his head in Heath's direction. "They must have stopped at the store to get him some new clothes. You can still see the store folds in his shirt."

She had noticed that but found it endearing rather than funny. Heath had made an effort to look nice for tonight. Tyler always looked polished and put together, but he showed extra attention to his appearance when negotiating business dealings. That's when he pulled out the custom-tailored suit, highly polished leather shoes, and six-thousand-dollar watch. "I want Heath to feel welcome here. Okay?"

Alex furrowed his light eyebrows, and a frown pulled down the corners of his mouth. "Do you think I was raised in a barn? Of course, I'll make him feel welcome. He saved your life."

She laughed and tucked her hand into the crook of her brother's arm. "We were both raised in a barn. Let's go see if we remember our table manners."

****

Dinner tasted delicious, the best thing Heath had eaten in the past year and a half. The beef was tender and moist. The bread was freshly baked and still warm. And the apple pie that Grace brought to the table after dinner left him so full he could barely move. "The meal was wonderful, Mrs. Murray."

Joslyn's smile beamed. "Thanks, Heath. I'm glad you could join us."

With the table cleared, the twins went off to play in another room. The adults lingered at the dining room table, recovering from overeating.

Over dinner, Heath realized that in this family, the dining room was the heart of the home. Cream-and-blue-striped wallpaper covered the walls, and a long mahogany table anchored the room. Pictures, along with a painting of the ranch, filled the space. He could almost hear the whispers of the countless stories shared around the table.

"Coffee anyone?" Grace stood to get the carafe on the sideboard. She poured the steaming liquid into white china cups before setting out the cream and sugar.

No use in denying his growing attraction. His feelings were harmless enough, even if they strengthened by the minute. Every time he glanced her way, his pulse quickened, sending hot blood coursing through his veins. Grace was charming and pretty, but more than that, her heart was genuinely pure. Tomorrow, he would leave to continue on his journey. And soon she would be a married woman.

The conversation flowed around the table, and Heath was content just to listen, only answering the occasional question thrown his way. Even though he was an outsider, they still made him feel like part of the family. That morning, when Bruce invited him to dinner, he'd first declined the offer. But he soon realized Bruce Murray would not take no for an answer. Now, he was glad Bruce had been so insistent.

The last time he'd enjoyed a meal like this was with John and Julie Ellis. In his head, Heath saw their cozy home at Fort Bragg. He had been a frequent guest, stopping by regularly for a home-cooked meal. Julie, with her curly, red hair and caring heart, was a very good cook.

Thoughts of his best friend tormented his already battered soul. They were his penance and reminded him of his failures, both professionally and personally. John would never eat another meal at home. John would never return to his wife and son. John would miss out on seeing his son grow up and become a man, strong and brave like his father.

"What do you do for a living, Heath?" Joslyn asked.

Heath's dark thoughts were thankfully interrupted by her question. He unclenched his jaw and took a few deep breaths through his nose to help him relax. "My last job was on an oil rig, ma'am. Before that I worked construction." He kept his answer as vague as possible. Even nice people judged him harshly once they realized he lived as a drifter. He'd been called many things—crazy, dangerous, deranged—but those words never stung, because he didn't allow himself to care about the people saying them.

"You revived Grace after you rescued her from the river," Joslyn said. "Do you have any medical training?"

He shifted in his seat and forced the words out of his mouth. "I served for twelve years in the Army, ma'am. Mostly as a medic."

Grace's eyes widened. "You were in the Army? I would never have guessed."

Strands of panic tightened around Heath's chest, causing him to strain for breath. He pushed back his chair. "Thank you for dinner, it was wonderful. I should be going."

As if on cue, the twins skipped into the dining room. One of them held a small box in her hand. "Papa, is it time to play?" She placed the box on the table.

Bruce laughed and lifted the small, red box, waving it at Heath. "Sorry, young man, but you can't leave just yet. We haven't played SOLO."

He glanced around at the Murray family, all looking back at him with wide eyes and raised brows, and he returned to his seat. A quick card game, and then he'd leave. Even though Grace's smile continually chipped away at his resolve.

Since he'd never played SOLO before, the twins sat one on either side of him during the first round and fed him instructions. For the second game, he switched seats and was placed between Lizzy and Grace. After several rotations around the table, he noticed Grace held only two cards. Since she'd won the first game, his mission became preventing her from winning again.

"Heath, it's your turn." Lizzy elbowed his side.

He'd learned to tell the twins apart by the color of the ribbon tying their ponytails.

"Draw Four." He slapped down his card on top of the pile.

Grace narrowed her eyes and picked four cards. "You will pay for that."

"Bring it on, sister." He smiled, because luck was on his side. He had another Draw Four and a Skip card in his hand. The muscles in his cheeks actually hurt from overuse.

"Nobody does that to Auntie Grace," Lizzy whispered in his ear. "She hates to lose."

"She doesn't scare me." Heath sent Grace a challenging grin. "She's going down." His index finger pointed to the floor.

Lizzy giggled and glanced at her cards.

He noticed that Grace was intensely studying her cards, maybe working out a new strategy. What a surprise to learn under her sweet and innocent exterior lay a cutthroat card player. For his next turn, he used his Skip card.

"That's not fair." Grace's hand pounded the table. "He's cheating." She narrowed her eyes at the others around the table.

The twins laughed. One of them gave Heath a high-five.

Bruce laid down a card, leaving him with only

three cards. "Seems to be working out well for me."

"Ugh." She folded her arms. "You guys are a bunch of traitors."

Soon, Grace held ten cards, while Heath palmed his last card. She even tried to peek at his card in a last-ditch effort to cheat. The flushed glow of her cheeks looked hot to the touch. He fought the urge to reach over and trail a finger along her jaw line, stopping at her full bottom lip. The same lip that stuck out in an attractive pout.

He pictured Grace wrapped in his arms, her head tipped back in ecstasy, as he ran passionate kisses down her neck and across her—*Not the time, man. Not the place.*

Lizzy tapped his arm, shaking out the seductive image from his mind.

"Your turn." Her sing-song voice fluttered.

When he placed his final card on the table, everyone cheered. Well, everyone except for Grace. Heath could almost see steam blowing out of her ears.

"I think that's enough SOLO for tonight." Grace bit her lower lip and glanced over at Heath. A smile twitched at the corners of her mouth. She collected the cards and put them back into the box. "You got lucky tonight, Carter. Next time, I won't go so easy on you."

"Guess I'm looking at a rematch," he said to Lizzy. His gaze followed Grace as she walked out of the room, her hips swaying under a loose black skirt.

"You're a brave man." Alex reclined in his chair and folded his hands behind his head. "We usually just let her win. Easier that way."

Heath stood and shook hands with Bruce and Alex. "Then that's my cue to leave." He said goodbye and walked to the front door.

"Are you leaving?" Grace materialized from the family room.

Backlight spilled from the room and illuminated her dark hair. Heath forced himself to look at the engagement ring on her finger, which served as a visual reminder to his wavering heart. She was off limits. "I'm heading to the bunkhouse. Thanks for the friendly competition."

She set a hand on one hip. The other hand rested loosely at her side. "Okay, then…goodnight. See you tomorrow."

He longed to give her a goodnight kiss. Instead, he settled for a solitary night in his bunkhouse—and a cold shower.

Chapter Five

A strong wind forced back Heath, and he grabbed onto the rappelling rope to steady himself.

"Thirty seconds to target." A voice crackled through his earpiece.

He was seated and strapped to a bench, which was secured to the outside of the chopper. Looking down past his dangling feet into the black abyss below, he ran the upcoming mission through his mind. The MH-6 Little Bird helicopter would hover over the target building, and the team would have a minute to fast rope to the roof. Next, they would secure the building and the surrounding courtyard. Taliban fighters would most likely be in the area, so they needed to be prepared. Their goal was simple—collect the target and get the hell out.

Moments later, when his feet hit the roof, he unhooked the rope, got into a kneeling position, and then provided cover for the second chopper. The beat of rotating rudders drowned out all other sounds. The smell of rotting waste made bile rise in his throat.

He entered the building through a hole in the roof. His heart pounded hard in his chest. As the team began sweeping and securing each room, the straps of his pack dug into his shoulders. He followed John down the hall, until John disappeared from view like he was swallowed whole by the dark mouth of the corridor.

From outside, a series of loud blasts sounded. The monster had awakened and he was ready to play.

Heath sprinted outside into the courtyard and saw bodies strewn across the ground. Approaching the nearest victim, he took off his pack and opened his medical supply bag. The soldier's face was turned away. Blood poured out of his mangled leg.

Around him sounded more screams and cries for help. He was surrounded by the dying and every time he refocused his vision, the victims multiplied.

"Heath, help me!"

Screams pierced his ears. He tasted smoke in the air, sour on his tongue. The coppery smell of blood filled his nose.

"Heath!" John's voice sliced through the chaos.

He crawled across the ground and found John slumped over with his back resting against the wall. Blood flowed from his mouth.

Bile rose in Heath's throat. *I won't let you die on my watch.*

"Leave! Get out of here now. Run!" John yelled, spitting blood.

Heath bolted upright in bed with a scream dying on his lips. Sweat dripped from his body, which hummed with delayed terror. After several deep breaths, he remembered where he was. Reality took hold. His body trembled, burning off the remaining adrenaline. Very slowly, his vision cleared.

Silver moonlight shone through the bedroom window, highlighting the bed. The sheets and blanket lay in a heap on the floor.

Every night, the same nightmare visited him, and each time, he woke up screaming. He never saved any of the soldiers who'd called out for help. Too much blood. Too much death. John's grimacing face was always the last image he saw. A reflection of anguish burned into his mind. His best friend who'd never returned home from Afghanistan alive.

Not wanting to slip back into the torment of sleep, he paced the cool floor of the small bunkhouse until the sun started its ascent over the field. The beautiful sunrise ignited a fire, which chased away the long, dark shadows. The golden light lifted his mood.

After a quick shower, he poured a bowl of cereal from the sparsely stocked kitchen and brewed a pot of coffee. He took his breakfast and sat out on the small front porch of the bunkhouse.

The screen door of the main house creaked, and he looked across the long stretch of lawn to see Grace step outside. She held her laptop in one hand and a large mug in the other. Taking a seat on one of the many rocking chairs that decorated the porch, she placed her mug on a side table and flipped open her laptop. Every once in a while, she'd take a break from typing to grab her mug, take a drink, and then set it down without looking.

He watched as she slid a rubber band from her wrist and drew her long hair into a ponytail. She was effortlessly beautiful, in white cut-off shorts and a red tank top. Her bare feet were propped on the porch railing. The large, white farmhouse surrounded her in a loving embrace. The Murray home was an old, rambling house, which looked like it had been added onto over the years. A wooden deck and multiple flower gardens filled the back yard. He wondered how many generations had called it home.

Home—a concept lost to him over the years. Aunt Linda had given him a loving home when he was younger, to make up for the fact that both his parents were complete failures. With a dad in prison and a mom who'd died from an overdose, he felt a deep gratitude for his aunt. His rebellious adolescence had forced the only person who'd ever shown him love to give an ultimatum—join the military or end up in jail, just like your dad.

In his gut, he knew he'd made the right choice all those years ago. The military had taken a troublesome boy and molded him into an admirable man. But sometimes, after waking from a nightmare, he asked himself if the sacrifice was worth the pain. Heath broke out of his reflection to notice Grace watching him from across the yard.

She gave him a quick smile before returning her attention to her computer.

Should he go over and say hello, or just let her work? He didn't question his instincts but strode over to the porch. Leaning against the rail, he cleared his throat. "Good morning." He removed his dusty baseball cap and tucked it under his arm. Her radiant smile stopped his heart.

"Good morning to you, too." She lowered the screen of her laptop.

Heath struggled to retain possession of his mind while in the presence of such a beautiful woman. *Don't just stand there and drool, you idiot.* "You have a wonderful office." He gazed around at their surroundings. From this viewpoint, he could see the horse stable and the barns, the animal corrals, a few of the flower gardens, and acres and acres of cattle pastures. A breathtaking sight.

"Yes, it is. I didn't realize how much I missed this place." Grace swept her hand in a wide arch. "I moved here from Dallas a few days ago, but only temporarily, until my wedding."

"When's the big day?" He didn't want to think about her getting married. He shouldn't care but for some reason, he did. A lot.

"At the end of August. We're holding the ceremony and reception at the ranch. So many things need taking care of, and all are easier to manage from here."

"Good luck. Well, I should let you get back to work." He didn't want to leave her but had enough sense left to know that's exactly what he had to do—for the sake of his poor, lovestruck heart.

"Thanks for coming over." She brushed a fly off her arm. The bug came back, and she swatted it away again. "You know…I think the ranch suits you. I'm glad you agreed to stay until your bike is fixed."

He placed his baseball cap on his head. "Yes, ma'am. Thanks for the hospitality." Pushing off the rail, he walked back to his temporary home.

Last night, inside the Murray house, he'd seen her engagement picture. Her fiancé had a smugness that rubbed him the wrong way. Tyler's buttoned-up attire and cocky smile didn't jive with easy-going Grace. Heath imagined Tyler tip-toeing around the ranch, not wanting to get cattle poop on his expensive leather shoes.

Returning to his motorcycle, he grabbed a socket wrench and got to work. Hours later, he sat next to his bike, swearing loudly. The ranch dogs ran around him, sniffing curiously. He'd counted four dogs around the property: two Collies, one German Shepherd, and a black one of questionable lineage. The old radio he'd found in the bunkhouse rested on the grass, crackling out classic rock. Today's weather forecast called for temperatures reaching 100 degrees—blast-furnace hot. The Texas heat reminded him of a desert a half a world away. His T-shirt was drenched in sweat and stuck to his body.

Jerry, from the auto-parts store, had stopped by earlier, delivering the parts Heath needed. The engine was now running but not smoothly. He'd counted out his remaining cash, which would last him only a few more days. If he left today, his bike might die while on the road and leave him stranded with a pricey repair. But he had to take that chance.

Bruce was over by the big barn, loading tools into a green ATV.

His overalls, cowboy hat, and work boots gave him the appearance of a man ready to spend the day working outside. Heath put down his wrench and walked over to give him a hand.

"Howdy." Bruce threw a bundle of wire into the bed of the vehicle. "You get her runnin' yet?"

"A few minutes ago. The engine isn't purring like it should, though. A professional mechanic would fix that, but I'm running out of cash." Hard thing to admit that he was almost broke, but his stress eased with the statement. Bruce made him feel comfortable, and Heath had gone a long time without someone he could talk to. "Time to get on the road and find a job."

Bruce got seated in the ATV. "I'm heading out to inspect some of the back fence. You want to tag along?

I'll give you a little tour before you leave."

"I'd like that." Heath adjusted his hat to shade his eyes from the bright sun. He sat in the passenger seat.

"Hold on tight." Bruce took off down the gravel drive and into the pasture.

When they hit an especially large bump, Heath nearly flew off. This rough ride reminded him of trips through the Afghan countryside. Only now, he was spared the threat of land mines and terrorists' bullets. That fact didn't stop his hyper vigilance. His gaze scanned the landscape around them in search of danger. A finely tuned skill that was now unneeded but too deeply ingrained to change.

He squeezed the side bar a little tighter as he rode past more Longhorn cattle than he could count. Some of the horns of the larger cattle were unbelievably huge, close to five feet tip to tip.

"You know," Bruce said. "I've trained them to respond to the horn of the ATV. I give a beep-beep, and they follow me into another pasture." After two short honks, all the cattle within view raised their heads and looked at the ATV.

"Smart cattle." He laughed and glanced around the field at the crowd of curious bovines. "They used the same trick with us in the Army, only their method included a blow horn and threats of extra PT to get us moving."

Bruce's wide mouth lifted with a smile. "Son, I never thanked you for your service, so I am now. You are a credit to your country."

Chest constricting his breath, Heath could only nod. When was the last time he'd felt pride for his military career? If Bruce knew the dark, deadly truth, he'd be repulsed instead of grateful. He turned his gaze and watched acres of fields roll past, spotted with ponds and rocky outcroppings, which hung over slow-moving streams. The ranch was nature at its most pure. While riding along the rough path, a peaceful world spread out before him, and the load on his shoulders lightened. An energetic green replaced the red that normally stained his vision.

They stopped at a section of fence that hung loose. Two dogs had followed them out and now darted through the pasture.

"Grab that wire cutter and gloves." Bruce lifted a roll of wire.

Heath labored alongside the rancher for over an hour, mending fence and working up a healthy sweat. Cicadas buzzed steadily. Their song punctuated by an occasional lowing of cattle. He raised his head to the clear, blue sky. Now, this was freedom.

"All this wedding business may drive me into an early grave." Bruce walked over to the cooler and grabbed a water bottle. "Joslyn and Grace have me working on so many projects. I hardly have time to work the ranch."

Heath accepted a water bottle from Bruce and took a drink. The cool moisture felt like heaven to his mouth and throat. "The wedding is at the end of August, right?"

"Yup, come hell or high water." Bruce laughed and wiped his brow with a red checkered handkerchief then tucked it into his pocket. "To tell you the truth, I'm not too happy about this whole thing. Tyler is a good man and he loves my daughter, but I wish they'd wait a bit. Not go rushing to the altar."

"How long have they known each other?" Heath gulped down another drink.

"Since elementary school. Alex and Tyler were good friends, and Grace had what you'd call puppy love. She'd get all dolled up whenever Tyler came over, but that boy never paid her any attention. I wonder if he's worthy of her love, after all those years of breaking her heart. He didn't appreciate the jewel hidden inside."

"Tyler must've recently changed his mind." Heath crushed the empty water bottle in his hand. The plastic container seemed like a safe outlet for his growing dislike of Grace's fiancé.

"A year ago, they ran into each other at a friend's wedding. Grace had grown up quite a bit since he'd seen her last. Now he was the one smitten. I give Grace credit. She made him work hard to win her hand." Bruce wrapped a length of wire around the wooden fence post and pounded several horseshoe nails over the wire to hold it into place. "I only hope she wants to marry the man Tyler is, not the version she'd put on a pedestal all those years."

"She seems to have a smart head on her shoulders." Heath handed Bruce the wire cutters. "And you're a good man for giving her a dream wedding."

Bruce laughed heartily. "It will either be a dream or a nightmare, depending on if I get all my projects done." He cut the extra wire and put his tools back in the bed of the ATV. "Heath, I could really use an extra pair of hands around here for the next two months. Between the wedding and preparing for the fall cattle auction, there's not enough time in the day. If you agree to stay, you can continue to use the bunkhouse, plus weekly pay. I know you had your heart set on leaving, but I hope you'll consider my offer."

He'd have a job here at the ranch, a roof over his head, and money coming in. He could get his bike fixed, and then stash the rest. True Horizon Ranch had been good to him so far. Here, the echoes of war filling his head had eased.

But then there was Grace. Could he handle being around her, knowing she was marrying another man? It would definitely be a challenge. And he never retreated from a challenge. "You got yourself a new ranch hand." He extended his hand.

Bruce gave it a crushing shake. "Welcome to the family."

****

"Why would you offer him a job?" Grace's hand jerked, causing her to accidently click on the wrong icon. She turned her gaze from her computer to her dad, who really did have a heart of gold. "Did he agree to stay?"

"I need the help, pumpkin. This wedding business is taking a lot of time, and our other ranch hands are busy already from dawn to dusk." Dad leaned a shoulder against the doorframe of her bedroom.

"Plenty of young guys in the area are looking for work." Grace stood from the desk and went to glance out her bedroom window. Heath would be living at the ranch. She'd probably see him every day. And who knew how long he'd stay—a week, a month, or even longer.

As if she conjured him from her mind, his tall form appeared outside. The sight made her skin tingle and her pulse race. Her body's reaction would have to stop for this arrangement to work.

53

"Heath is already here, plus he's worked construction. I'm putting him in charge of building the fancy gazebo you and your mother got planned."

Grace watched Heath as he walked into the horse stable. "Are you sure we can trust him?" Part of her feared him. He forced her off balance. Dark shadows churned behind his eyes. He was hiding something. She'd bet her new designer purse on it.

Dad scanned the room and stopped at her collection of riding trophies on the bookshelf, and he smiled. "I'd never ask someone to stay at the ranch who I didn't trust. Heath is a little bit of an odd duck, I'll give you that. But I believe that underneath his rugged appearance, he's a respectable man who jumped into a river to save a stranger."

She walked over and gave her dad a hug. He had a solid point. She owed Heath so much more than a job. "Okay. You're right. I'm glad you have the help."

"Don't fret too much. Things have a way of workin' out the way they should."

When her dad left her room, she went to work on her computer. The beauty of her job was all she needed was Wi-Fi and her laptop. Tyler's company had contracted her to run a security sweep of their data servers. That would keep her busy for the rest of the day. Hours later, when she heard the crunch of tires on gravel, she glanced out the window and nearly jumped out of her chair. She closed her computer and checked herself in the mirror before running downstairs and out the door. "Tyler." She flung herself into his open arms, which wrapped around her like sunshine. His body felt solid and real. "I didn't think you'd be here tonight."

"I finished my meetings early." He kissed her

softly on the cheek.

Tyler looked like he'd stepped out of a men's fashion magazine. His Italian suit only had a few creases from the car ride. A yellow tie lay over a crisp white dress shirt. As he walked to the trunk of his silver sports car, he stepped carefully so he wouldn't dirty his expensive shoes. Pulling out a garment bag and suitcase from the trunk, he followed Grace into the coolness of the house.

Joslyn came out of the kitchen, wiping flour off her hands.

Tyler greeted his future mother-in-law with a kiss on the cheek. "I hope you don't mind if I join you for dinner."

Her fiancé was such a charmer.

"Of course not. You are welcome any time. I cleaned out the second bedroom on the left. You can put your things up there." Joslyn retreated into the kitchen. "Dinner will be ready in thirty minutes," she called out.

Standing in the entryway, Tyler wrapped his arms around Grace's waist.

His embrace grounded her back to reality. What she had with Tyler was the real deal. He represented her future. She ran her fingers through his perfectly styled blond hair.

He leaned in and kissed her hard on the mouth. "You taste like strawberry shortcake."

"Hope you like it, because that's tonight's dessert." Resting against his solid body, she nipped at his neck. When the bitter taste of Tyler's cologne landed on her tongue, she had to suppress the urge to gag.

"Yummy. I can't wait until dessert. You will be

mine."

Hand in hand, she led him upstairs.

When they reached the privacy of her room, he yanked her close. This time, his kiss was urgent and strong.

Some disconcerted feeling inside her gut made her hold back. Tyler's usual demanding passion suddenly instilled panic. Her chest squeezed, leaving her struggling to breathe. She pulled away. Grace stroked his smooth face, free of even a millimeter of beard hair. In her adolescence, she'd spent hours making up stories about Tyler. She'd hidden in the hay loft and imagined her wedding. In her mind's eye, she would be a beautiful bride, and Tyler was the love-struck groom. Not once during all those daydreams did she ever expect them to come true.

Now those dreams were becoming reality.

"I can't wait until I can claim you as my wife," Tyler whispered in her ear. "No more separate bedrooms at your parents' house."

The term 'claim' bristled against her firmly instilled sense of independence. He probably didn't mean to sound like a caveman.

Even so, Tyler was still perfect, she reminded herself, and he was all hers.

Chapter Six

When they finally came downstairs, Grace took one look at the formally set dining room table and knew her mother had pulled out all the stops for that evening's dinner. She always put in extra effort for Tyler. After so many years of desiring her mother's approval, Grace was glad to know she'd finally done something right.

"Another fabulous dinner." Tyler folded his hands behind his head and reclined his body. "I don't think I could eat another bite."

"Thank you, Tyler." Joslyn's face glowed as she began clearing the table. "I always enjoy when you join us."

"So, Bruce, have you given any more thought to that oil contract?" Tyler's body leaned toward Bruce. "I can have a copy of the paperwork sent to your lawyer. I believe you'll be pleased with the terms."

Grace recognized the gleam in Tyler's eyes. The one he always got when talking business. His body appeared relaxed, but she saw the tension he held in his jaw and the muscle tic on the lower part of his left cheek. Tyler Ross was a lion in the arena of deal negotiations, and her stomach tightened with worry for her dad.

"Haven't had time to think about that." Bruce shrugged. "Too many other things to do."

"I know you're busy." Tyler rolled up the long sleeves of his pristine, white dress shirt. "But I don't want you to miss out on this opportunity. My men can start prospecting the site as soon as you sign the agreement."

"I'm not keen about drilling platforms on my land." Bruce folded his thick arms across his chest.

A hundred-year-old oak tree would be less unyielding. Grace placed a stilling hand on Tyler's thigh. "Let's put off this conversation until after the wedding."

Tyler wore his best salesman smile. His attention remained directed at Bruce. "You have over a thousand acres. Only a few would be affected by the drilling. Trust me...it's a small inconvenience for large profits. With the extra money, you could secure the ranch's future and never have to worry about drought, low cattle prices, or high taxes."

As he stood, Bruce's chair scraped against the wood floor. "We are doing just fine here. We don't need a big oil company coming to our rescue. I'll give you an answer, but not until after the wedding." With a stiff back and long stride, Bruce left the room.

Seconds later, Grace heard the back door bang shut.

"I'm sorry if I upset him. But I really think that deal is the best thing for your family's future." Tyler laid an arm on the back of Grace's chair and combed his fingers through her hair.

She knew that was more for his comfort than hers. In business, Tyler liked to win, and with her dad, victory wouldn't come easy, if at all.

"Bruce is a proud man." Joslyn rested a hand on

the back of Bruce's empty chair. "And stubborn. He'll come around. I know you have our family's best interest at heart."

Needing an escape from the tension lingering in the room, Grace picked up a few empty bowls and brought them to the kitchen, with her mom following right behind her.

"You leave the cleaning to me." Joslyn lifted the handle to the faucet and began filling the sink. "Go take a walk with Tyler before nightfall."

Of course, Mom was right. Her attention should focus on Tyler and keeping his mind off of business for the rest of his stay. Grace waited out on the front porch while Tyler changed his clothes. The sun hung low in the sky, highlighting cotton candy clouds that swirled with shades of purple and pink. Leaning over the porch rail, she was struck by how long she'd been gone—four years of college, and then another five working in Dallas. Coming home for the occasional holiday or family celebration wasn't enough. This homecoming was only temporary, but she needed to make the most of it.

Tyler came to stand beside her and lifted a lock of her hair, running it between his fingers. "You are stunning."

She took his hand and led him across the lawn to the large, red barn. "I remember when you and Alex would be out here playing basketball." The hoop hung lopsided off the barn wall, now providing a good nesting spot for a family of birds. She pointed to the small window up in the hayloft. "I would hide in there and watch you."

Tyler laughed. "Really? I was too busy beating

Alex to notice a little caterpillar dangling above us." He pulled her toward him. "You must have liked it when I took off my shirt."

His warm breath tickled her ear. "That was my favorite part." Grace leaned against the wood siding of the barn. Even as a teenager, Tyler had had a body that made girls swoon. And she'd done her fair share of swooning. "I would have given anything for that sweaty, shirtless boy to have noticed me and kissed me silly."

He rested his hands on the barn, one on each side of her body, pinning her against the wall. "If I could go back in time, I would've kissed you silly, braces and all. I guess now I have to make up for lost time."

She sighed at the tingling sensation of his light bites. He nibbled down her neck and over her collarbone. His lips came to meet hers, firm and demanding. Grace wrapped her arms around his neck and ran her fingers across his broad shoulders.

Suddenly, a force slammed into them, sending Grace tumbling to the ground.

"*Hmpf*." Heath peeked over the pile of horse blankets he was carrying. "I'm sorry. I didn't see you when I came around the corner." He tossed the blankets on the ground and extended his hand to help up Grace.

"Are you okay, sweetheart?" Tyler stepped forward to block Heath and took her hand, pulling her off the dirt.

She could smell the familiar and comforting scent of the horse stable on Heath. He wore it like his filthy clothes, which was probably the result of mucking out the stalls. His baseball cap covered damp hair. For Grace, he carried with him the sweet smell of her youth.

Grace stood still while Tyler stepped away, as if he was avoiding contamination from Heath's grime.

"You really should watch where you're going," Tyler said.

Tyler looked at Heath, obviously sizing him up, and Grace fought the urge to roll her eyes. *Men.* Heath wiped what she could only imagine was horse poop onto his pant leg and held out his hand for Tyler. In Heath's eyes, she caught a glint of smug humor, making her almost laugh out loud.

After the handshake, Tyler glanced at his hand and frowned. "You must be the Murray's new ranch hand."

"Started today." Heath hooked his thumbs in the front pockets of his jeans.

"This is the man who saved me from drowning." She hoped Tyler would feel some sense of obligation and at the very least be civil.

Tyler's gaze went from inspecting his hand to Heath's face. "I'm Grace's fiancé, Tyler Ross. Pleasure to meet you. Thanks for saving my future wife."

"Heath is helping out Dad until the wedding. He's staying in one of our bunkhouses." She glanced from Heath's dirty boots to Tyler's white sneakers. As different as a draft horse from a thoroughbred. Neither better than the other. Each just served a different purpose. And she knew enough to appreciate both.

A dark expression clouded Tyler's face. "I need to go wash my hands before we can finish our walk." He kissed her cheek and went back to the house. His legs carried him with long strides.

"So that's the infamous Tyler." Heath watched Tyler with narrowed eyes.

"The one and only." She brushed off dirt and bits

of straw that were speckled over her bare legs. "How do you like farm work so far?"

"If you're asking if I mind the dirt and smell, then no, it doesn't bother me. I've had much worse. Plus, your dad's a great boss."

"Good." She found the smudge of dirt streaking across his cheekbone strangely appealing. Her fingers itched to clean it off but only because she wanted to touch his skin. She talked with him for another minute, until Tyler returned and possessively took hold of her hand.

"Let's go." Tyler pulled her along with him.

"Bye, Heath," she said. "And go take a shower." Grace finally let her built-up laughter escape.

"Will do, ma'am." Heath tipped the brim of his baseball cap at her.

He strode away, smiling like a naughty schoolboy. Tyler increased his grip on her hand and led her toward the pasture.

"What's his deal? Don't get me wrong, I'm thankful he saved you, but what was your dad thinking? Hiring a stranger and letting him live here. I don't think it's safe."

A strong hint of annoyance filled his voice. "Dad trusts him, and so do I." She strolled with Tyler along the fence line and when she stopped, she reached over to rub the nose of a yearling heifer.

The bovine licked her hand, and then shook its head.

"Hey, little lady." She stroked the heifer's silky, brindle-colored coat. "Your horns are growing so big. You must be proud."

Tyler grasped her shoulders and spun her to face

him. "I'm only worried about you. When I leave, I need to know you'll be safe."

Tyler's fingers dug into the flesh of her upper arm. She shrugged out of his hold. Why was he acting so aggressive? This dominant, territorial behavior was unlike him. "I'm in more danger from my own clumsiness than anything else. Heath saved my life, don't forget."

A scowl soured his expression. "I don't like him. He's the type of guy you can't turn your back on."

The heifer moved toward Tyler, who stepped back to avoid a lick from a long, gray tongue. "Gross," he muttered.

"I wouldn't mind it if you spent more time here. You could protect me from the boogie man." She slipped her hands into his back pockets. What could she say to convince him to work remotely from the ranch?

Tyler cleared his throat before kissing her gently on the cheek. "I found out this week that I have to travel to Mexico. I'll be there for the next month. I'm sorry, babe. I hate to leave you for so long right before our wedding."

Her gut churned. How could he leave now and shrug off the burden of planning their wedding? She opened her mouth in protest then snapped it closed. As much as she didn't want him to leave, this business trip was good for his career. She was marrying an oil executive, so she couldn't balk at his busy travel schedule. "I understand. When do you leave?"

"I leave Tuesday." He stroked her back. "This trip could mean a huge promotion. I'm doing this for us. I want to give you the kind of life you deserve."

His soft touch helped release her tension. She

didn't want a rich, fancy lifestyle, but those feelings would be lost on Tyler, so she kept them to herself. Sure, she liked nice things but could be just as happy without them. Her time spent at True Horizon had proven that. "Well, I'll be so busy with wedding plans to miss you." She softly pinched his nose.

"You better miss me," he growled into her neck.

The sun had disappeared behind the horizon, and thousands of stars started their nightly show.

Would spending a month apart right before the wedding weaken their bond? She already started to feel a crack in their relationship. Did he feel it as well?

She held his hand against her heart, hoping the contact would soothe her doubts. "Let's just enjoy the time we do have together."

****

Lying on his bed, Heath reached over and opened the paisley curtains, exposing the night sky. He shifted his weight and put his hands behind his head, causing the metal springs to squeak underneath him. He was transfixed by the view through the window, countless stars shone brightly, seemingly only for him. Without city lights, the night got truly dark—just like in Afghanistan, where he'd spent so many nights.

His time in the Army had given him some good things: friends, adventure, weapon skills, and travel— all wrapped into a neat, camouflage package. But along with the good came the bad. The experience had shaped him into the man he was today—a partially defective human being.

The sound of muffled screams drifted through the open window. Instinct had him bolting out of bed. His highly trained ears strained to identify the direction of

64

the noise, which seemed to come from the direction of the stable. The screaming was getting more frequent and louder. Grabbing his pants and shirt, he yanked them on before slipping on his boots. While passing through the kitchen, he grabbed the two-foot length of steel pipe he'd earlier discovered, which probably was part of some long ago neglected plumbing project.

Following his instincts after years of specialized military training, he approached the building with short, cautious steps. He scanned the surroundings. Everything appeared normal.

The large, main door was closed, but light shone through the side door. Heath slowly opened the door and peered inside. Quiet for now, besides the occasional neighing of horses and the pounding of his heart.

A dim light glowed at the back of the barn.

Crouching, he hustled toward the low wall that divided the rear from the main section. Another scream sounded, and Heath instinctively darted forward, expecting to find a murdered body. Instead, he found Grace, curled up on several haystacks. A series of high-pitched squeals came from the television she'd propped against the wall.

Grace turned her head toward him, jumped, and let out a blood-curdling cry. "Holy cow! You scared the living daylights out of me." She flapped her hands. Tears pooled at the corners of her eyes.

"You?" His heart thudded hard, threatening to burst out of his chest. He pushed down the desire to pull her into a protective embrace. "I thought someone was getting murdered back here. What are you doing?"

She grabbed the remote and clicked pause. A mutilated face froze on the screen. "I'm watching a movie." She tipped her head to meet his gaze. "Zombie Slayer 4."

His relieved laugh sounded almost hysterical. "You're out here watching a scary movie, alone, at night? You're nuts."

"The Zombie Slayer movies are my favorite. I haven't had a chance to see the new one yet. Tyler was tired and went to sleep. I used to watch scary movies out here all the time when I was younger." She lifted her chin.

He became totally absorbed by the vision of her, bundled up in a black-and-yellow blanket despite the heat. She'd made a lounge chair out of stacked hay bales. The seating arrangement actually looked comfortable. A black, shaggy dog lay next to her, its head resting on her lap. With the flat screen against the barn wall, this was a perfect spot for watching horror movies.

"I didn't know they made a fourth Zombie Slayer." Heath studied the empty DVD case. "We used to watch these in Afghanistan."

"Bring over a bale and join me." She patted the spot next to her. "The movie just started. Sasha woke up from her coma. Remember at the end of the third movie, when she got hit on the head by Zach's machete and fell into the zombie pit?"

"I thought she died." Heath pulled a horse blanket off the shelf and got comfortable.

Grace offered him the popcorn bowl.

For a split second, he questioned whether this was a good idea, sitting so close together in the dark.

She was too trusting, too pretty, and too enjoyable to be around. And she was very much in love with another man. So he grabbed a handful of popcorn.

Grace started the movie. "When Sasha woke up in the pit, all the zombies were gone." She picked up a big cup and took a sip out of the straw. "Now, she's trying to locate her sister. She's met a group of survivors who took her in, but she doesn't know if she can trust them."

"Who's the dude with the mullet?" He tossed more popcorn into his mouth. This was the good stuff, air popped with real butter. Not the microwave kind he always overcooked, making awful-smelling smoke and a snack that tasted like burnt plastic.

She laughed, and then groaned. "I guess it doesn't matter anymore. The dude with the mullet's arm just got ripped off by a zombie." Another person got bit, and Grace squirmed.

"You okay?" He enjoyed watching her cute face scrunch up with each disgusting scene.

"I really do love this." She smiled. "I'm so happy to share my love of all things zombie. Tyler hates these kinds of movies, and my parents won't let me watch them in the house. That's how I ended up with a movie theater in the barn." While the man on the screen struggled to fight off Hollywood zombies, Grace's startled cry broke into laughter.

He enjoyed the next two hours at her side, and he frequently caught himself staring at her. Luckily, she was too engrossed in the movie to notice. She had an air of innocence about her, and he hoped the world would never take away that. Grace needed to stay safe from people like him.

Earlier, when he'd seen her wrapped in Tyler's embrace, he'd wanted to rip her away from the prick. The strength of that desire had frightened him. Anger

67

was a common feeling. Jealousy, on the other hand, was brand new.

When the ending credits started rolling across the screen, Grace turned off the TV, shaking her head. "That movie was as silly as it was scary. My favorite is still the second one."

"That came out when I was at Fort Benning. I remember a few of us organizing a first-run showing for the base."

"How old were you when you enlisted?" She sat with her legs crossed and tucked beneath her.

Her wide eyes looked like melted dark chocolate. They were so deep and inviting, he imagined drowning in them. "I was eighteen, right out of high school. I've been out for the past year and a half."

"That must be a tough transition." She pulled a piece of hay out of the bale and twirled it between her fingers. "Do you ever wonder why things happen the way that they do? Take my accident, for instance. For some reason, you stopped in Liberty Ridge. You were there to save me."

"In regards to my own fortune, I don't believe in luck. But I'm glad I came to Liberty Ridge that day, even if it meant a broken bike and a pause in my travels." And the chance to be here, sitting next to Grace.

"What are you searching for? Or what are you running from?" Reaching over, she touched his arm.

She looked at him like she was peering into his soul. A shiver ran through his body, and he stood, brushing hay off his pants. "You really don't want to know. Don't lift the hood to get a closer look. It's not good…what's inside."

Chapter Seven

After a week of working on the ranch, every muscle in Heath's body ached. At the end of each day, he crawled into bed and was asleep within seconds. Last night, for the first time in years, his sleep had remained undisturbed by nightmares. That morning, he'd awakened energized and refreshed. Out in the fields, he could think clearer. Was that the result of the fresh air or the physically demanding work? Whatever the reason, he hoped it signaled the catalyst for a fresh start.

He had just finished putting on his shirt when a knock sounded. Opening the front door, he saw Grace walking back across the yard.

She looked over her shoulder and smiled. "You're too skinny. Eat."

His minimalist lifestyle had lent to a significantly slimmer frame since leaving the Army. How much weight would he put on if he continued to stay, between the home-cooked breakfast and lunch he was provided every day?

He pulled his gaze off Grace long enough to see the breakfast tray placed on his porch. They'd fallen into a routine. Every morning for the past week, Grace would leave his breakfast on the bunkhouse porch. Then, she'd tell him to eat up because he was too skinny—the only words she'd spoken to him since the night they'd watched the zombie movie in the barn. Besides bringing him breakfast, she'd kept her distance.

He wondered if that night, he'd been truthful enough to scare her away. As much as he hated to admit it, he enjoyed her friendship. After all this time alone, he'd forgotten how good having someone to share a joke with felt. But was that selfish, knowing she might not be safe with him?

He carried his food inside and ate in a hurry. Plenty of chores waited. Once he was finished, he stood and grabbed his empty plate, causing the rickety kitchen table to wobble. Heath looked out the front window to see Grace sitting on a rocking chair with her laptop. She wasn't looking at her computer, but staring across the yard in the direction of his house. A part of him wanted to go over there, kneel in front of her, and come clean. His soul yearned to be unburdened. Would she grow to fear and hate him? Probably, and that wasn't a chance he was willing to take.

Tomorrow, he had a day off. With his motorcycle now fixed, he might ride into town. See what trouble he could find in Liberty Ridge.

Another knock sounded at his door. Thinking it was Grace again, he smoothed back his hair with the palm of his hand. "Who are you trying to impress, stupid?" he muttered to himself.

He opened the door and saw Bruce standing outside, holding two rifles.

"You finished with your breakfast, son?"

"Yes, sir. I was getting ready to head over to the paddock and check on the bull." Did the man know Heath had just been ogling his daughter? With a gun in each of Bruce's meaty hands, he sure hoped not.

Bruce descended the porch steps with a scowl on his weather-lined face. "Never mind the bull. You're coming with me."

As Heath sat on the ATV, he fought the urge to chuck his breakfast. Bruce drove through the pasture. Minutes slowly ticked by in silence. Ahead, he saw a dark spot resting on a small hill. It appeared to be a rock, until the vehicle got closer. Not a rock, but a dead calf.

"Coyotes," Bruce said as they came to a stop. "The monsters come back every summer and hunt my calves and pick off weaker members of my herd. The dogs do a good job of running 'em off, but they can't be everywhere."

Heath hopped off the ATV and followed Bruce over to the calf. The smell of decaying flesh made him sick to his stomach. He breathed in through his mouth to avoid inhaling anymore of the awful scent. "What do you need me to do?"

"Last night, this poor little guy's mom scared away the coyotes before they could drag him off. Now, we'll wait for 'em to return. Coyotes can't resist an easy meal." Bruce pulled out the rifles and handed one to Heath. "I figured you must be a good shot, so we're goin' hunting."

The familiar weight of the cool metal settled in his hands. The rifle was similar to the semi-automatic he'd used in the Army. He looked through the scope, scanning the terrain. "It's been awhile since I've shot a rifle. Not sure how my aim will hold up."

The men returned to the ATV and drove around to another hill, one which placed them downwind and gave them a good view of the carcass.

71

Taking a prone position, Heath waited patiently, just as he'd been trained. Ranger school seemed so long ago. On those courses, he'd covered himself with branches and earth-colored face paint, and then waited in the woods for hours. Slowly, he would creep inch by inch until he lined up his shot. Sometimes, he'd work all day to reach his goal unseen. Nothing like the Rangers to teach a man patience.

Even though they were in the shade of a mesquite tree, the air was still hot. The tree's long, narrow pods littered the ground. Heath swatted at the fire ants crawling and stinging his arm. A few thunderheads hovered to the west. Besides the insects that buzzed around their heads, all was still. Not a coyote to be found.

After two hours without action, they took a break for lunch. Bruce lifted out a red cooler from the ATV and unpacked the food, which was cold chicken, cucumber salad, and fruit. While they ate, Bruce talked about Alex.

"I was disappointed when he came to me with dreams of culinary school instead of working with me on the ranch. He bought the old Wagon Wheel restaurant in town and totally gutted the place. It's called the Desert Rose now, and they serve the best food in town." Bruce put on his wide-brimmed hat and grabbed hold of his rifle. "You live here much longer, and I'm buying you one of these." He pointed to his weathered Stetson. "It keeps the sun off your face and neck. Better than those baseball caps."

Heath slipped his old cap on his head. "I'm pretty attached to this hat. Belonged to a good friend."

"Must've been a good friend. The thing's seen

better days."

"He was the best." John's face flashed in Heath's mind. The two of them in Afghanistan, walking across the base, and that beloved Warrior baseball cap resting on John's head. The hat had been a Christmas gift from John's wife. Now Heath wore it in memory of his friend's loyalty, right up to the very end.

After they finished eating, they got into position, and the minutes crept along.

Suddenly, a lone coyote came upon the hill, sniffing the air. It let out a yip, and two more appeared. They began circling the dead calf.

Bruce nodded and held his rifle in position.

Heath lay still and studied the animal's movement through his scope. One was acting as lookout, while the other two ate. Heath leveled his rifle at the coyote on the left.

Bruce gave him the thumbs-up and aimed at his own target.

The center of the animal's body lay in his crosshairs. Heath slowed his breathing into a controlled, steady rhythm. His finger gave slight pressure on the trigger. Blinking once, then twice, he fired. Bruce's shot followed immediately.

Both coyotes dropped, and the third one ran off.

The men rode over to the other hill and tossed the dead coyotes in the bed of the ATV.

"I'll have one of the other guys come out here with the tractor to haul away the calf carcass. Thanks for your help," Bruce said.

When they returned to the barn, Heath finished his work for the day and took a long, hot shower. The sound of gun shots still rang in his ears. His hands shook from the ghost feeling of the gun. The experience had breathed life into memories he'd just as soon forget.

He checked the time—still too early to head out for the evening. So he lay in bed, only meaning to shut his eyes for a minute. His eyelids grew heavy as the weight of his body lifted. The room suddenly felt hot and dry. He was no longer in the bunkhouse but in a dirt hut surrounded by scared women and children. "Where is he?" he screamed in English.

The group huddled in the corner, shaking their heads and shivering.

He grabbed hold of a young boy, maybe five or six years old, and held him by the collar. "Tell me where your father is."

The boy's mother cried and reached out for him.

Heath pulled him closer, out of her reach. Still holding the boy's dirty shirt, he walked outside and stepped into the blinding sun. His eyes slowly adjusted to the light. Spread out before him on the ground were the bodies of women and children—all dead.

Flies buzzed around the carnage. The smell made him gag. He ran over to a small bush and emptied the contents of his stomach. The boy he'd been holding only seconds before was lying on the ground dead, next to his deceased mother. His vacant eyes stared up at Heath. His mouth twisted in pain.

Standing in a sea of death, Heath felt a familiar panic rise, making him want to run, but he found his boots stuck in mud. He screamed for help. All was quiet. Looking at the ground, he saw hands ascend through the mud to grab hold of his leg.

A scream broke from his lips right before he awoke

in the bunkhouse. Taking a few deep breaths to calm the tremors racking his body, Heath focused on the room around him. *This is real, not the dream.* He rolled out of bed and headed to the bathroom. Standing in front of the sink, he splashed cold water on his face. After drying off, he stared at his reflection in the mirror. "Murderer." He acted as judge and jury, pronouncing guilt and a life sentence in one breath.

Once he shook out the last web of the dream, he grabbed his wallet and left the house. His Harley rested under the shade of an ash tree. He straddled the bike and hit the ignition. The deep, throaty sound of the engine drowned the screams still echoing in his head.

He rode fast and careless down the country roads. If he crashed and died, who'd care? The world might be better off without him. Pain and regret clawed at the hole in his chest.

Finally, he drove across the Hickory River Bridge and toward the brick buildings that comprised downtown Liberty Ridge. The Damn Yankee bar sat in sharp contrast to the otherwise quiet street. People milled around on the outdoor patio, and a constant stream flowed in and out the door. He parked his bike on the street and went inside, searching for a much-needed release.

****

A buzzing sound startled Grace out of a good dream. She blindly reached over, slapped down her hand on her nightstand a few times before making contact with her cell phone. "Hello," she said in a raspy voice, still half asleep.

"Hey, it's Molly. Can you come to the police station?"

Now she was wide awake. She pushed her hair away from her face, and then had to go back to remove a few strands stuck to her lips. "Why? What happened?"

Molly cleared her throat. "Your dad hired Heath Carter, right?"

Grace glanced at the clock. Why would Molly call in the middle of the night to ask about Heath? "Yeah, he's been working at the ranch."

"I know he saved you from drowning, so I'm calling you first. He's sitting in one of my holding cells."

Grace sat up like she was spring loaded. "Was he arrested?"

Noise sounded in the background, and the phone crackled.

"No, I put him there for his own safekeeping," Molly said. "I'm hoping you can talk to him and reason with him. He might listen to you, plus I thought not involving your dad was for the best."

"What did Heath do?" Did she really want to hear the answer? After flipping on the light, she held the phone to her ear while slipping on a pair of shorts.

"I'll explain everything when you get here."

"Leaving now. See you soon." Her breath came out in short, shallow bursts. Nervous tension buzzed inside her belly. She hoped whatever he'd done wasn't too bad. And took comfort in knowing Molly would have not called Grace if she thought Heath was dangerous.

Twenty minutes later, when Grace walked into the Liberty Ridge Police Station, she approached the young male officer behind the front desk. "I'm here to see Molly Hernandez."

The officer flashed a toothy smile. "You must be Grace. I'll let her know you're here." He picked up the phone and made a call.

Molly quickly appeared from out of the police bullpen and escorted Grace to her desk.

She lowered herself onto a chair and scooted her bottom to rest at the edge of the padded seat.

Molly pulled her chair forward, resting her folded hands on top of a tall stack of paperwork.

"Spill, Molly. What happened?"

"Heath was in an altercation tonight." Molly sighed. "At the Damn Yankee. He could have been seriously hurt."

Grace's stomach dropped to her feet. "So, he's all right?"

"From witness statements, he was drinking heavily. Then picked a fight with three Navy boys. The match was not fair, and Heath's lucky he got out of there in one piece. A couple other guys stepped in to break up things. When I got to the scene, Heath was sitting on the curb outside the bar. The guys who broke up the fight were keeping an eye on him to make sure he didn't get into any more trouble."

Mild-mannered Heath had started a bar fight? That couldn't be true. During his time on the ranch, he seemed like a quiet, gentle man. She'd forgotten she didn't know a lot about him. His calm exterior could be hiding danger. "He wasn't arrested." Grace folded her arms around her churning stomach. "That's good…right?"

One of Molly's dark brows lifted. "No one is pressing charges, but I held him for a few hours to allow him to calm down and sober up. I hope you'll take him to the ranch."

"Let me talk to him." Uneasiness gripped her. What kind of condition was he in? And would he accept her help?

Molly led her through several corridors, the sound of their footsteps echoed in the quiet hall. After Molly unlocked a door at the bottom of the stairs, they entered the small room that held four jail cells. Only one cell was presently occupied, with its door closed.

Grace approached, her insides twisted with nervous jitters. She looked into the cell and saw Heath lying on his back on a low cot. An arm slung over his face.

"Heath," Molly barked. "I'm willing to release you to Grace if you agree to go directly home. No more trouble."

Besides the small rise and fall of his chest, Heath lay perfectly still. He gave no sign that he'd heard Molly.

The remainder of Grace's patience evaporated. What an ingrate! He was ignoring them. First, she'd been awakened in the middle of the night to come to the police station. Then, Heath didn't even have the courtesy to acknowledge her. Her temper flared, but she quickly reined it in. She might be crazy for agreeing to see him home but she did owe him her life.

"You're acting like an idiot," she snapped. Letting her anger show might be the only way to get through to the thick-headed fool. The good cop approach obviously wasn't working. "Get up. I want to head home and get back to sleep."

Molly's dark brown eyes widened. Her jaw hung slack. "You go, girl," she whispered.

Very slowly, Heath lifted himself to a sitting

position and set his feet on the cement floor.

Dried blood caked one eyebrow and the side of his beard. Marks dotted his arms, and a dark shadow covered his left eye.

"I didn't ask you to come."

His voice was hoarse. "You look terrible." She smiled like she would for a willful child, which was exactly how he was acting. Where was the gratitude? "You either come with me, or I call my dad. Which do you prefer?"

When he stood, he grunted, and then walked toward them on unsteady legs. "Let's go." His hands gripped the bars.

Molly placed the key in the lock then hesitated. "You promise to go straight home with Grace?"

"Yes." He sighed and rolled his eyes upward, staring at the ceiling.

He was the one acting exasperated when in all fairness, Grace had every right to leave his sorry butt in jail. She recoiled at the smell of alcohol wafting toward her.

Once the door was rolled away, Heath followed her out of the holding cell area.

When they arrived at the front desk, Molly turned to face Grace and Heath, hands on hips. "Heath, I don't expect to see you around my police station again. And Grace, call me when you get home."

"Yes, Officer." Grace hugged her petite friend.

Heath mumbled something and opened the door.

She stepped out into the warm night air, followed by Heath. The fresh air instantly soothed her irritation and worry. "My car's parked over there." She pointed to the lighted parking lot next door.

Around her, the town was silent and dark. The sidewalks and streets were empty of activity. A block away, one stoplight blinked red in a one-sided conversation.

Grace began walking toward her car. When she turned her head to look over her shoulder, she saw Heath headed in the other direction. "Where are you going?" she hollered after him. Her question didn't cause him to hesitate, but he actually quickened his gait.

"I'll go to the ranch but not with you. I'll walk."

If she'd had something hard to throw at his head, she would have. Anything to get through his thick skull. "The ranch is ten miles away, and you're hurt. Stop being difficult and come with me."

"Go home. Leave me alone." Heath continued down the empty street.

Grace followed. The decision to chase Heath was the definition of stupid. She knew that. But deep inside, she trusted him. Rational or not, she couldn't imagine him ever hurting her. On the ranch, she'd dealt with willful animals. She knew how to get them to yield and relent to her direction. Would those same skills work on Heath? Or was his stubborn anger a whole different beast?

As he stepped on to the Hickory River Bridge, she reached out to touch his arm. *Time to find out what you're made of.*

Chapter Eight

Without hesitation, Grace reached out and tapped Heath's arm.

In an instant, he swung around with his fist in the air until recognition dawned in his eyes.

Heath yanked down his arm to lock it at his side.

Her heart thumped inside her chest. "It's me." Grace stepped away out of self-preservation. Luckily, he seemed to be returning to the present. The urge to touch him again burned her fingertips, but she restrained her hand. Not a good idea to poke a grumpy bear. "Please let me take you home. I don't understand why you won't come with me."

"My problems aren't for you to understand." He stared into the dark river, a deep scowl furrowed his brow and pulled at the corners of his lips.

"I want to, if you'll let me in. Tell me what's wrong." She reached over to touch his arm but pulled away.

He turned to face her.

Even in the dark, she could see the storm brewing in his hazel eyes.

"No," he snapped. "Go home. I don't want your help."

Grace stood still and firm, not willing to give in. He reminded her of an angry bull, ready to direct its rage at whoever crossed its path. She remembered when she was thirteen and Dad had instructed her to stay out of the east pasture. Of course, she didn't listen. When he went into the barn, she snuck through the fence and darted across the field, which was the quickest route to her tree house. She made good time until Slash, their large bull, appeared in her path.

He grunted and swung his head, his massive horns cutting the air—*swoosh, swoosh.*

She stopped mid-stride, standing in the middle of the pasture, alone and scared. Dad once explained the bigger the show, the bigger the fear. Don't submit and whatever you do, don't run away. But Slash, standing thirty-feet away, didn't appear the least bit afraid.

Grace gathered every single scrap of courage, puffed out her small chest, and moved slowly toward the fence. She knew not to turn her back on the bull. Thankfully, Slash lowered his head to munch on sweet-grass and let her go in peace. After that day, she had never ventured near that bull or that field again.

Now, as she watched Heath, she replaced her fear with determination. She'd get him into her car, even if the process took the rest of the night. "Why did you pick a fight with three men? Do you have a death wish?"

"I don't owe you an explanation." His words were slightly slurred. "You're the kind of person who sees the best in everything. You think the world is full of sunshine and roses. Well, it's not. You have no idea what's out there." He took a step to leave, but his boot hit an uneven board and sent him stumbling forward.

Grace reached to steady him and pulled him upright. His skin felt hot to the touch. Empathy swelled inside her. "You're right. I haven't seen the things you

82

have. But that doesn't make me any less capable of helping you. Everyone needs people in their life who care about them, so don't walk away from the ones who do."

"I don't need anybody, least of all you." His shoulders slumped, and he stared at the wooden floorboards.

"Well." She set her hands on her hips and looked around at the empty bridge. "Sorry, but I'm all you got right now."

"Go home, Grace. Leave me alone."

His voice held a deep sadness. Tears welled in her eyes. "I'm not letting you wander off in the middle of the night, still tipsy and injured."

His arm extended toward her, sending her heart fluttering wildly, like the wings of a hummingbird.

"Oh, Grace." He ran an index finger down her bare arm. "Don't…."

Heath's soft touch flickered sparks across her skin. His long hair was a disheveled mess, and he was still bloody from the fight. To anyone passing by, he would have looked like a menace to her safety. She held out her hand.

He placed the palm of his over her upturned one. His finger slowly traced the lines on her palm.

A light but electric touch. "Don't what?" She kept the tone of her voice calm and gentle. For the first time since she'd met him, she saw his protective wall start to break.

"I'm not worth your worry." He lowered his arm and took one step backward. "You shouldn't be around someone like me. You're so beautiful." Closing his eyes, he sighed. "And I'm…tainted."

She wrapped her fingers around his hand and searched his face in the light of the crescent moon. "Nobody is beyond repair. Your life is valuable, Heath. Don't ever tell yourself otherwise." Still holding his hand, she led him across the bridge toward her car.

The digital clock in her car read three a.m. when they pulled onto the long, gravel driveway of the ranch. She parked in front of the garage. Next to her, Heath was asleep, quietly snoring. "We're home." She tapped him on the shoulder.

He looked around with half opened lids and opened the door. "Thank you."

She watched him weave his way across the lawn to the bunkhouse and disappear inside. He was safe, for now, and she was exhausted. With heavy steps, she climbed upstairs to her own bedroom and flopped on the bed.

As tired as she was, one word kept tumbling around in her mind and kept her from getting to sleep— tainted. Is that how he saw himself? What had happened in his past that made him feel that way?

The answers she sought might be as close as her laptop. In mere minutes, her fingers were tapping across the keyboard, typing the name *Heath Carter, US Army* into the web search bar. Clicking a promising link, she was shocked by the picture now on the screen. Looking back was a man she hardly recognized. In his official Army photograph, Heath looked the classic American soldier. His short brown hair was mostly hidden under a green beret. Without his beard, Heath looked years younger, and she noticed a deep dimple on the left cheek of his serious face. His handsome appearance stole her breath.

Heath Carter was listed as a Sergeant First Class and member of the Army Special Forces.

Grace scanned through a few more links before she found an article from a Florida newspaper, telling of their hometown hero. The story said that after joining the Army, Heath quickly climbed the ranks. He served as an Army Ranger, and then earned the rank of Sergeant and finally joined the elite Special Forces. He was awarded the Bronze Star for his heroic actions during a firefight in Afghanistan. While taking enemy fire, Heath broke cover to help four wounded soldiers who were lying exposed. After moving them to a secure location, he rendered medical aid, consequently saving all four lives.

The article went on to quote his aunt, Linda Carter, along with a former high school teacher. At the bottom of the screen was his high school yearbook picture. His cocky, crooked grin was charming and really showed off his cute dimple. He looked like a very mischievous youth.

If she'd met him in high school, would she have fallen for bad boy Heath instead of clean-cut Tyler? That question was better left unanswered.

She clicked out of the website and closed her laptop. From what she'd read, Heath had been a model soldier and hero. He'd spent years moving through the ranks to be sent to the front line on the war on terror. That was his goal, right? To be the first one called for the toughest missions and put his life on the line to save others in need. He'd jumped into a river to save her, a stranger, and she'd be forever in his debt for that heroic action. Somehow, she'd have to find a way to repay him.

Nothing she uncovered explained what had turned him into the lost soul he was today. The only person who could tell her that was Heath. She thought of him as a computer program guarded by a firewall. All she needed was the time and patience to find a way through. If she was to help him, she'd have to gain his trust and get him to talk. And that task would not be easy.

****

Heath's natural alarm clock buzzed inside his head, demanding he get out of bed. *Fine*. Time he opened his eyes and faced the reality of what happened last night. Or at least, what he could remember.

He propped himself up on his elbows in an attempt to sit. The room spun in one direction then the other. Immediately, he returned his head to the pillow and closed his eyes. A groan sounded from somewhere deep within his aching chest. The bedroom curtains acted as gatekeepers, keeping the bright sunlight confined to a narrow slice that shone along the edges.

Lucky for him, he had the day off of work. The memory of last night remained foggy, but his body happily filled him in on the details. His nose throbbed, most likely broken. When he flexed his fingers, the scrapes on his knuckles stung. And his right eye, well, he was pretty sure it sported a tender bruise. Instead of crying in pain, he laughed, which made his ribs shoot off a stabbing pain.

Why did he find so much happiness in feeling so miserable? Maybe he was crazy. Or maybe pain was the only way he could be sure he was still alive. Probably a combination of both.

The red rage that had receded over the past week

reappeared last night, raising its ugly head. A reminder that he couldn't become too comfortable. His calm life at True Horizon Ranch could implode without warning.

Very slowly, he inched his body toward the edge of the bed and, after a minute, rose to a sitting position. He touched his feet to the cool wood floor and crept toward the bathroom. The thought of the food tray most likely left on his front porch almost sent him to his knees with nausea.

After a long shower, he felt almost human again. He pulled back the curtains covering the large picture window in the front room and squinted into the brightness. Sunlight streamed inside and chased away the gloom.

His new home was small, with a combined sitting room and kitchen in front. A bedroom and bathroom were set in the rear. The interior was decorated in the western style—what he'd expect on a Texas ranch. Practical, and for the most part, comfortable.

He brewed a pot of coffee and poured a cup. Once seated on the small sofa, he took sips of the lifesaving brew while reading yesterday's paper. The stories were mostly about high school football and the weather. A drought threatened to increase feed prices and subsequently shrink herd sizes. Heath wondered how Bruce made a living, year after year, off the unpredictable land.

His grandparents had lived in a small town like Liberty Ridge. They weren't ranchers, though, but one of the few wealthy families in their town and had cut ties with Heath after disinheriting their only child, his mother. Now, the only thing he had to remember them by was the contents of the envelope sitting on top the dresser. And for the time being, he would ignore the letter from his grandparents' lawyer.

The caffeine from his coffee started activating his brain. He washed out his empty cup and slipped on his boots. Heath walked outside. A nice breeze blew from the west, taking some of the sting out of the hot air. When he was halfway to the barn, he heard his name called. His gut wrenched with memory. Grace had been with him last night. She'd brought him home. He prayed a sinkhole would open underneath him and swallow him whole—anything to avoid facing her.

With a cheery expression on her pretty face, she ran to catch him. Her dark braid swung behind her back, and he was having a hard time not staring at her long legs. His attention became fixated on a small oval mark on her thigh.

She caught his gaze and smiled, pointing to the birthmark. "I hated that mark until my mother started calling it an angel kiss."

Good lord, could he make any bigger fool of himself? Probably, but best not make an attempt. He gulped and pulled his awareness to her dark brown eyes, which were safer to look at than her legs. "Good morning. Sorry, I didn't eat my breakfast. Didn't have much of an appetite."

She laughed. "More like good afternoon, and don't worry about the food. The pigs appreciated the extra treat."

He stood, shifting his weight between his wide-spread legs. He jammed his hands into the front pockets of his jeans. Much to his chagrin, he remained tongue-tied, unable to think of anything to say.

The shaggy, black dog that followed Heath around

the ranch came running toward them and pushed his nose against Grace's leg.

Heath was grateful for the distraction. "Thanks for getting me home last night," he finally blurted out. "You could have just left me in jail. I deserved it."

She shrugged. "No big deal. What are friends for?" Bending over, she gave the dog a scratch behind his floppy ear.

Is that what she thought of him—a friend? He stepped away, ready to continue his walk to the barn, when she reached out and touched his arm. A spark shot straight to his heart, and he involuntarily flinched. Did Grace notice the effect she had on him? Hope not. She'd tell her dad. If Bruce knew Heath's intense attraction to his only daughter, he'd toss him out on his rear.

The dog moved from Grace to Heath and licked at his hand, and then sat at his feet with his pink tongue lolling out the side of his mouth.

"Shadow's been with us since he was a pup." Grace tilted her head toward the dog. "My dad brought him home from the shelter ten years ago. You give him a little love, and he'll be your best friend."

Heath rubbed the dog's shaggy head. "Pretty soon, I'll have more friends than I'll know what to do with."

Shadow looked at him with amber eyes and barked.

"Seriously, though, thanks again for last night. The events are somewhat hazy, but I do know I'd still be wandering the countryside if not for your persistence." He grinned, causing a burst of pain inside his busted nose. "Would you mind giving me a ride into town so I can get my bike? The poor girl will develop a complex if I keep abandoning her."

Grace laughed. "Sure, but you'll have to make it up to me."

Her smile was pure innocence, but the spark in her eyes told a different story. "Is that so?" A slow smile emerged as he crossed his arms. "Name it."

"Do you know how to ride? Horses, that is."

"That's a negative, ma'am."

"Well, I guess it's time you learn." She rubbed her hands together. "The ranch is fun to explore on horseback."

"As grateful as I am that you sprung me from jail, I'm not interested in death by horse. Is there anything else I can do? Wash your car? Paint your nails? I'm building your wedding gazebo, don't forget." His internal temperature rose along with his panic. The thought of riding one of those huge beasts made his nausea revisit with full force.

"You were in the Army, right?" she asked.

Afraid of where this line of questioning was headed, he nodded.

"You jumped out of planes? Fast roped out of helicopters? Was shot at?"

"Affirmative."

"But you're afraid of riding a sweet, tame horse?" A smirk formed on her face.

"I didn't say I was afraid." Too late, he realized his assertion of fearlessness was tantamount to surrender. How would he get out of this situation with his male pride still intact? *News flash, soldier—you're not.* Grace was on the offensive and showed no signs of surrender.

"Great! I'll go change and meet you in the stables." She smiled and took off toward the house, her spry legs moving quickly across the lawn.

He forced his gaze away and slowly walked to the stables. "I survived multiple tours in a war zone only to be ensnared by a bewitching siren and lured to my death on horseback," he muttered to himself.

Bruce exited the stable and gave Heath a hearty pat on the back. "Ain't that the way it goes, son? But if you're lucky, she won't let you escape her net."

Chapter Nine

Inside the stable, Grace went about preparing the horses, while Heath stood silently watching her like a cornered cat. She led out a chestnut mare and handed him the reins.

"This is Daisy." Grace rubbed the fury patch between the horse's nostrils. "She's a sweet girl and will take good care of you. I'll get her saddled."

Heath folded his arms across his chest. His widened gaze darted from Grace to the horse.

Grace found Heath's reluctance to ride a horse very surprising. He seemed fearless, to the point of recklessness. The twist and turns of his personality continued to intrigue her. She went to the tack room to grab a saddle and when she returned, he was gently rubbing the horse's nose and whispering something she couldn't hear.

Daisy obviously could, because she snorted and shook her head.

Her curiosity got the better of her. "What are you telling Daisy?"

"We made a deal." He scratched the horse behind one velvety ear. "If she's kind to me, then I'll treat her to a juicy apple."

She laughed and tossed a red blanket across the horse's back. "And what about me? What's my treat if I'm kind to you?"

"You can have an apple, too."

His smile lit the dusty stable. A fat, orange barn cat strolled past them and rubbed its body along his leg.

She lifted the saddle onto the horse's back and tightened the cinch, tugging the end to make sure it was secure but not too tight. She could just picture Heath sprawled on the ground because the saddle slipped. With one black eye already and a swollen nose, he didn't need any more injuries.

Finishing with Daisy, she patted the horse on the rump. "I'll be right back." She handed the reins to Heath.

Grace entered Silver's stall. A long time had passed since she had ridden her favorite mare. Golden strands of sunlight filtered through the cracks in the barn siding, highlighting the horse's gray hair. She slipped the bridle over the mare's head, fastened the buckles, and took hold of the reins. When she brought Silver into the wide aisle where Heath waited, she saw Daisy nudging him with her velvet muzzle and blowing warm breath onto his face.

With Daisy's stamp of approval, Grace knew without a doubt Heath was a good man. "I think she likes you." She saddled Silver with an efficiency that came with years of riding. Then, she turned her attention to Heath. "Okay, let's get you in the saddle."

"You're really making me do this? I just remembered…Bruce wanted to talk to me about a few of the heifers."

The raveled edge of nervousness sounded in his voice. Setting her hand on a flaming skull tattoo that decorated Heath's arm, she softened her expression. "Do you trust me?"

He looked at her for several seconds before swallowing hard. Sweat beaded from the deep creases of his forehead. "Yes," he finally said. "Yes, I do."

"You'll be all right." She guided both horses out of the barn with Heath following and keeping a good ten feet of distance. Stopping by a section of fence surrounding the horse paddock, she tied up Silver and Daisy. Then, she reached down to grab the stirrup hanging from Daisy's saddle. "Slide your left foot in here and grab hold of the horn up on top."

Heath followed her directions, looking awkward as he stood on one foot and leaned against the horse.

"As you pull yourself up, swing your right leg over the horse's rear," she instructed.

He completed the motion in one easy stroke and grinned. "I did it!"

"See, you're a natural." Grace placed the small, soft-sided cooler filled with their lunch into the saddle bag on Daisy.

He squeezed the saddle horn so hard, his hands had turned an unnatural shade of white.

When Daisy took a few steps forward, Heath's head whipped around and his widened eyes stared in her direction. "She's taking off," he yelled.

Laughing, she swung herself onto Silver and directed the horse toward the open field. Daisy and Heath fell in line behind her.

Heath gave a startled shout.

She turned to make sure he was still on his horse. "Loosen your grip on the reins," she called back. "Daisy knows what to do." She made a few clicking sounds, and Daisy trotted to catch up. She watched as Heath bumped and swayed in the saddle. Thankfully, he remained upright.

"How am I doing so far?" He managed a small smile through clenched teeth.

"You're doing great." She ran her hand through the silky mane of her horse. "We're going through the main gates and into the cattle pasture. Once we cross the creek, there's a small gate that leads to a trail. I know a nice spot by the lake for a late lunch." She guided them at a slow pace across the field, with their horses side by side. Grace pointed out several cows with their young, grazing nearby on tall grass.

"You seem happy here on the ranch. What made you decide to leave and live in Dallas?" Heath asked.

"I needed to move away and mature into a lady, or at least that's what my mother said." Grace visually took in the rolling landscape around them. For her, nothing could ever be as beautiful as the Texas prairie. If she'd had more backbone, she would have never left. "Being away at college, and then living the big city lifestyle helped me grow out of my awkward phase. I do miss the country life, though. And I sometimes miss the person I used to be."

Heath slackened his hold on the reins and leaned forward to pat Daisy's neck. "We all change over time. If we're lucky, it's for the better, but sometimes change is for the worse."

The lowing of cattle and the occasional bird song echoed across the hills. A yellow butterfly fluttered in front of her face before darting away. The sweet scents of grass and flowers filled her nostrils. "As you already know from Alex's stories, I had the biggest crush on Tyler when I was younger." She swayed in the saddle in time with Silver's gait. "But he barely paid any attention to me, though, until a year ago. When our paths crossed again, I wasn't that same gangly girl who used to follow him around. See…I had to move away to become the person I am today. After all those years, my dreams are coming true."

But after her wedding, she'd move away again. Since she'd quit her job in Dallas and become her own boss, she didn't have the demands that had kept her away in the past. She now had the freedom to spend more time at the ranch.

Heath adjusted his weight in the saddle. "Just don't lose that fire I see burning behind those brown eyes. I'd hate to see you become ordinary."

Laughing, she tipped her head. Small, puffy clouds floated above her in a baby blue sky. "I don't think there's any danger of that. Walking a straight line really isn't my style."

The wide open prairie spread out before them, dotted with Texas bluebells, ranging in color from purple to white. For a while, she enjoyed riding in silence. When she crossed the shallow, pebble-bottomed creek, the horses' metal shoes clinked against the stones. Cold water splashed from the creek, dampening the denim just above her boots.

Shadow ran ahead before stopping to wag his bushy tail as he waited for them to catch up. Every so often, he would approach a cow and bark a brief greeting, but always stayed clear of swinging horns.

Heath's shoulders had relaxed into a more natural position, and he held the reins with slack. His knuckles had returned to a ruddy bronze. When he looked over at her, his smile twinkled in his eyes, which were framed in impossible thick, dark lashes. She could barely make out the dimple in his cheek because it was hidden by that shaggy beard. What she wouldn't give for a razor. She'd shave off that horrid thing.

Up ahead, the gate appeared, along with the entrance to the forest trail. Grace decided now was as good a time as any to approach the delicate subject of what happened last night. "So…will you tell me how you ended up in Molly's jail cell?"

"Not much of a story…drank too much, ran into a trio of rowdy sailors, and spent a few hours in jail." He shrugged. "I've had worse."

He may very well have had worse nights, but none that involved her. His vague answer didn't touch the heart of her question. "I guess what I want to know is why. You were clearly outmatched, so why did you pick a fight?"

"You want the simple answer? I'm not a very nice guy." He stared down at his scraped-up fists holding onto the reins. "I drink more than I should. I get into fights."

"I don't believe you." Everything she'd learned of Heath Carter told her he was a man of honor. She'd seen his gentle manner with the ranch animals. For her, the way a person treated animals was a good indication of the quality of their soul.

"Well, sometimes the truth is hard to accept."

"Stop using those lines as an excuse." She narrowed her eyes. "You must have had some reasonable explanation for why you went after three Navy guys last night."

He remained quiet for several seconds before letting out a long breath. "Those sailors." He spat on the grass. "One of them was a local boy. They were heading to San Diego for BUD/S training."

"What's BUD/S?" She hopped off Silver to open the gate.

"It's the Navy SEAL's training program. They were talking tough and acting like they were better than everyone else in the room, even though they hadn't yet seen a lick of action. Hanging out on a ship in the ocean is different than having your boots on the ground in the middle of a war."

Grace walked her horse through the open gate, and Heath's horse followed. She closed it behind him before swinging back onto her horse. "I can understand how that would've gotten under your skin."

"I listened for an hour or so, rattling off a lot of BS. Blood and glory. I know how easily that can turn into a nightmare."

"Why didn't you walk away?" She flicked her wrist to pull the reins to the right, and she started through a green tunnel. Trees and low shrubs enclosed a wide path. The crunch of gravel under the horses' shoes played a rhythmic beat.

"I don't know what came over me." His gaze drifted into the woods. "The sailors got up to leave, and the waitress handed them their bill. One of them told her it should be on the house. They were training to become SEALs and shouldn't have to pay. She called after them, saying if they didn't pay, the money would come out of her paycheck. All she got for her trouble was an unsolicited kiss." He shifted and looked straight into her eyes. "The next thing I remember, I'm throwing punches."

"I'm glad you weren't seriously hurt. Just a few bumps and bruises." She glanced over at the deep purple bruise covering his left eye and cringed. *That can't feel good.*

"Those boys didn't have much fight. They were full of hot air." His loud laugh startled Daisy. As the horse jerked forward, he tightened his grip on the reins.

They approached the end of the trail, and the trees gave way to a wide field full of white and yellow wildflowers. A pond sat directly ahead.

Shadow took off to chase after the ducks, which waddled into the water, quacking.

This small patch of heaven used to be her favorite spot. Growing up, she would often come here to be by herself. Now, she hoped Heath would find peace as well. Grace brought Silver to a halt and turned to Heath, who was at her side. "See, you survived! Time for lunch."

****

Heath followed Grace's lead and tied his horse to a section of old wooden fencing. He unstrapped the bag resting behind Silver's saddle and carried it over to the shady spot where Grace had spread out a blanket. If he let his guard down, even for a moment, he could slip into loving her. Part of him wanted to pretend, just for this afternoon, that she was his.

He trusted her, even after he'd sworn that part of his soul was a dead zone. She had him opening parts of himself that had been sealed shut. Maybe, the soothing tempo of the horse ride or the serene landscape had lowered his guard. Most likely though, the reason was Grace's kind and caring personality. She didn't buy his canned lines or his excuses. Grace pushed him to be truthful and along with that, forced him out of the shadows.

The dog now lay on the grass with his head resting on his front paws, watching the ducks swim in the pond.

Grace sat with her long legs stretched out. She opened the bag and pulled out a container of fried chicken and a plastic bag that held three biscuits. Then she grabbed a plate and filled it with food. "I brought some leftovers from Mom's dinner last night. I hope that's okay. Did you get back your appetite?"

He appreciatively took the plate Grace handed him. "This is perfect." His stomach had finally stopped churning. Now, it was empty and growling for food.

"Thanks for taking over building my wedding gazebo. It's one less thing my dad has to worry about." Grace split open the biscuit and smothered the insides with strawberry jam.

"He gave me the plans yesterday, which don't look too complicated. Good thing. There's not much time between now and your wedding." The corners of Grace's mouth tilted down, liked she'd tasted something sour. Shouldn't a soon-to-be bride glow when she spoke about her wedding? Grace appeared less than thrilled.

"The big day will be here before I know it. I'm starting to get nervous that something won't go right. I have so much to keep track of. Maybe having both the wedding and reception at the ranch wasn't such a great idea. I could have saved a lot of trouble and run off to Vegas."

"How would your mother react to that?" He took another bite of fried chicken and groaned in satisfaction. Joslyn Murray might have the makings of a Five Star General and to be honest, she scared him a little, but the woman was a queen in the kitchen.

Grace shook her head and smirked. "Oh…she'd never forgive me." A light breeze lifted several strands of her hair, and she brushed them off her face. "Have you ever been married?"

"A long time ago. We were both too young, and it was short lived." He hadn't thought about his ex-wife, Jessica, in a long time. Their marriage had provided him with a sense of home, and he'd given her a military husband. In the end, she had wanted more than just a man in uniform stationed a half a world away. "Our marriage lasted less than a year. She served me divorce papers while I was stationed in Iraq."

Her eyes widened. "I can't believe someone would do that."

The purity of her reaction was what he'd grown to expect from Grace. He sensed her nature was to do the right thing, even if the harder option. "Truthfully, it didn't come as a surprise. We hadn't known each other very long before we married. Then, I was sent overseas one month after the wedding."

"I'm sorry it didn't work out." Finishing her lunch, she set down her plate and lay on her side, propping her head on a hand. Her bare feet stuck out past the frayed edges of her jeans. Across her tan shoulder and chest rested a long, dark braid.

Heath's gaze roamed over her curves. Needing a distraction, he tossed Shadow the last corner of his bread and got a slobbery lick as payment.

"I think he'll be your shadow from now on." Grace smiled.

"In Afghanistan, dogs ran wild around the villages. We brought a few back to the base. My favorite mutt,

Moe, ended up going home with a soldier from Kansas."

Anxiety at the memory of war made his muscles tighten, so he stood to refocus his energy. He looked across the wide field. The grass around them was knee high and swayed with the wind. Small brown sparrows and yellow finches darted from the grass and flew across the blue sky.

"You see the hill on the other side of the pond?" She pointed at a small mound in the distance. "That's the first dwelling on the ranch. It's a home built into the side of the hill. Would you like to take a look?"

He meandered with her over to the spot. As he got closer, he could see a low opening cut into the hill. "This structure looks like some of the rudimentary dwellings I saw overseas."

"In the mid-1800s, my father's ancestors bought this plot of land in hopes of making a living. They were a young couple having a hard time fitting in with society. He was a white man, and she was full-blooded Cherokee."

An image formed in his head of Grace's Cherokee ancestor, a woman who probably looked very much like Grace. "You're part Cherokee."

"You thought I was adopted, didn't you?" She gave him a light punch on the arm. "I know...I look nothing like my parents or my brother. Every few generations, the Cherokee genes make a strong reappearance. I look just like my dad's grandmother when she was my age."

He must have been staring because her cheeks grew red. But how could he stop? Between her breathtaking Native American beauty and the wonderful person she was on the inside, she was special, and his heart was a goner. Heath walked over to get a closer look at the earthen house. The front was covered in logs, which supported the structure. A dirt roof provided a good habitat for the tall grass and flowers that grew on the sloping hill.

"You want to come inside?" Grace bent to step into the opening. "I think it's still safe."

He followed her into cool, damp air, which came as a relief from the heat outside. He breathed in the stale smell of dirt and decayed wood—scents that reminded him of Afghanistan, and tried not to panic. Beside the light coming in from the doorway, the space was dark. He had to feel his way forward.

A burst of light came from a candle in Grace's hand, filling the small room with a warm glow.

As he studied his surroundings, he calmed. The interior was framed with logs and stone. Standing inside this ancient dwelling, he felt like he'd stepped into another time.

Chapter Ten

Once upon a time, the old dugout had been her escape. When the teasing had gotten too much, or the expectations were too great, she would get on her horse and ride out here to hide. When Grace had been twelve, she'd first discovered the dugout. She'd spent weeks working up the nerve to step into the time-worn structure. But once inside, she'd felt safe and protected. Now, she watched Heath look around.

He picked up a piece of carbonized wood and a few shards of clay pots scattered on the ground. "This is pretty cool." Heath stood and bent his neck forward to avoid hitting the hand-hewn ceiling beams.

"They lived here while the permanent house was being constructed. That log house isn't standing anymore. Eventually, the family built the current main house." She'd seen faded black-and-white photographs of the original log house. What incredible strength someone must possess in order to create a home from raw materials. Her ancestors' homestead had been small and humble, but she was proud of their determination.

Heath examined the crumbled fireplace. "Someday, this whole thing will collapse. I hope nobody's in here when it does."

"I'm the only one who ever comes out here." The toe of her boot traced the outline of a heart in the dirt floor. "I used to pretend I was a pioneer woman, and this was my little house on the prairie." She laughed at the memory of spending hours here, lost in her own imagination. He gave her a smile that had no hint of judgment. A gift of acceptance for the insecure, daydreaming girl she'd once been.

As he studied the construction of the wall, his hand glided across a long plank set into the dirt wall.

What would his calloused hand feel like caressing her—running over her bare leg? Shaking her head, she tried to remove the thought, without much luck.

"Have you ever noticed this recess in the wall?" He slid several large stones off to the side. "There's a wooden box in here. Looks rotted." He slid the box into the middle of the floor.

The box might have been used for storing root vegetables. She opened the lid, which creaked on its rusty hinges. Using the candle for illumination, she glanced inside. "A metal case is in here. Can you get it out?"

Heath tipped the rotten wood box and pulled out the metal container. The metal was flat and dull, blemished with only a few rust spots. After setting it on the ground, he pried the lid with his fingertips, but the thing wouldn't budge. "This is in good condition for being so old."

The metal box was square in shape, as tall as it was long. Its secrets pricked at Grace's imagination. The box was a leftover from another time, maybe holding nothing of value but might provide a window into her ancestors' early life together on the ranch.

"This lid is locked tight." Heath lifted it with a grunt. "And it's heavier than it looks."

"Can't you pick the lock?"

"Do I look like the type of guy that knows how to pick a lock?" he asked, followed by a beat of deep laughter. "Wait, don't answer that. Let's take it home. With the right tools, I can get it open."

She left the dugout with Heath following. Sunshine and heat greeted her, chasing away the chill she'd gotten while inside.

He bent to set the box under the protection of the framed doorway. "I'll come back later with the ATV."

"Thanks, Heath." She studied the box again, now in the sunlight. "What do you think is in there?"

"You'll have to be patient." He winked.

In that moment, her fiancé seemed so far away. Heath was there, standing right before her, making her heart beat way too fast. No doubt her feelings for Heath were dangerous. Not because she was worried about her safety. He had this unsettling effect on her, like her heart didn't feel balanced in her chest.

She imagined what his lips tasted like, or how the hard angles of his body would feel under her touch. All the tattoos covering his arms were incredibly sexy. Did he have more hidden under his shirt? She was the moth, and Heath was the flame. Could she enjoy the heat without getting burned?

"We should probably head home." Needing to look away, she turned her back to him. "I'm sure you have things you wanted to do on your day off." Grace started strolling toward their horses, grazing on the tall grass by the fence.

"Nothing too important." He walked at her side. "This was nice, Gracie. Thanks for twisting my arm to make me come."

He'd called her Gracie. Dad had used that

endearment and only when she'd been a little girl. Once she had reached the mature age of thirteen, she'd insisted to be called only by her given name. But now, coming from Heath's lips, Gracie didn't sound childish. The name sounded kind of sexy. "I'm glad you finally acquiesced without too much of a fight." She grabbed Silver's reins and led her out to the open field. "Do you remember how to get on, or do you need a boost?"

Before she could finish, he'd swung himself up into the saddle.

The smile on his face was borderline cocky. His eyes glistened with a smug challenge. *Let's see if you can ride at a trot, tough guy, without hollering like a little girl.*

"You might make a cowboy of me yet." With a light tap with of his heels and a firm hand on the reins, he got Daisy moving toward the path.

"I could picture you as a cowboy." Her gaze swept over his body, appreciating his athletic physique. "Just swap out the baseball cap for a Stetson and your work boots for Justin Ropers. I could teach you how to cut cattle on horseback."

"Cut cattle? That sounds brutal." One eyebrow arched.

"No actual cutting is involved," she said with a laugh. "You are only separating a calf or an adult from the herd. I did it competitively when I was a teenager and have the trophies to prove it."

"While I appreciate the offer, I'm still a greenhorn." He clicked his tongue, which Daisy took as direction to increase her speed. Heath let out a holler and whipped his head around. His face twisted.

His attitude had switched from over-confidence to

sheer panic. Watching him bounce down the path and disappear around the corner, she couldn't stop her laughter. "Wait for me!"

****

After Grace drove Heath into town, she slowly made her way back home. Once Grace walked into the house, she spotted her mother darting out of the kitchen.

"Have you completely lost your mind?" she asked. "What were you thinking going out with that man…all alone?"

Grace noted the red flush on her mother's cheeks and her high-pitched voice, not a good sign of what was coming her way. "Last time I checked, I'm an adult and perfectly sane."

"We hardly know him. He could have hurt you."

"He's not a threat." She held the end of her braid in her hand and twirled it back and forth, a habit formed during the many clashes of opinion with her mom. "I've always found riding therapeutic, and I hoped Heath would feel the same."

Joslyn let out a long sigh. "Just because he works for us doesn't make him our problem. You should be focusing on your wedding to Tyler, not playing amateur shrink to a troubled vet."

That statement was her mother in a nutshell—don't worry about fixing the world, just fix yourself. "I owe him my life, Mother. Tyler's in Mexico and the wedding plans are all under control. I can help Heath. He trusts me."

"Heath is not the type of person you should be spending time with, Grace Ann." Joslyn reached out and took hold of Grace's dirt-stained hand. "Oh my.

You need a manicure."

"I'm twenty-six, not sixteen. You need to trust me. I can take care of myself." She loved her mother, she really did. Sometimes the woman was utterly exasperating.

"Okay." Joslyn raised her hands. "But be careful. Promise?"

Grace gave her mother a hug. "Of course. Careful is my middle name."

"Your middle name should have been Prudence. Then maybe you wouldn't have been such a wild child." Her mother headed down the hall and into the kitchen. "Do you plan on joining us for dinner?"

She followed and entered her mother's domain. A large island topped with white marble dominated the room. Huge windows draped in floral fabric looked over the back yard. Amazingly, her mother had designed the kitchen to ooze sophistication, yet still remain true to the history of the farmhouse.

Her brother spent more time in here growing up. He preferred working in the kitchen to tending the animals. They'd often swapped chores, since she loved being outside and was totally useless in the kitchen. She'd supported Alex when he'd followed his dreams and attended culinary school. "No, I'm meeting Molly. We're going to the Beach Boys tribute band concert in the park." She noticed the time glowing on the stove's digital clock and shoved off the counter. "Yikes, I need to get ready."

Joslyn came out of the pantry holding a jar of canned green beans. "Go upstairs and get yourself clean. Those barn clothes do nothing for your figure.

****

Heath sat on the porch of the bunkhouse with a glass of cold water in his hand. "Well, that was quite the adventure," he said to the dog at his feet.

Shadow, true to his name, had not left his side all afternoon.

Heath relaxed on the creaky rocking chair and enjoyed the cool breeze. His stomach growled, lunch long forgotten. He'd become used to a large breakfast and lunch, and today's hadn't quite measured up. Maybe he'd go to Alex's restaurant, The Desert Rose, for dinner. Surely, he could stay out of trouble for one night.

His time with Grace proved a natural medicine for his troubled soul. The voices that plagued his subconscious were quieting. For that afternoon, he'd forgotten about war and death. The ice usually flowing through his veins had melted with the warmth of Grace's smile.

Earlier that week, he bought a cell phone at a convenience store in town. The need to make a few phone calls weighed on his conscience. First would be to Julie, John's widow. He had promised to stay in touch, and until now, he'd been doing a bad job. Next call would be to his grandparents' lawyer. *Time to stop hiding from the world and face my fears.*

The slap of a door closing made him look up to see Grace striding across the lawn.

She glanced over at him and waved.

Her face glowed with a wide, genuine smile. When his gaze drifted to her dress, he had to rub his eyes to make sure he wasn't having a vision. She wore a coral dress which flowed softly in the breeze. Copper bracelets adorned her tan arms. A belt cinched her small waist, and impossible high heels capped off her legs. In his life, he'd never seen a more attractive woman. Grace's true beauty could only be appreciated by those privileged to know her. Her loveliness radiated and spiraled outward from its source, her gentle heart.

She walked across the gravel driveway, heading to her car. "Have a good night," she called out.

"You, too," he answered. The sight of her, dressed in all her designer glory, served as a wake-up call. On some level, she was still a country girl who'd spent her childhood on a ranch. But now, most of that person was erased.

Grace's life had taken a different direction. After spending the afternoon with her on horseback, he'd forgotten she was a sophisticated woman—more model than farm girl. Grace had no room in her life for someone like him.

Shadow gazed upward with amber eyes, and Heath rubbed his head. "Way out of our league, dude."

The dog barked.

Maybe in agreement. He watched Grace drive away, down the dusty driveway. "I'm gonna rustle up some grub. See you later." Heath patted the shaggy dog before standing to stretch his legs. After going inside to get his wallet, he mounted his bike.

As he drove the winding country roads, his thoughts of Grace crept into his mind. Soon, she'd be married and living in Dallas. Her future was all laid out before her. For this brief time, his life intersected with hers, and he was thankful. She'd shown him the world was not all darkness. Light could be found in the most unexpected places.

Acres of farmland flew past his peripheral vision.

Wire fences, strung parallel to the road, made an unending line of metal. Cattle hung their heads low, grazing on abundant grass. The power of his bike was under his control, unlike the horse he'd been astride earlier. Given time, he could see himself content at the ranch. The wide open space didn't leave him feeling confined like all his other jobs had.

He entered the restaurant, wearing a new pair of jeans and clean shirt, but he still felt out of place. A petite blonde hostess showed him to a small table by a window which faced Main Street. When he noticed other diners stealing glances his way, he self-consciously smoothed his unruly hair.

A waitress appeared at his side. She was really cute and probably college age. Way too young for him to be interested in.

"Hey there," she said. "I'm Berry. What can I get you to drink?"

"Iced tea with a slice of lemon."

"Sweet or regular, honey?"

"Regular." Sweet things didn't appealed to him, well, with the exception of Grace.

"You got it. Here's a menu. Our chef's special tonight is a fire grilled T-bone steak served with rosemary fingerling potatoes and sautéed asparagus. It's really good." She looked him over before walking away.

Heath noticed Alex standing across the room, talking to a middle-aged couple seated for dinner. He liked what Alex had done to the place. The Desert Rose was quaint, with intimate tables and high-backed booths, which gave diners a sense of privacy. Perfect for a romantic night out. The menu was heavy on regional fare, with plenty of local beef and seafood from the Gulf.

Berry, his perky waitress, returned with his iced tea. "You ready to order?" she asked with a smile.

"The T-bone special cooked medium rare." He forced himself to make eye contact. *No time like the present to start polishing your social skills.*

"Smart choice. You won't be disappointed." She took the offered menu from his outstretched hand. "You're new around here, aren't you? I saw you last night at the bar. You caused quite a stir."

Best to avoid her line of questioning. "Will you tell Alex I'd like to speak to him when he has a minute?"

Her smile drooped. "Sure. I'll go turn in your order."

Heath knew this type of woman all too well. She saw him as exciting, rough, and dangerous—the perfect combination to spark a woman's imagination. He wasn't interested in being someone's fantasy, because he really was anything but. He'd tried those kinds of relationships in the past and quickly learned they were more trouble than they were worth.

Moments later, Alex joined him and reached out to shake hands. "Hey, man, good to see you. How's the family treating you?"

"Really good. Ranch work is tough, but I like the physical activity."

Grimacing, Alex sat on the other side of the table and adjusted the knot in his purple tie. "I hated farm work so I used to bribe Grace to do my chores. If she cleaned out the chicken coop, I'd let her sit in the rear seat of my car when I drove Tyler to school."

"Using your sister's feelings to get out of doing

your chores…that's low, man." If Heath had been around when Grace was in high school, he would have made sure she'd only had eyes for him.

"I know, I know." Alex raised his hands in mock surrender. "I was an appalling big brother. What made it worse was Tyler couldn't stand her tagging along. He acted like he didn't notice her, but he did. He used to make fun of her and call her names behind her back. On our last day of senior year, he called her a mutt. I finally had enough and punched him in the face."

"Why would she want to marry someone who'd hurt her like that?" Heath wanted to punch Tyler in the face, too. He knew Tyler was a jerk, but a mean-spirited bully? His heart hurt for a young Grace—the object of her affection openly mocking her.

"That's Grace for ya." Alex spun a sugar packet in his fingers. "When Tyler saw her again last year, he realized how foolish he'd been to dismiss her. My sister is a lot like my dad. They love everybody, no matter if the people deserve it or not."

"Some people don't deserve that kind of love." Heath put himself into that category and shuddered.

"Well, Grace would argue about that until the end of time." Alex laughed. "Tonight, dinner's on the house. I need to go to my office and balance a few spreadsheets." He gazed at the kitchen doors. "Some days, I wish I didn't have to spend my time dealing with cost and profit sheets, employee schedules, and supply orders. I'd rather be in the kitchen. But, I guess you have to take the good with the bad."

"Thanks for dinner. I appreciate it." Heath really did. Not only for the steak dinner, but also for his friendship.

Alex stood to leave.

"Wait a sec." Heath glanced around to make sure he wasn't overheard. "I have one quick question. Is Tyler good enough for her?"

A slow smile emerged on Alex's face. "I don't know, man. I honestly don't know. Tyler and I were best buds growing up, even though I knew he could be a real jerk. I know he's changed a lot since then, and he really loves Grace and wants what's best for her."

"Would he move to Liberty Ridge in order to make her happy?"

Alex shook his head and laughed. "Anything but that. Tyler couldn't stand living in a small town." He walked toward the back of the restaurant and disappeared into his office.

His waitress appeared, placing his dinner order on the table.

Filling up most of the plate was a large, sizzling steak. The food smelled out of this world delicious—a heady combination of smoky meat, cooked vegetables, and fresh baked bread.

While Heath ate his meal, Alex's answer gave him plenty to think about.

Chapter Eleven

Fourteen-year-old Grace had sprinted toward the house, her boots splashing through muddy puddles. "Hey, Molly." She waved to her friend and pounded up the stairs. Molly had wisely remained on the porch, protected from the rain.

"Hurry, Grace. The festival starts in less than an hour." She pointed to Grace's muddy boots. "You better take off those before you go in the house or your mom will have a cow." Molly fluffed out her short, brunette hair which bordered her jaw line.

She did as her best friend suggested, and the girls hustled to Grace's room. They did their hair and makeup in between singing along to the pop music blasting on the radio. Grace needed to look her best today. Molly laced her hair into a long French braid. Then Grace applied foundation to cover the multitude of red blotches on her face.

"You look fabulous." Molly stood next to Grace in front of the mirror.

"Do you think Tyler will be there?" She twirled to get a better look at herself. The temperature was predicted to reach ninety-five degrees today. Whatever she wore needed to be cool and comfortable. After much debate, she decided on jean shorts and a Garth Brooks T-shirt.

"Yeah, he should be." Molly picked up a can of

hairspray and released a cumulonimbus-sized cloud over her head. "The football players are in charge of the carnival games. He's on the JV team so he should be by the dunk tank."

Grace coughed and stepped back. The idea of seeing Tyler today left her giddy with excitement. "I can't believe we'll be freshmen this fall." She squealed with a release of nervous energy. Finally, she might have a shot at catching Tyler's attention and maybe even his heart. "Let's find my dad so we can get going." She found Bruce sitting in his easy chair in the family room, reading the paper.

"Hey, butterfly." He peered over his newspaper and smiled. "Hi, Molly. You girls ready?"

"Yeah. Come on…let's go." Grace grabbed her dad's beefy hand and hauled him onto his feet.

Bruce laughed and put down his paper. "Okay, okay…but first, let me get the keys to your carriage."

Grace sat between Molly and Dad in the front bench of the truck. As soon as he parked along one of the side streets bordering Snowfield Park, she nudged Molly to jump out, and then she ran off with her best friend toward the festival.

"Have fun," Bruce yelled after them.

With the rain gone, the sun now shone hot and bright. She moved past crowds of children and their parents until she reached the dunk tank. Grace's heart beat rapidly when she saw the cutest boy alive—Tyler Lee Ross. This was it. The moment she'd waited all summer for. *Please notice me for someone more than Alex's pesky little sister.*

"Come over and try to dunk my buddy, Ryder." Tyler called out challenges to people passing by.

"Three chances for a dollar."

Over the noise around her, all Grace could hear was Tyler's voice. As she and Molly approached Tyler, Grace handed him her money. He placed three baseballs in her hand and directed her toward the red line, the whole while barely looking her way. Grace cocked her arm back and threw. The ball curved wide and landed in the grass about five feet from the target.

Warm breath suddenly brushed over her neck.

"You want a turn in the tank?" Tyler whispered.

His nearness made Grace almost faint from excitement. "Sure," she croaked, not even certain of what she had agreed to. She was too distracted by the scent of his spicy cologne to listen to what he said.

He took her hand and walked her to the dunk tank. "Hey, Ryder, time for a break. Alex's little sis wants a chance."

"Cool," said a boy wearing a red football jersey. He wiggled his way out and jumped down.

"Climb on in, sugar." Tyler held her arm as she climbed the ladder.

His touch seared her skin.

A blonde cheerleader approached Tyler and put her arm around his shoulders. "What's goin' on?" she asked.

Grace knew the perky cheerleader, Colleen Gardner, because she'd been at a few of Alex's parties. No denying the girl was outwardly pretty. Colleen was the object of many boys' affections. But Grace had also seen on several occasions a side of Colleen that wasn't so attractive—her mean temper and vicious tongue.

Tyler whispered a reply in her ear, and the girl let out a giggle.

Then she said something to him.

As Grace watched the interaction too quiet to overhear, her jealousy bloomed like a magnolia tree.

"Baby, you need to be patient," he said to Colleen. "You'll get me alone on that Ferris wheel soon enough." Tyler went back to the red line and grabbed three balls.

"If you dunk Alex's sister, he'll kill you," Colleen said with a smile.

Tyler threw the first ball, a weak underhanded toss, and missed.

Shivering with nerves on the seat above the tank of water, Grace sighed with relief. She watched as the second toss hit closer but not the bull's eye. *Just hurry up and get it over with.*

As he held the last ball in his hand, Tyler smiled at the crowd of teenagers who gathered around.

"Cut it out, Tyler." Alex's voice sounded through the crowd as he marched up to Tyler. "Leave Grace out of it. I know you're mad at me for not giving you a ride today, but geez, don't be such a jerk."

"No worries, bro." Tyler glanced at Grace out of the corner of his eye.

For a moment, she thought she saw a spark of interest. Maybe after all this time, she would get her chance. As she watched him rocket the last ball toward the dunk tank and hit the bull's eye, her wish shattered. The scene played out in slow motion. She dropped like a rock into the cold water.

Sputtering, she climbed out of the tank, dripping wet. Grace wanted to shrivel up and die. Surrounding her were kids that she'd soon be attending high school with, all of them laughing and pointing. Her hair was now plastered to her face. And she was sure her make-up washed away in the water.

She could barely breathe, and the food she'd eaten earlier threatened to expel from her stomach. Clenching her lips shut, Grace willed her body to calm down.

Molly shoved her way through the crowd. "Come on, Grace. Let's get out of here." She took Grace by the hand and pulled her away from the dunk tank.

Tyler flung his arm around Colleen's shoulder, and they started walking away.

Alex ran up to Grace. "I'm so sorry. That was rotten of Tyler."

"I'm fine." She sniffed. "It's only water." Her dreams of a happy-ever-after with Tyler dissipated before her eyes.

Grace and Molly made their way to the bathrooms.

At the exit to the game area, her dad stepped in front of them holding a towel. "You get dried off," he said. "I'm gonna have a nice talk with that Tyler boy."

"Don't, Daddy." She grabbed onto his arm. "I'm embarrassed enough already. He was only getting payback on Alex. Please promise you won't talk to Tyler?"

"All right, but if I ever see that boy treating you like that again…"

Grace could only imagine what he would do. Her dad's face was as red as a beet.

He looked mad enough to lasso Tyler and tie him on top of a fire ant hill. She forced herself to smile, concealing how hurt she'd been by Tyler's stunt.

"Thanks for the towel, Mr. Murray." Molly put her arm around Grace. "I'll take her in the bathroom to get her dried off."

Once inside the bathroom, Molly pointed a finger at her. "Next time he tries something like that, just say NO! He's not worth it. When will you learn?"

Now, back in the present, that question echoed in her mind. The incident with Tyler and the dunk tank was so many years ago, but she still carried some of the sting.

"Okay, Grace. I'm back."

Tyler's voice sounded from her computer. His handsome face appeared on the screen. He was wearing a black suit with an aqua tie and a smile only for her.

"Sorry, I had to answer that call," he said over video chat. "Rick had a question about a contract I gave him. I'm all yours now."

He was all hers until the next important call. Grace picked up the nail file she'd earlier abandoned by her computer and resumed shaping her nails. "I was thinking about your dunk tank stunt. The Founders' Day Festival is today."

Tyler scrunched his face and shook his head. "You'll never let me live that down, will you?"

"Nope." She grinned. "I'm still plotting my revenge."

"Ah, come on." He placed a hand over his heart. "The weather was hot, and I figured you'd appreciate a dip in the cool water."

Did he think the innocent school boy act would work on her? Maybe when she was in high school but not anymore. "No way, I'm not buying that for a second." Her engagement ring sparkled on her left hand. Tyler had insisted on getting her the largest and best ring he could afford, which in Grace's opinion, was too extravagant. "Come home soon, and we'll call it even."

"Done."

His laughter sounded canned through the computer's speakers.

"I wish I could go with you to the festival today. I thought I'd have a little fun while I'm in Mexico, but so far, it's been all work."

"I miss you so much." She took a deep breath to control her jumble of emotions. She did miss him, but unfortunately, she was also getting used to him not being around. "Be safe, and I'll see you soon."

"Miss you, too, love. Only two more weeks, and I'll be home." Tyler's gaze shifted from the computer screen to the cell phone in his hand.

"Hurry." She wished he wasn't thousands of miles away. The physical separation had created emotional distance in their relationship. Not good, if they were to be married soon. "Life's not the same without you."

****

Heath drove the old reliable tractor across the field, bouncing along on the seat. He steered the green machine through the pasture gates and finally into the barn. The trailer was empty of the alfalfa bales he'd scattered through the fields. While making the rounds, he'd checked the water lines and made sure the troughs were full and clean. *Keeping busy is keeping sane.*

Bruce had told him to take off the rest of the day to come to the Founders' Day Festival. He'd insisted that the annual summer celebration was a lot of fun, with good food and music.

The thought of being surrounded by large groups of people he didn't know left him anxious. He planned to finish his chores and borrow a fishing pole, and then head over to the pond to waste away the rest of the day.

Without turning his gaze to the door, he sensed had Grace entered the barn. The hairs on his arms stood on end, like immediately before a lightning strike. He couldn't explain how he always felt her presence before he caught sight of her. Maybe his mind was once again working at a heightened state, similar to when he was in combat. He knew her floral scent and recognized the beat of her stride.

"Hey there." Leaning against one of the tractor's large tires, Grace crossed her arms.

She looked perfect in a plaid shirt, which was tied up to reveal a peek of skin. His body flushed with heat. His hot flash had nothing to do with the temperature in the barn. "Hey, yourself." He hung the tractor keys on a small peg board attached to the wall.

"You coming to the festival today?" she asked.

"Probably not." He hooked his thumbs in the front pockets of his jeans.

Chicken clucking echoed through the barn. A rooster crowed.

"You should come." Grace tugged at the sleeve of his T-shirt. "I promise you'll have fun. You can hang out with the family. Alex, Jenny, and the girls will be there. I know the twins would love to see you."

"I don't like big crowds." He had to decline the invitation without hurting her feelings. "But tell those two troublemakers I said hello."

Grace kicked a puff of hay. "Okay, but if you change your mind, come find me. I'd really like it if you came."

Her smile was tempting. Heath could see himself agreeing to anything she wanted with that smile. Jump off a cliff—sure, how high?

He exited the barn with Grace by his side.

At the beginning of the gravel path that led to the bunkhouse, she halted and lifted her gaze. "Have you had a chance to pick the lock on the metal box we found in the dugout?"

"I got it open but haven't looked inside it yet. I thought you should do the honors."

"Can we go look at it now?" Her eyes widened under arched, black brows.

She grinned like a kid at Christmas. "Sure, come over to the bunkhouse, and I'll bring it out. I'm surprised you haven't asked earlier."

"I've been so busy lately, between wedding errands and my work duties. I had my dress fitting yesterday, and the invitations went out earlier this week."

Her face lost some of that carefree smile. Heath's stomach clenched at the image of her wearing a wedding dress meant for Tyler. "I notice you're on the computer a lot. What exactly do you do for work?"

"I recently started my own cyber-security business. I left my former employer when they asked me to run data mining on some companies who had contracted us to protect their networks and data. I told them no, and then walked away."

"I don't see you as a techno geek." She looked more like a supermodel. But then again, who said a girl couldn't be smart and pretty? "What made you go into that line of work?"

"Computer Engineering was something I just stumbled across when I was a sophomore in college. The classes came easy, so I went with it."

He was impressed. Computers baffled him. "You

seem like such an outdoorsy girl."

"Owning my own business gives me a lot of flexibility." She sighed. "I'll find it hard to leave next month."

Heath went inside his bunkhouse and came out carrying the box. He set it at her feet. "Here you go, ma'am."

She gently opened the lid, peeked inside, and pulled out a book wrapped in a yellowed cloth. "Look at the embroidery on the handkerchief." She fingered the old fabric then lifted it to show Heath. "The stitching is so delicate. These are Cherokee roses. And look at these initials—EB & KB, and they're encircled within a heart."

Grace laid the handkerchief on her lap and peeled it open to reveal an old Bible. Inside the cover of the leather-bound book was a faded inscription.

Ezra Burchfield
Born October 29, 1820
Married June 12, 1842

As we live our lives in peace, we grieve for all those we lost on the great journey. My love for the Cherokee people is as strong as my love for my dear Kamama. She is the light after seeing so much darkness, goodness to defy evil. God bless our children and their children, throughout the generations. May they never forget the sacrifices of their ancestors.

"A family Bible." She traced a finger over the words.

Heath leaned over to get a closer look. "The Bible's in good condition for being so old."

"What do you think Ezra meant by the great journey?" she asked.

He scratched his beard. "I don't know. Maybe they had a long, hard journey when they moved here to establish the ranch."

"I wonder if Granny knows more about Ezra and Kamama." Grace reached inside the box again and took out several copper bracelets. They were tarnished and dull, but their engravings were still clear. "These must have belonged to Kamama. How gorgeous." She slipped them over her hand and onto her slender wrist.

"This is a real find." He watched Grace paging through the Bible. Did the words inside hold meaning for her? His faith was shaky at best. Though each day here at the ranch with Grace rebuilt his spirit and his connection to forces greater than himself.

"Well, I should get going. Hope to see you at the festival later." She hopped down the porch steps with the precious finds in hand.

She gave him that smile again, the one that pierced straight to his heart. He knew right then and there he'd be joining her later at the festival. He'd go to the moon and back for her. Cursing his own weakness, he watched until she disappeared behind the creaky screen door. Apparently, a pretty face and a smile would turn him against his better judgment.

"Well, I better take a shower," he mumbled to himself. "Can't go to the festival smelling like a horse."

Chapter Twelve

Heath drove past Snowfield Park, seeing the place buzzing with activity. After a brief search, he found a side street with an empty spot for his bike. He slipped the key inside his pocket and followed the flock of people heading in. Instead of the ratty jeans and T-shirt he normally wore, he had on nice khaki shorts and a new button-up shirt. The clothes felt slightly stiff and itchy, but he didn't want Grace to be embarrassed about being seen with him. He even left the old Warrior baseball cap at home. What a guy won't do to make a good impression? And he really wanted to look good for Grace.

The sprawling park sat beside the Hickory River, with the wooden bridge at the north entrance. The sight of the rushing river gave him chills. He remembered the panic he'd felt swimming through that water to save Grace.

When Grace told him this weekend festival was a big deal for the town, she wasn't kidding. Tents and stages were scattered around the park, and carnival rides and games filled the paved parking lot. A Ferris wheel, covered in blinking lights, stood high above the crowd, tirelessly spinning countless customers. Music from a country band filled the air, along with delicious smells coming from dozens of food stands.

From the looks of it, every man, woman, and child

living in the county was in attendance. He weaved through the crowd, conscious of the growing nervous tension in his gut. His eyes scanned for danger, along with any sign of Grace and her family.

The unmistakable sound of her laughter caught his attention. He turned to see her sitting on a blanket next to Alex and Jenny. Along with Lizzy and Kara, they watched a magic act being performed on a small stage. The second he saw Grace, his heart rate increased like a stampede of wild horses. Why did he struggle to act like a normal person around her? He hadn't wanted anything this badly in a long time—to just have fun and fit in.

When Grace noticed him, she waved him over. She scooted to the side and made room on the blanket.

The twins both greeted him with energetic hugs, nearly squeezing the life out of him.

"Hi, Heath!" they sang in unison.

"I'm so glad you decided to come." Grace patted him on the shoulder.

He took a calming breath. *You're just a normal guy, enjoying the day with a pretty girl. You got this.* "So, what did I miss?"

Lizzy filled him in on all the cool tricks the magician had done so far.

He noticed Kara studying his tattoos through narrowed eyes.

Scrunching up her nose, Kara touched his arm. "Did those hurt?"

Her small hand lightly brushed his skin like a warm breeze. "Just a little. When I was in the Army, I was expected to look tough. Most of my friends got tattoos, so I did, too." He saw both girls now scanning the artwork on his arms. "I hope they aren't too scary."

Lizzy giggled and touched the ink design of an open fan of playing cards. Her small finger traced the Ace of Spades. "I think they're silly."

He smiled at the girls. "Good. Because now I'd rather look silly than scary."

The realization suddenly struck—for the first time since leaving the Army, he felt like part of a family. His mind whirled with questions that, for many years, had been left unanswered. How much longer could he bear living a life of solitude? When he finally stopped running, would anyone be there for him? Someday, would he desire a wife and children of his own?

Not since he'd been served his divorce papers had he given any thought to marriage. Up until this point in his life, he'd been happy being single. Right now, he'd make a terrible husband. But years in the future, would his solitary existence be enough, or would he want something more?

Jenny stood and took Lizzy and Kara by the hand. "Let's go play some games. Who wants to join us?"

"I have to judge the barbecue competition." Alex interlaced his fingers, stretched out his arms, and then cracked his knuckles. "I'll join you when I'm done."

"We'll come." Grace peered at Heath. She stood and reached for his hand, pulling him up.

The blazing heat from her touch left him temporarily speechless. Heath followed Grace, Jenny, and the twins to the fishing game. Kids ran around, darting between booths. Their laughter was contagious.

Grace pointed to a small field set behind the carnival games. "Look, they're starting the potato sack race. You game?"

"Are you sure? Because I will beat you."

She huffed a loud breath and shook her head. "Honey, I've been doing that race since I started walking. You don't stand a chance."

By now, he knew how to rile her competitive streak. "Put your money where your mouth is, princess." His gaze wandered to her pretty mouth and the smile pulling at the corners. "If you win, I'll shave off my beard. If I win, you clean horse stalls for the next week."

They shook hands on the terms and lined up for the race. She looked fierce in her potato sack, and he was sure she was plotting some kind of strategy to take him down. The horn blew, and all the competitors took off toward the red ribbon marking the finish. Grace and Heath were side by side, at the head of the pack, when his foot hit a bump, pitching him forward. Luckily, he caught his balance before he face-planted on the grass. The rascal had tripped him. *This means war.*

He put his whole heart into the last fifty meters, and his lungs burned with the effort. The finish line was within reach. Heath took one last long hop and passed Grace, who let out a sound of defeat that reminded him of an irate rooster.

Once across the finish line, he fell next to Grace, laughing so hard tears streamed down both their faces. "You're a little cheater," he said once he finally caught his breath.

"I had good motivation." She reached over to place the palm of her hand over the scruff on his cheek. "You really need to lose the beard."

He sat in silence and stared until the world around him disappeared. Heath put up his hand to cover hers, which still rested on his face. Her delicate fingers tickled the sensitive skin under his beard. He was having a hard time continuing to deny his growing feelings. She surely saw him only as the man who'd saved her life and now returned the favor. But for a few seconds, he wondered if she saw something more.

Grace finally broke the spell by pulling away and wiggling out of her potato sack. A few people came over to them and congratulated Heath on his win. A man in overalls handed him a large blue ribbon.

"We should find a game where we could be on the same team." She led him away from the crowd, stopping under an ash tree.

"We'd be nearly unstoppable." The two of them competing side by side was the best idea he'd ever heard.

"Why don't you ever let me win?" She tilted her head.

Her wide-eyed expression was as innocent as a child, but he knew better. He laughed at the question. "Why would I? Does Tyler always let you win?" Speaking the name of her fiancé left a bitter taste in his mouth.

"Every time." She raised her chin to meet his gaze.

"I'm not Tyler," he said with more force than he wanted. The way she looked at him, with wide-eyed wonder, left him breathless. He was plummeting down the rabbit hole, grabbing at anything to stop the freefall. Guess that's why they called the feeling falling in love, and he didn't stand a chance.

****

Grace couldn't believe that Heath'd beaten her, even after her little trip maneuver. Now, she faced a week of cleaning horse stalls, something she hadn't done in over eight years. Seeing Heath shave off his beard had been her main motivation to win. She'd have to craft another plan to make the scruff disappear. He used his facial hair as a mask, and she wanted the world to see the real Heath Carter.

They were standing under a tree, talking, when out of the corner of her eye, she saw Tyler's parents approach.

"Grace, darling," Marion Ross called. She gave Grace a polite kiss on each cheek.

"Hello, Marion, Dr. Ross." After that race, she must look a sweaty mess. How embarrassing. She smoothed her hair and clothing.

Tyler's dad raised a hand in greeting.

Both Tyler's parents were overdressed for a festival. But they were one of the more important families in Liberty Ridge, and Grace knew they always dressed to impress. "I hope you're enjoying yourself. We lucked out on the weather this year."

"This event keeps on getting bigger and bigger every year." Marion turned her attention to Heath, and her penciled eyebrows arched up her smooth forehead.

"I'd like to introduce you to Heath Carter." Grace stepped closer to Heath. "He's the man who pulled me out of the river. Heath, these are Tyler's parents, Dr. Ross and his wife, Marion."

Tyler's parents shook Heath's hand then slowly looked him up and down. Both wore expressions of well-bred neutrality. Despite their politeness, Grace saw through their act like a thinly woven white skirt.

"We are so grateful to you for saving Grace's life," Dr. Ross said.

"Are you staying in the area?" Marion asked him.

"I'm working at the Murray ranch for the time being," Heath said. "Helping out until the wedding."

Marion's brows rose even farther in obvious disapproval, and Grace wondered with one more surprise, if they'd disappear under her hairline.

Returning her attention to Grace, Marion smiled. "Speaking of your wedding, you looked absolutely divine at your dress fitting yesterday. I can't wait until Tyler sees you walking down the aisle. You will be such a beautiful bride." One hand fluttered over her heart and the other brushed away a small tear.

Grace smiled, wanting to appear grateful for her future mother-in-law's compliments. The truth was she'd been less than excited at her bridal fitting. The wedding dress had fit like a satin glove. The train flowed behind her, gloriously long, and her tiara and veil completed a breathtaking picture. *Oohs* and *aahs* sounded all around the room. But for Grace, she felt shockingly little joy when she saw herself in the full-length mirror.

When Tyler had proposed five months ago, she thought all her dreams were coming true. Now, doubts popped up like dandelions. She'd wanted to marry Tyler since she'd first seen him at twelve years old. Why had she suddenly developed cold feet?

"Hello, hello, hello," her dad's voice boomed. He shook Dr. Ross's hand.

Grace saw Heath tighten in anticipation of Bruce's now-expected pat on the back. The physical action was Dad's way of showing his affection, along with testing the measure of a man. Judging from the respect Dad showed Heath, he had proven solid on all fronts.

Instead of a smack on the back, Bruce gripped Heath's shoulder with his large hand and gave him a fatherly squeeze. "Good to see you, Heath."

As Bruce and Dr. Ross started a discussion regarding the town's plan for rezoning a large parcel of land, Grace wanted an escape. "I'm taking Heath over to visit Mrs. Hernandez's tamale stand. Enjoy the rest of your day." She walked away with Heath, feeling the laser-focus scrutiny of Marion's gaze. After all her dealings with the prim and proper surgeon's wife, she knew Tyler's mother excelled at stirring up gossip.

Marion would be on the phone with her son the second she got home tonight. Heath was not the type of person she'd find an acceptable escort for the woman engaged to her only son.

"I should probably get going. Thanks for the race. I had fun beating you." Heath shoved his hands in his pockets and walked away.

"Wait." She reached over and grabbed his arm, not ready to say goodbye just yet. "You can't leave without trying a tamale. Molly's mom has her stand right over there. Come on."

With a shrug, he turned to follow. They walked past the dunk tank on their way to the tamale stand. A flock of high school football players and cheerleaders called out to passersby.

"When I was that age, I didn't fit in with that group." Heath pointed his chin toward the kids.

If I would've known Heath Carter in high school, those days would have been full of amusement. "Tyler was popular. The star football player. Everyone wanted to be in his circle. I, on the other hand, hung out on the edges."

"Popular kids," he huffed. "Definitely more fun to be the class troublemaker."

"You, a troublemaker?" Widening her eyes, she placed her hand over her opened mouth in mock surprise. "I find that hard to believe."

Laughter was his only reply.

When she passed the dunk tank, she saw the red-and-orange striped tent. Nearby, a short man plucked at a banjo, sending a bluegrass song drifting through the air.

"Mrs. Hernandez is right over there." She wasn't surprised by the long line of people in front of the tent. Over the years, word of Mrs. Hernandez's food had gotten around. Eating at her stand was a tradition when attending the festival.

At their approach, a tiny Hispanic woman greeted them. "¡*Hola, mi hija*! So happy to see you." After shuffling around a table topped with trays of delicious-smelling tamales, she wrapped Grace in a loving hug.

"*Hola, Mamá*." Grace gave her a kiss on her soft cheek. "Meet my friend, Heath. He's working on our ranch."

Heath had to bend over to receive the kisses Mrs. Hernandez placed on both his cheeks.

At the rear of the tent, Molly, dressed in casual street clothes, waved to Grace. Molly pulled out a steamy tray from the heat box and brought it to the table. "Hello again, Mr. Carter."

"What a pleasure to see you again, officer." Heath's face turned serious, but only for a few seconds. His tight set mouth soon lifted in a grin.

"You doing okay, Grace?" Molly's scowl stayed firmly in place.

Grace mouthed to her friend to go easy on Heath. The poor guy didn't need another person making him uncomfortable. "We're having loads of fun. He beat me at the sack race, but only because I let him." Grace patted Heath on the arm and winked. "I wouldn't let him leave before he tried one of your tamales."

"Come, sit." Mamá Hernandez took Heath by the elbow and led him over to a small table with two folding chairs. "I'll be right back with something good to eat." She returned shortly and placed two paper plates on the table, one for Grace and another for Heath. Each plate was topped with packets wrapped in corn husks. A small container of green chili sauce sat next to the tamales.

As he studied his plate, his brow furrowed. "Do you eat the corn husk?" Heath picked at the tamale with his plastic fork.

"Um...no. Peel off the husks. The good stuff's inside." If he planned on staying in Texas, he'd have to get more familiar with the local cuisine. Her mouth watered as the familiar smell hit her nose. Grace demonstrated with her own, revealing a baked masa shell filled with seasoned chicken.

Heath took a tentative first bite.

Before she knew it, his plate was empty, except for a layer of corn husks.

He leaned back in his chair with a satisfied grin and groaned.

Mamá Hernandez came over to their table and pointed to his plate. "Did you like?" she asked Heath with a wide smile.

"Where have you been all my life?" Grinning, he took her tiny hand and kissed the top.

The light brown skin on her face blushed rose. "*Bromista*." She squeezed his hand. "You call me Maria, you handsome tease."

Molly, who stood in the tent nearby, rolled her eyes. "*Mamá*, stop flirting. Geez, you're as bad as Aunt Consuela during happy hour."

"Leave us be." She waved away her daughter. "You'd do good to find a man like this."

Molly let out a loud groan. "Oh, *Mamá*, if you only knew."

Heath smiled at Maria Hernandez and winked. His dimple peeked out from behind his beard.

Grace was totally amazed at how much Heath had changed since she'd first met him two weeks ago. Back then, he barely spoke more than a few words at a time. Now, he was openly flirting with a woman old enough to be his mother.

She liked his quirky sense of humor. The more time she spent with him, the more she appreciated the inner strength he carried. He was confident without being overbearing and funny without being demeaning. She was glad others like Mamá Hernandez could see past the long hair and tattoos to appreciate the good man inside.

After talking with Heath a little longer, *Mamá* went to serve her other customers.

Grace and Heath lingered at the table, drinking lemonade and sharing stories. While Heath talked, her mind drifted to the dream she had last night. In her dream, they had been alone in the barn. She remembered the feeling of his arm wrapped around her waist, pulling her close and the tickle of his beard as he kissed her neck. Her gaze now drifted to his lips, and she thought about how they had tasted in her dream, like bourbon and honey. Desire took over her body, and she sipped her cold lemonade, quelling the heat. "*Phew*." She fanned her face with her hand. She knew her cheeks were probably bright red from her improper thoughts. "It's really hot out today."

He cocked a brow and tilted his head. "Are you okay?"

"Heath, there you are." Bruce approached their table at a jog. "You're needed at the pie contest, pronto. We could use one more judge."

"If I'll eat loads of pie then lead the way." Heath stood, his gaze never leaving Grace. "Thanks for the tamales. I'll find you when I'm done."

"Go." She shooed him away. All this social interaction was good for him. Plus, he'd get to eat a truckload of pie. "Your fellow pie-loving countrymen need your taste buds. See you later." Grace stayed behind to talk with Molly. She pulled her away from the tamale stand to walk through the art exhibits.

"Be careful, Grace." Molly gingerly set down a hundred dollar hand-made glass bowl. "I know Heath's type, and they're loaded with problems. You may want to help him, but you won't fix him. You'll only be hurt in the process."

She considered what her friend said, but Molly had seen Heath at his worst. "Maybe you should get to know him better. Why not come out to the ranch sometime? We can hang out, and you can see Heath isn't a menace to society."

Molly gave an uncommitted mumble.

An hour later, the late afternoon sky turned a bright shade of orange. The air buzzed with renewed activity with the arrival of an older evening crowd. Molly returned to help her mom, and Grace found Heath with her dad and Alex, sitting at a picnic table. Jenny had taken the twins home so they could go to bed.

"How did Mom do this year?" Grace sat next to her dad. "She had big expectations for her pecan pie."

"Blue ribbon," Alex said with a wide grin. "Mrs. Nelson's mixed berry pie gave her a run for her money, though. I think Ma got nervous when they were handing out awards."

"She always manages to come out on top," Grace said with pride.

Heath sat across from her, wearing a relaxed smile.

He had stayed. He looked happy. Warmth spread through her, settling in her heart. No matter where their lives would take them in the future, she'd always have the memory of this fun day. Molly's warning flashed in her mind. She reassured herself the feelings she'd developed for Heath were merely a response to seeing someone in need. But she knew Molly was right about one thing. Heath's issues were more complex than a bird with a broken wing. His demons were stronger than she could mend. Her mother came toward them, wearing a smile that could be seen from space.

In her hand was a large blue ribbon. "There y'all are. Another year…another win."

"Congratulations, Mom." Grace recognized the triumphant smile on Joslyn's face. The same smile she'd worn a time or two. She couldn't deny that was one thing she'd inherited from her mother—a fierce competitive streak.

"Heath did a fine job as judge." Bruce rested his folded hands over his midsection. "He ate so much pie that at one point I thought he might split in half."

"He obviously has good taste." Joslyn sat at the table next to her husband.

In the sky, a flash lit up the twilight, followed by a deep boom. Blue and red sparks glittered above.

Heath hunched his head low.

Grace saw his face turn a milky white, and perspiration beaded on his forehead.

"I need to go," Heath muttered. He jumped off the bench at the same time another firework exploded overhead. The next second, he dove to the ground and covered his head with both arms.

Bruce knelt next to Heath. "Grace." He put a hand under Heath's arm to help him stand. "We need to get him as far away from these blasted fireworks as possible."

Watching Heath, the sad truth hit her like the touch of a live wire and her stomach clenched. The fireworks must have triggered a panic response. In Heath's mind, he was at war, where bombs meant death. She ran over to help, understanding the urgency to get him out of the park.

Chapter Thirteen

As Grace and Bruce stood on either side of Heath, moving him through the crowd, the fireworks continued a non-stop barrage. His whole body shook, and she could feel the effort needed to simply put one foot in front of the other. Grace sensed a crack growing inside of him. She hoped they'd get him to a safe place before the flood was released.

"Grace, I want you to drive him home," Dad commanded.

"Okay." She tried so hard not to break down into tears at the sight of this strong man, crumbling like a dried clump of earth.

He had slipped out of reality, into another place and time. Heath lost his footing.

The weight of his body was more than Grace could support.

He fell to his knees and raised his hands to cover his ears. A groan came from deep inside him.

The sound ripped apart her soul. She knelt and gently cupped his face in her hands. "Heath," she whispered. "Look at me. You're in Texas. You're safe."

His wild gaze met hers with a glimmer of comprehension.

Bruce grabbed Heath's arm and helped him to his feet. "Grace will drive you home. Just hold on…you'll be out of here soon."

Bruce opened the door of her car, but Heath's stomach gave way.

Grace jumped back and frowned.

"Once he feels safe, he'll calm down," her dad said over the boom of more fireworks.

With Heath now in the car, she turned the ignition key and peeled out of the parking lot. Her hands and wrists ached from her tight grip on the steering wheel. The drive home was a blur, with her mind going in a million different directions. Admitting that she cared for Heath was easy. But realizing how deep those feelings had become was a difficult pill to swallow. His pain had become her pain. Could time and love heal his broken spirit?

She turned onto the gravel drive and drove under the True Horizon sign. Besides a few outdoor lights, the house and grounds were dark. Turning off the car, she sat quiet and still. The metallic ping of the cooling engine echoed in the car.

Heath continued to stare out the window. He turned to face her. "Thank you."

His voice sounded as rough as stone. "Will you sit on the porch with me for awhile? The night air will help clear your head."

After a nod, Heath followed her onto the porch and sat on a white rocking chair.

"Would you like a drink? Something to smooth out your nerves?"

He nodded before staring out into the darkness.

When she returned, she placed a short glass of whiskey in his hand and a bottle of water on the table. In her other hand was a damp towel. "You have a little mess on your face." She knelt before him. The moment

she started washing his face, his whole body slackened.
****

Slowly, Heath returned to reality. Grace served as his anchor and her calming presence soothed his troubled mind. The warmth of her hand on his face relaxed him more than any shot of whiskey. Grace's dark hair, backlit by the porch light, made her look like his personal angel of mercy.

"There." She laid the washcloth over the porch rail before taking a seat in the rocker next to him. "You look better."

"I'm sorry about what happened." He cleared his throat. "I hope I didn't embarrass you and your family." The ringing in his ears dimmed to a low-pitched buzz. At the park, he'd been caught completely off guard. His shock had turned so quickly to panic. If not for Grace and her family, he would have been utterly lost.

"I won't pretend to understand what you're going through. But I'm a good listener, if you ever feel like sharing your burden."

Needing a physical connection, he took hold of her hand. Her engagement ring dug into his palm, stinging his skin. "I couldn't save him. My best friend died because I failed."

"What was his name?" she asked.

Her voice was calm and soothing, like wind rippling through prairie grass. "John Ellis. We were friends for over eight years. Both of us were Green Berets, assigned to the same team. He was a weapons specialist, and I was trained as a medic. We were as close as brothers…no, even closer." His memories of John had been locked away, kept private to ward off the pain. Now, his complete trust in Grace helped him unburden some of the weight crushing his chest.

"How did he die?"

"We were on a highly classified mission." Heath slipped backward in time and saw the events unfold before him. "Our team was in pursuit of a highly valuable target. John was shot several times. I tried to treat him. We were taking enemy fire…we had to fall back." He took a long drink, the liquid burning a path to his stomach. A rogue muscle in his cheek twitched in time to the pounding of his heart. "By the time the medevac chopper arrived, it was too late."

"And you blame yourself."

Her words were more of a statement than a question. "Every single day," he answered without hesitation. "I was trained to save lives, and I couldn't save my best friend. He died on my watch."

Grace squeezed his hand. "You were in combat and were forced to make quick decisions. With the hindsight you have now, could you have done anything different?"

Heath rubbed his face with his free hand. "I don't know. I would give anything to have another chance. John left behind a wife and young son. For over a year, Julie didn't know how her husband died because of the classified nature of the mission. I let her suffer, until I finally got the nerve to tell her the truth."

The crickets played their evening melody.

Heath looked over to see a frown on Grace's face. Panic hit him like a punch in the gut. Did his failure change her opinion of him?

She sighed. "When good men die it is a tragedy, especially so when they're young. You would have done anything to save him, even risk your own life. I think what happened that day was well out of your control."

He shifted in his seat to face her. "Guilt is the price I have to pay. I'm here…and he's not." He paid every day. The guilt may recede but it never went away, even in his sleep.

A tear glistened in the corner of Grace's eye. She entwined her fingers with his. "If he was your friend then he would want you to be happy. He'd be mad if he knew you still carried all this guilt, right?"

The idea of John returning for one last fight made Heath smile. "Yeah, he'd probably whack me upside the head with the end of his rifle."

"How many lives do you think you've saved over the years?" Grace lifted her gaze to look him in the eyes.

As he flipped through his memory bank, the question hung in the air. So many battles were fought. Too many injured teammates to count. "I'll never really know," he said. "But that was my job. I was there to save lives."

"Because of you, countless men and women are alive today. I want you to remember that whenever you feel guilt over John."

In his mind, he pictured a scale. A side for the good he'd done and a side for the bad. In the end, he couldn't deny the bad side would always carry more weight. John wasn't the only one who'd been hurt by his failures. So many other people had died because of him. He could never tell Grace the entire story. If she knew the truth, she'd hate him.

"Twelve years was a long time to serve." Grace rocked back and forth in the chair. "Leaving the Army must've been a tough transition."

"When I drove through Fort Bragg's gate and saluted the MP on duty for the last time, I was an emotional wreck. The first week I spent with my Aunt Linda in Florida. She'd taken me in when I was eight years old and is the only family I have left. After that, I drove to Georgia and checked into a motel, and then spent the next two weeks stone drunk." To her credit, Grace's face remained relaxed, with no hint of judgment.

He swallowed hard, pushing down the lump in his throat. "I wanted to die. My body hurt from the abuse received over the years in the military, and then I had voices in my head, telling me my life wasn't worth the struggle. I took out my gun and pressed the barrel against my head. I couldn't stand another day of living with myself." On that day, he'd sunk into a deep darkness. The same pit as so many other warriors, some who'd never made it out alive. "I just couldn't pull the trigger."

"Thank goodness you didn't." Grace sucked in a breath. "You deserve your life, Heath. You deserve to be happy."

The light touch of her finger moved over a long scar on his arm. The simple action spread warmth throughout his body. "After I sobered up, I decided to take a road trip. First, I went to see John's widow, Julie. Then I came to Texas. I've been working odd jobs ever since. Being here, working at the ranch, I finally feel useful again. I enjoy caring for the animals. I like the freedom, the fresh air, and the open space."

"I think you were meant to find your way here." Her rocking chair continued to produce a rhythmic squeak against the plank wood floor. "We don't know each other very well, and I'm not a therapist, but I promise to listen if you ever need someone to talk to. I care about you."

All the air emptied from his lungs. He searched her eyes until his gaze dropped to her parted lips. All sane thoughts left his mind.

Grace leaned forward.

She smelled sweet, like a strawberry, and he lost the fight to maintain control. He didn't care that she wore another man's engagement ring, that he worked for her father, or that he wasn't good enough for her. Every cell in his body screamed to take her in his arms and kiss her. He brushed a trembling thumb across her bottom lip.

Grace made a low, throaty moan.

His lips were inches away when the sound of tires on gravel brought him back to reality. Headlights cut the darkness, and he leaned back.

The car came to a stop. Bruce and Joslyn got out and headed straight toward the porch.

"How are you doing, son?" Bruce placed a hand on his shoulder.

"A lot better, sir." Heath stood to put some more distance between Grace and himself, leaning against the porch rail. "I'm so sorry about what happened…I find my behavior hard to explain."

Shaking his head, Bruce waved his hand. "I'm the one who should be sorry. You had no idea those fireworks were coming. I did."

Joslyn stepped next to her husband, her petite frame only reaching Bruce's shoulder. "My dear boy, I can't even imagine what you've been through in service to our country. My older brother fought in Vietnam. I saw what that did to him. Don't ever apologize for things that are beyond your control."

Heath looked around him, at people who cared about his well being. Their kindness touched his soul. "Thank you, ma'am. I should turn in for the night." Shoving his hands in his pockets, he descended the porch steps. When he was halfway across the lawn, he turned back to see Grace still standing on the porch.

Her smile beamed across the dark empty space between them before she turned and went inside the house.

He could barely contain his emotions. When he entered the bunkhouse, he slammed the door behind him and braced his back on its sturdy surface. Years of unshed tears flowed from his eyes, which acted like a cleansing rain, washing away anger and pain. He cried for John, his lost brother, and for all the innocent people he'd seen die. Lastly, he cried for himself and the small seed of hope at a second chance.

Grace's face swam into view. The kiss they'd almost shared pricked at his conscience. She'd soon be married, and he'd inserted himself into her life, with so little regard for her future happiness. He'd let his own strong feelings for her totally supersede all other considerations. His attraction needed to stay locked away in his heart. She would be a friend—nothing more.

The time was well past midnight before he finally crawled into bed. Bomb blasts flashed behind his closed eyes. *Please, don't drag me back to the land of death. Tonight, let me dream about a dark-haired girl dancing across the Texas prairie.*

Chapter Fourteen

Boy, last night had been one for the record books. Grace rolled out of bed and dressed. Not only had she come to the aid of a former soldier suffering an all-star panic attack, she'd almost kissed him as he poured out his soul. While he'd talked, her focus remained on the shape of his full lower lip or how the ridges of his scars felt under her fingers. Might as well make it official— she'd completely lost her mind.

Her heart was like a laundromat dryer, and Heath the red sock that repeatedly tumbled past the window. The harder she tried not to think about him, the more often she did. Tyler had been slowly pushed to the recesses of her mind. He was away, working in some far-off location. And Heath—he was the one she couldn't wait to see each morning.

She'd known Heath for two weeks, and now she dreamed about him every night. Looking at her mirrored reflection, she saw the slow creep of a blush at the memory of last night's dream. This infatuation had to stop, which could possibly jeopardize her future with Tyler.

One year ago, she'd bumped into Tyler at his cousin's wedding. Alex had told her that Tyler would be there, so she'd dressed to kill. The formal gown she'd bought for the occasion was an attention grabber. The black dress clung to her body, with a modest cut in the front. But the reverse side dipped low and pooled around her lower back, exposing a lot of skin.

At the reception, she entered the room and purposely sauntered past Tyler, who was in deep conversation with several high school buddies. The heat of his stare followed her across the room. That night, Tyler asked her out on their first date. Before the month ended, he'd won her heart.

Tyler was everything she had imagined all those years ago. When they were together, he made her feel like a princess. He had swept her off her feet and never put her down. For her birthday, he'd planned an elaborate dinner, taking her to one of Dallas' finest restaurants. When he had gotten down on one knee during the middle of dinner, she'd practically screamed yes. That night was one of the happiest of her life.

Grace picked up their engagement picture sitting on her dresser. Next to Tyler's handsome face, she still viewed herself as awkward. She might have grown out her hair and learned to apply makeup in order to accent her best features, but inside her mind lurked the same insecurities. No amount of expensive clothing or trips to the salon would change that.

With a long sigh, she left the photo on the dresser and went downstairs. When she entered the hallway, Grace halted at her parents' voices echoing from the kitchen.

"Stop encouraging Grace to spend time with Heath." Mother's voice sounded firm and commanding. "Either you or Alex could have just as easily taken him home last night. I know what you're doing, Bruce Murray, and I don't like it."

"Havin' Grace take him home only made sense.

Besides, I knew she'd calm him better than anyone else."

"Don't make him Grace's responsibility. My brother had some of the same issues. The war destroyed his marriage and his family."

Grace stood frozen, her heart pounding in her chest.

"Darling, I know how you struggled watching your brother self-destruct when he came home from Vietnam. I've seen the way Heath is with Grace. She connects with him like no one else. He's coming out of his shell and—"

"Grace is getting married in six weeks. Tyler is the type of man she deserves. I think it's nice that both of you want to help Heath, but her focus should stay on Tyler and her wedding. Tyler is her future. He will give her a wonderful life."

"Remember the first time we met? At the rodeo parade," Dad said. "You were such a pretty little thing, Miss Longhorn and all. I only had five dollars in my pocket and worked for my pa on the ranch. I didn't have anything to offer you."

Still in the hallway, Grace heard the soft sound of her mother's laughter.

"You were so handsome that nothing else mattered. A bandit who stole my heart."

"Thank goodness, you looked past the skinny boy with no money and saw what was in my heart. I'm not saying that Grace shouldn't marry Tyler, but the girl needs the freedom to make her own decisions. Our kind-hearted daughter sees something worth saving in Heath. Let her figure out her own path."

Grace sighed and leaned against the hall closet

door. Were her feelings for Heath so transparent? Had her parents noticed the longing in her eyes whenever she'd looked at him? Not wanting to overhear more of their conversation, she walked into the kitchen. "Good morning," she called out in a cheery voice.

"Morning, butterfly." Dad reached for the newspaper on the table. "Your ma and I were just talking about how much fun we had at the festival yesterday."

"Was that all you were talking about?" Opening the refrigerator door, Grace pulled out the jug of orange juice. She poured a glass and sat on a stool by the kitchen island.

Joslyn set a plate filled with scrambled eggs and bacon in front of her and kissed the top of her head. "Eat up, honey. I'll take Heath's breakfast out to him." Seconds later, the screen door closed behind her.

"How much did you hear?" Dad asked.

"Enough." Grace picked at the scrambled eggs on her plate. She had to give her mother credit. The woman had the nose of a Bloodhound. She'd sniffed out Grace's attraction to Heath, which must have her very worried. Tyler was the apple of her mother's eye. If Grace told her the truth about her growing uncertainty, her mother would definitely freak.

He reached out a hand and stroked her back. "Your mom is concerned about you, that's all. She sees in Heath the same ghosts that still haunt Uncle Mike."

"She doesn't need to worry." Grace tried her best to sound nonchalant. "It's not like I'm planning to run away with him."

Her dad bellowed out a deep laugh. "Well, don't put that idea in her head."

As Grace chewed on a piece of bacon, she wondered what her dad's reaction would be if he knew she'd dreamt that very thing. In her dream, when she'd hopped on the back of Heath's motorcycle and wrapped her arms around his waist, the rest of the world had slipped away. They drove together for what seemed like hours, finally finding a quiet spot to stop. And, well, she couldn't think about what happened next. Not sitting across from her father.

"I know you, Grace." He pointed a finger in her direction.

Had he just read her mind? *Yikes!* Her blood pressure spiked. "What do you mean?"

"You want to help Heath, and you're good for him." Her dad stole a strip of bacon off her plate and waved it in the air. "Heath's been dealt a crap hand, but I know he's a fine man."

She smiled. For a man so big and strong, her dad carried a sensitive heart. "I want to understand him better. I hope that someday he can put behind the past and live a full life."

Dad placed his hand over hers. "You do what's in your heart."

"Thanks, Daddy." Grace rested her head on his broad shoulder. "I just want a marriage like yours, still madly in love after all these years." She remembered the story of how her parents met. Joslyn had been Miss Longhorn, and her dad had driven her in the parade. He'd been smitten by her mother's beauty but was too shy to approach her. He'd waited weeks, saving money and building up the nerve to ask her out. Little did he know, she'd been struck by the same bolt of attraction. After that first date, they'd become inseparable.

"Do you think marrying Tyler is the right decision?" Grace finally put into words the worries weighing on her heart.

"Pumpkin, I can't tell you that." Dad's eyebrows knitted together. "You need to decide what's right for your life. Just remember, real love isn't about looks or how much money you have in the bank. Real love is finding that one person who is the other part of your soul. You become two halves of the same whole."

Joslyn reappeared in the kitchen, coming through the back door and holding an empty tray. "What kind of advice are you dishing out, Bruce?"

He walked over and kissed her cheek. "Only what I've learned after thirty years of marriage to the most wonderful woman on the planet."

Her mother giggled like a schoolgirl.

"Perfect answer."

Grace rolled her eyes and laughed. "Did you see Heath outside?"

"I did, and he looked much better than last night. He's waiting for the lumber yard to deliver the wood for the gazebo."

While her mother was distracted with the dishes, Grace slyly scraped the remains of her breakfast into the trash. "I'm glad he's feeling better." She put the empty plate in the dishwasher. "I'm visiting Granny today. I want to show her the family Bible Heath and I found in the dugout."

"Tell Granny I say hi," Dad said before his grin withered into a frown. "From now on, stay out of that dugout. I wouldn't want you trapped inside when it finally collapses."

"I'll stay out, promise." She passed him at the

door, heading outside. She had to find Heath. After almost kissing him last night, she wanted to see if a spark truly existed between them or the attraction was a figment of her wild imagination. The only thing she knew for sure was that her feelings for Heath were getting harder to ignore.

****

After scarfing down his breakfast, Heath strode out to the barn to check on a loose board on the pig sty fence. So many chores to do. Added to his list was today's lumber delivery. *Good. Less time to dwell on what happened last night.*

Building the wedding gazebo would take top priority for the next few weeks. Grace deserved to have a perfect wedding, and he'd work hard to insure that happened.

He looked out toward the meadow that sat behind the house, picturing the completed gazebo draped with flowers. The image made Heath's heart ache—Grace adorned in her wedding dress, standing there with Tyler, promising to love him forever. She would soon belong to another man, blowing out of his life as quickly as she'd blown in.

He was lost in thought when he felt a hand grab his shoulder. Instinctively, he swung around, fist clenched and ready to strike.

Grace jumped back and stared with wide eyes. "It's just me," she squeaked out.

"I'm sorry." Regret squeezed his chest. He'd been so close to hitting her, for no other crime then approaching him from behind.

She stood perfectly still. The undeniable energy of fear rolling off her body.

"I didn't hear you approach." He stuffed his hands into his pockets, knowing no amount of apologizing would make up for his outburst.

"It's my fault. I should know better than to sneak up on a soldier." Grace took another step away.

His hair-trigger reaction frightened her. *I can't be trusted not to hurt the ones I love.*

He couldn't look her in the eye, so his gaze dropped to her red sneakers. "Maybe you should wear bells on your shoes." A lame attempt to lighten the tension. "Speaking of shoes, those don't look like barn-cleaning ones."

A hint of a smile appeared on her face. "You really making me do that? Cleaning out horse stalls is the worst."

"I won fair and square." He followed her outside. "Besides, I'm too busy to clean the horse barn. I'm starting your gazebo today." Approaching the ATV, he hopped on, resisting the urge to pull her close and breathe in the fresh scent of her hair. What were the odds he could get away before she mentioned anything about last night?

His military training had taught him to be tough. They'd turned him into a killing machine, capable of doing a lot of damage. But what happened last night, seeing Grace kneel before him and wash his face, had broken through his hard shell. Her soft touch had been more disarming than any weapon he'd ever encountered.

Last night's episode was bad, but he hadn't fallen as deep as usual. When the fireworks had blasted, and he'd felt himself slip away, hands had been on the other side, ready to pull him back.

Grace stood beside him. "Well, I should let you get to work. See you around." She hesitated. Her mouth opened, and then closed. Without another word, she turned and walked toward the house.

For the best. Mere words couldn't describe how precious she'd become. Something she would never know. Heath drove out into the pasture. Shadow, his ever-present companion, trailing alongside. The dog stayed by him throughout the day and slept at the foot of his bed at night, often waking him from bad dreams.

As he rode, the hills lay out before him. The abundant Longhorn cattle made for an inspiring show. Over the weeks working on the ranch, he'd come to know some of them by name. One of his favorites was a white cow with tan spots. When she heard Heath coming, she ran over to greet him, always bumping him for a treat. He also had become particularly fond of a new mom who had a gorgeous red coat and horns that were probably close to six feet in width. Her baby liked to stick his nose in Heath's pockets.

When he was done with his ride around the pasture, he returned to find the lumber truck had arrived. *Perfect timing*.

They'd unload the truck, and he could get to work.

He organized the lumber boards into neat piles. Noticing the time, he decided to eat lunch before getting out the power tools. Heath surveyed the area of land he'd build on. The natural beauty would make a perfect backdrop for a wedding. Instead of imagining Grace standing next to Tyler in the gazebo, he pictured Grace waiting for him in the middle of the field, surrounded by wildflowers and wearing a simple wedding dress. She would be draped in white, a symbol of purity. Could he reach out his hand to take hers without soiling it?

Who was he kidding? What type of husband would he make? The answer left him chilled. Grace deserved so much better than what he could provide.

As he walked to the bunkhouse, he noticed Grace's car was gone. Wonder where she went? Probably running errands for the wedding. Heath kicked a stone, sending it bouncing along the dry ground. He had to keep stop thinking about her wedding. If he kept busy, his mind was less likely to wander onto subjects better left alone.

The gazebo project would take up a lot of his time. This project would be a labor of love for the woman he couldn't have.

Chapter Fifteen

As Grace pulled her car into the senior apartment complex parking lot, she noticed three elderly women enjoying a morning stroll. Her great-grandmother had been a resident here for the past ten years. At ninety, Evelyn Murray was still energetic, always ready for a fieldtrip to the casino. Grace hoped that if she lived to be as old as her granny, she'd have half as much spunk. "Good morning," she said to a silver-haired gentleman sitting by the entrance doors.

The man looked up from his position on a park bench and gave her a friendly smile. "Good morning, dear. Who are you visiting today?"

"Evelyn Murray. I'm her great-granddaughter, Grace."

"Evie and I are card buddies." His long, age-spotted hands clapped together. "We play Gin Rummy after dinner every night. She'll be so happy you came. Her hip's been bothering her lately. I'm Ed, by the way."

She tucked the box under her arm and moved the paper bag to her left hand. Reaching over, she shook his hand. "Very nice to meet you. Have a good day." Grace gave him one last smile. The automatic doors swished open, and she stepped inside.

The lobby was spacious and comfortable, with a large grouping of upholstered seating in floral fabrics.

Four tall palm trees along with various plants helped bring the outdoors inside. Grace walked past the dining hall.

Inside the craft room, a group of ladies sat around a large table, working on a colorful quilt.

Down the carpeted hall was the door to her granny's apartment. She rang the doorbell and waited.

"I'll be right there," Granny said from the other side.

The sound of shuffling feet drew closer, and her barely five-foot-tall granny opened the door.

"My Grace," she said, taking her hand. "Come in. I'm so happy to see you."

Grace bent over to give the older woman a kiss on the cheek. "Good morning." She presented a brown paper bag. "I've brought two of Mom's blueberry muffins."

A smile brightened Granny's already cheery face. "Yum. I told your mom a long time ago she should open a bakery."

Grace followed her into the pint-sized kitchen. She grabbed two plates from the upper cabinet and opened the bag containing the muffins. The delicious smell of warm, sugary goodness filled the air. "I hear your hip is bothering you."

"Oh, just a few aches and pains." Granny poured two cups of coffee with a tremor in her hands. The carafe clinked against the ceramic mugs. More than a few drops landed on the counter. "Just part of getting old."

Grace wiped up the spills before grabbing the coffee mugs. "I'll take these into the living room."

"I'll carry the muffins." Granny moved to the

living room. She placed the muffins along with two plates on the coffee table then got seated in her recliner.

Grace sat on the sofa and filled in her granny on the latest wedding details. As they talked, Grace noticed her granny's yellow dress blended in with the yellow floral fabric on her recliner. The plate in her hand was decorated with painted yellow roses. She made a mental note to order a yellow corsage for Granny to wear at the wedding. Grace talked about cake options, DJ services, renting tents and chairs, flowers, and dresses.

As she listened, Granny bobbed her head. "Seems like a lot of work. In my day, we didn't have so much fuss. Your great-grandfather and I had two people in attendance. We went to the church then had a nice dinner. Everything now is too complicated." She wagged her finger.

"You're right." Grace sighed. How could she explain the heavy apprehension growing in her heart? "But these days everyone expects a big show. Tyler's parents are inviting a lot of their friends, so Mom's worried about impressing them."

Granny waved her hand and quietly grunted. "Who cares what those hoity-toities think? It's your day. I say do whatever makes you happy."

Smiling behind her mug, she took a drink of coffee. *Probably time to change the subject.* Granny was old-school and down to earth, and might not approve of her mother's grand wedding plans. She lifted the old Bible lying at her side. "I found this family Bible the last time I was in the dugout on the ranch." She extended the worn, leather book.

The old woman's wrinkled hands ran over the leather, and then opened the front cover. The stiff spine crackled. "Ezra Burchfield." Granny's finger traced over the inscription. She picked up her reading glasses and put them on. "Burchfield is my maiden name. Ezra was my pa's granddad and Kamama was his grandma. They lived in the dugout for the first year, while Ezra built the log cabin."

"We found the Bible and some copper bracelets locked in a metal box. Why do you think they left them after they moved?" Grace asked. The story of her ancestors was growing more and more intriguing.

"For safekeeping. If there was a fire in the log cabin, everything inside would've been destroyed. I'm sure they kept important things stored in the dugout. As a young girl, I used to play in that dugout. I'm surprised it isn't in ruins by now." Her brown eyes sparkled. Silently, Granny read the words Ezra had written in the Bible.

Amazing that even with a sixty-plus year age difference, she and Grace looked so much alike. Granny's long hair was now silver, but back in her youth it had been the same shade of black as Grace's. Remove the wear of time, and Grace saw her own dark brown eyes. The pictures on the wall showed a young Evelyn, many included her husband. In their wedding picture, they both looked young and in love. The grainy black-and-white photo did not do justice to Evelyn's beauty.

"Ezra wrote about a journey," Grace said when her Granny finished. "Do you know where they came from? Kamama was a full-blooded Cherokee, and Ezra was white. At that time, how would their paths have crossed?"

"If I remember right, they moved here from

Oklahoma. The Cherokee tribes often traded with the whites. Ezra could've met her that way." Granny gripped the arm of the chair and gradually stood. "I remember my dad telling us stories about them. They had a rough start, starting both a family and a ranch. Those were hard times." Granny disappeared down the hall, followed by the sounds of drawers opening and closing. Finally, she returned, carrying an old file folder. After placing it on Grace's lap, she returned to her recliner. "Those are some old family pictures, plus a few letters and such."

Grace opened the folder and slid out a stack of black-and-white photographs. "Since I've found that Bible, I want to learn more about our family's history, especially the Cherokee portion."

"Knowing where you come from is important." Granny tapped over her heart. "If you start to get serious, you could visit the Cherokee History Center in Oklahoma."

Grace looked at the pictures in her hand. Old images that chronicled a hundred years of her family's past. Two images stood out. First was one of Granny as a young girl. She stood under the arch for True Horizon ranch. That little girl was a mirror image of Grace as a young child.

The second was of a beautiful, older woman in a simple dress. The photograph was faded with time. She sat stiffly in a Victorian chair, unsmiling, and her long hair hung in two thick braids.

"Is this Kamama?" Grace whispered. She couldn't stop staring at the woman who was no doubt her ancestor. They shared the same high cheekbones, eye shape, and wide mouth. The image provided her with a strong connection to the past.

"Yes, this is Kamama." Granny's age-worn face softened. "My dad said it was taken about a year before she died. She'd already lost her husband. The man who took this image was a traveling photographer who'd come to town. Gave her a copy as payment for sitting for a portrait."

After paging through the stack of pictures, Grace gently slid them into the folder. "Would you mind if I took these home and scanned them into my computer?"

"I don't know what you mean by scan," Granny said with a laugh, "but they're yours to do with what you want. My gift to you." She took an embroidered handkerchief out of her pocket and blew her nose. "Did you know Kamama means butterfly in Cherokee?"

"That's what Dad calls me." Grace smiled at the coincidence. Or maybe it wasn't. "I should be going. I have a work project that needs my attention today. Thanks for the information, and the pictures."

Granny walked Grace to the door. "Say hello to that handsome man of yours. I got my dress for the wedding."

"Is it yellow?" Grace gave her a gentle hug, hiding her smile.

"How did you know?" Her eyes widened, allowing the surrounding creases to momentarily smooth.

"Lucky guess." Grace felt incredibly blest to still have her great-grandmother in her life. With her growing uncertainty about the upcoming wedding, she needed to stay close to the people who loved her and would support her, no matter what.

****

Heath sat at the worn, rickety table in his tiny

kitchen, reading over his sloppily written notes one more time. Seven million dollars—an unbelievable sum of money for someone who, until now, had his life savings stuffed in a cereal box. He'd just gotten off the phone with his deceased grandparents' lawyers and scribbled down words like benefactor, trust, probate, and estate tax. His grandparents hadn't tried to contact him in over twenty years, so the fact they'd willed their entire net worth to him was a shock, to say the least.

His mom's parents never approved of their only child running off with a troubled loser—the man who'd eventually become his father. They'd finally cut her off when Heath was four years old. His father was serving a life sentence in federal prison, and his mother had become addicted to first painkillers, and finally heroin. That was a dark time in Heath's young life. He didn't remember much, only the feeling of being alone and unloved. Then his mother lost her battle with drug addiction, and her parents avoided her funeral.

After her death, Heath went to stay with his dad's sister, Linda. He'd only seen his mother's parents a few times. They were practically strangers to him. Last year, when he'd found out they'd died in an accident, Heath had felt no reaction or loss.

Come to find out his grandparents had actually cared, a little. They'd just had a funny way of showing it. Along with the will, they'd left a letter. The lawyer indicated once Heath retained a lawyer of his own, he would fax over all the paperwork, and they could get the ball rolling. Heath had no idea where to find a lawyer in Liberty Ridge.

Thankfully, he'd waited to learn about the will until his life was somewhat stable. The peace of the ranch would help him make the right decision about the money. Maybe, he could use it for good. But in the end, all the money in the world wouldn't atone for the blood on his hands.

Bruce might recommend a good lawyer, though Heath wouldn't share the details of why. No one, except for the lawyers, would know he was a multimillionaire. While the ghosts of war still chased him, a simple and uncomplicated life was best.

Stepping outside into the heat, he smoothed back his hair and put on his baseball cap. His scratchy beard was growing too long and bushy, even by his standards. What had started out as an act of rebellion and toughness was now hot and annoying. But shaving it totally off, that idea sent panic through his veins. *Maybe give it a little trim. One step at a time.*

He saw Bruce standing by the horse paddock and went over to say hello. The high-noon sun beat down unmercifully. As he walked past the door to the horse stable, he turned his head to look inside. What he saw shot a lightning bolt to the chest. For several seconds, he stopped breathing.

There stood Grace, leaning against a manure fork, looking dirty and incredibly sexy. Gone were the expensive clothes. They'd been replaced by a black tank top and faded denim overalls. Scuffed work boots covered her feet. She wore the small version of a Stetson—her dark hair pulled in one long, glorious braid. Grace must have sensed he was standing there, because she looked over and gave him a small smile.

"You're lucky I still fit into my barn clothes," she called, waving at him. "I haven't worn these since high school."

Bruce approached with heavy steps. "I can't believe my eyes." He wiped his forehead with a red handkerchief, and then pushed it into his back pocket. "My fancy daughter is cleaning the stable. You must have lost a bet, girl."

"I did." Grace sighed. "And Heath has no mercy. I forgot how horrible a warm barn can smell."

"Well, bust my gut." The sound of Bruce's laughter echoed through the barn, disturbing a pair of doves nesting overhead. They cooed and flew out the door.

Heath was too busy catching his breath to say anything coherent. He stared wide-eyed and muttered something that didn't even make sense to his own ears. Taking a step backward, he tripped on a rake lying across the ground and landed flat on his rear.

Grace dropped the pitchfork and walked over to him, while he sat like a fool on the ground.

"Are you all right?" Her eyes narrowed. "You don't have heat stroke, do you?" She reached out and grabbed his outstretched hand, pulling him up.

"Ah…no." He refused to meet her gaze. "Wait, what did you ask?" *What's the matter with me?*

Laughing, Bruce shook his head. "Heath, you mind giving me a hand with the feed delivery? I'll give you a minute to pull yourself together. Meet me behind the white barn."

"Sure." Heath mentally kicked himself for losing his cool. Especially in front of Bruce. Seeing Grace dirty and sweaty had done things to his mind, and his body. He gathered the nerve to look at her again. And got hit with another jolt of attraction. "Good job in there." He cleared his throat. "Let me know if you need any help."

She stared, her gaze scanning up and down. "I won't need your help, but thanks. See you around." With a laugh, she turned and went back to work in the stable.

Heath kicked a clod of dry dirt and started toward the white barn. *You're acting like you've never seen a woman before.* He remembered returning stateside after a long deployment in the Middle East to the sight of Western women. His reaction to Grace had been one thousand times more intense.

She belonged here, maybe not cleaning out a barn, but at the ranch. Why had she chosen to live in a big city, away from a lifestyle she clearly loved?

Heath went to give Bruce a hand with the feed, which was the least he could do after he'd literally fallen for his daughter.

The large man grabbed a bag and only carried it a few feet before it slipped from his grasp. "Darn it," Bruce muttered.

Heath bent to pick up the bag and noticed Bruce shaking his hand and flexing his fingers. "You feeling okay?"

"Yeah, yeah. Only a little bit of tingling in my hands every once in awhile. Nothin' to worry about."

As they loaded the feed bags onto the bed of the truck, Heath kept an eye on Bruce to make sure he was really all right. "I've just learned I've been left a small inheritance by my grandparents. I need a lawyer to help with the details. Would you have a recommendation? Someone from Liberty Ridge."

Bruce tossed the last bag into the truck. "Well, the town's got a couple good lawyers. Mine is Milton

Prescott. His partner, James Garza, is a nice guy, too. I'll get you their office phone number later." He motioned Heath to get into the truck.

The two men drove into the east pasture.

"An inheritance, huh." Bruce gripped the steering wheel with one hand. His other fist rested on his lap. "That will give you a bit more freedom to decide what you want to do."

"Yes, it will." Heath knew the money was the key to his freedom.

"Whatever you decide, I have faith you'll choose the right path. Sometimes, it's unclear and may take some time to figure out. You know, you're welcome to stay here as long as you want."

"Thanks, sir. I appreciate the offer." Heath looked out the window, his gaze scanning the horizon. "For years, I didn't believe I had a future. A life outside the Army was hard to imagine." His heart constricted with memories of days filled with hard work and camaraderie. "At times, I thought I'd never make it back alive."

"And now, you build a life in honor of those who didn't." Bruce came to a stop and got out of the truck.

Heath stepped out, and then leaned on the hood of the truck. A sharp pain spread across his chest, stealing his breath. "I lost my best friend in Afghanistan. Most days, I feel I don't deserve to be here, alive…living my life as if nothing happened. Like I didn't lose everything that ever meant anything."

Bruce crossed his arms over his chest. "My ancestors had a purpose when they named this ranch True Horizon. It's a nautical term—a true horizon is the line between heaven and earth when you take out all obstacles, like if you were on a boat, staring across the ocean."

Nodding in understanding, Heath looked across the pasture, to the horizon line.

"See, I learned a long time ago," Bruce said. "To look past the distractions to see the important stuff."

Heath couldn't see the unbroken horizon line because too many obstacles blocked the way. The guilt, anti-social behavior, and his hard heart—all things that stood in his way of a clear view of his future. When he removed those things, he was left with only pure desires. He saw a family of his own, a wife, and children. Peaceful nights free from nightmares. And at the core stood Grace, holding the key to his happiness. With that thought, the whole illusion crashed down.

"Those are words of wisdom." Heath's vision blurred with unshed tears. "I'll just have to wait to see what's in store."

For years, he'd closed off his heart. Now, by allowing himself to feel again, all his old wounds had begun to fester. After spending so much time running from his emotions, they refused to be ignored and threatened to rip away his new sense of contentment.

Chapter Sixteen

Thank goodness, this is the last day of paying off that stupid bet. Grace shoveled another urine-scented load of straw into the wheelbarrow. Earlier in the week, the job hadn't seemed so bad, only a few hours of hard work. But now, seven days later, her muscles ached and her hair had the impermeable scents of barn, horse, and poop.

She grabbed the handles of the wheelbarrow and walked to dump it onto the pile outside. She'd saved Stargazer's stall until last. The gelding sure knew how to make a mess. After emptying the wheelbarrow, she had to stop and fill her lungs with fresh air before heading back. Inside the barn was so hot and stuffy, that she struggled to breathe. Grace noticed her boots were covered in horse manure, and her jeans streaked with some horrible green goo. Her shirt was soaked with sweat and stuck like a second skin.

An hour later, when she was finally done, she walked outside into the bright sunlight and blinked a few times. Was that Tyler's car parked in the driveway? He was supposed to be in Mexico.

She saw him standing on the porch, watching her with a wide grin. "Tyler!" She ran toward the house. As he came down the steps, she launched herself into his arms.

"Whoa, hold on there." He raised a hand to push

her away. "Why are you so dirty? Were you rolling around in the horse barn?" Tyler scrunched his nose and picked a long piece of straw out of her hair, letting it fall to the ground.

"I was cleaning horse stalls." *Wow*. Irritation made her already warm body boiling hot. After two weeks apart, he worried more about keeping his clothes clean than holding her. "Why are you home already? I thought you'd be in Mexico for a few more weeks."

"My boss let me have three days off. So I got on a plane to come see you. I missed you so much." Tyler leaned over to give her a kiss on the cheek, keeping a good foot of distance between his body and hers.

Her throat tightened with sentiment. "I've missed you, too. I'm almost done with the horses, so hang tight."

"I'll wait in the house. I'm sweating just standing here." He went to kiss her hand but recoiled at her dirty work gloves. After a brief scowl, he walked into the house.

The look on his face left her cold. Standing there in her work clothes, she forced back tears. She'd forgotten that he only knew the cleaned-up version of Grace. The way she looked now was a carbon copy of what she'd been as a teenager. The girl he'd no attraction to.

She quickly brushed aside her hurt feelings and went to finish her work. After a nice cool shower, she slipped on a baby-blue sundress. She'd washed her hair three times, and it now smelled like wildflowers and honey, a huge improvement.

As she brushed her straight locks, her mind drifted to Heath. Since the night of the Founders' Day Festival, he'd been avoiding her. After he'd opened up, she'd thought he'd come to think of her as a trusted friend. She couldn't have been more wrong. Maybe he felt bad for almost hitting her that next morning in the barn or embarrassed for sharing intimate details of his life. But for whatever reason, he treated her like the plague, and since she didn't know what she had done wrong, she didn't know how to fix things between them.

Although Heath was trying hard to avoid her, she still saw him every day, working around the ranch. Yesterday, when she was scooping out horse manure, she had caught a glimpse of him loading bales of alfalfa onto the flatbed. She couldn't help but notice he'd put on some weight, mostly muscle. Her heart had skipped a beat, watching him work with his shirt off, muscles rippling.

"Okay," she said to herself. "Time to pull your mind out of the gutter and go back to your fiancé." One more image of his tattooed chest and scars flashed through her mind. She slapped her hair brush on the vanity and rose. This obsession with Heath had to stop. Later, when she was snuggled against Tyler on the sofa of the family room, she laid her head on his shoulder.

He kissed the top of her head and inhaled deeply. "You smell good enough to eat."

"Better?" She studied his full mouth and felt only a small stirring of desire.

"Yes. Why were you working outside? Didn't your dad hire help for that?"

Grace considered for a moment telling Tyler about her bet with Heath, but that would lead to the potato sack race at the festival. She didn't think he'd be happy to hear that story. "I wanted to help. I like getting my hands dirty once in awhile. Everyone's doing extra chores to get ready for the wedding. I wanted to do my share."

"Soon, my love, we'll be home in Dallas, and you won't have to subject yourself to ranch work." Tyler said those last two words with disdain. He took her hand and rubbed it between his palms. "No calluses should be on these gorgeous hands."

She liked working outdoors, and Tyler would never understand that side of her. When she and Tyler had children, she hoped they would come here and learn the value of a hard day's work outdoors.

"How is your work in Mexico going?" she asked.

"Good. Our acquisitions department is working overtime to keep up. Which reminds me, did your dad ever review that paperwork I emailed over?"

She leaned back and narrowed her eyes. "He hasn't said anything to me. To be honest, I don't think he's interested in leasing to the oil company. He doesn't see the need."

Tyler stood and paced the room. "I don't understand why not. It's a good opportunity. After looking at the maps, I can tell your family is likely sitting on millions of dollars in profit."

"Dad has been clear about our family not needing the money. My parents don't need a lot of fancy things to be happy." She waved her hands around the modestly decorated space. "There's no rush, right? The oil will be here, if and when my dad decides to allow drilling." The room became uncomfortably silent.

Tyler stood still, looking out of the large picture window that overlooked the meadow. Hot pink flowers from a bougainvillea plant spilled across a trellis outside, framing the view.

Moving from the sofa, she went to him and wrapped her arms around his waist. Her lips brushed the small scar her brother had given him when they were fifteen. They had fought over a girl, and Grace remembered Tyler had eventually come out the winner. He'd dated that girl, Colleen Gardner, for the next two years.

Tyler turned in her embrace and firmly kissed her lips. "Let's go out and do something fun. You look too pretty to stay home."

His kiss left her head spinning. He still had that effect on her, a crazy rollercoaster ride that left her breathless. The feeling reminded her of why she wanted to marry Tyler. He was the love of her life. He was everything she'd ever wanted. At least, that's what she kept telling herself.

****

Standing in the shadows, Heath watched as the expensive sports car drove away, kicking up dust. So Tyler was here, staking his claim on Grace. A blazing jealousy filled him. He wanted to be the one she'd looked at with those large, adoring brown eyes, not Tyler.

A wave of sorrow washed over him. Ever since the night of the festival, he'd kept his distance. He was in no position to offer her anything good. So, he decided to go about his life as if Grace Murray didn't exist. Unfortunately, that plan had been a complete failure. He couldn't ignore her any more than he could ignore the sun in the sky.

That morning, for instance, he'd come across her raking out the horse stalls. He had gone into the stable to get a shovel. She'd looked dirty, sweaty, and totally irresistible. Her shirt had clung to her body, showing off all her curves. After Heath had spotted her and regained his senses, he'd stealthily made his escape without being noticed. Guess his Special Forces training was still good for something.

For a while longer, he let himself brood then hopped on his motorcycle and drove into town. After crossing the Hickory River Bridge, he parked in front of a two-story brick building set on Main Street. Heath took a deep breath and opened the glass door imprinted with the title—*Prescott & Garza.*

Inside sat a petite receptionist, her red hair in a high ponytail. "Hello," she greeted. "How can I help you?"

"My name is Heath Carter. I have an appointment with Mr. Garza."

She gave him a warm smile and handed him a clipboard with a sheet of paper attached. "Here is our privacy statement. Please read it over and sign at the bottom…oh, here's a pen."

Heath took the clipboard and pen, and then went to sit on one of the brown leather chairs in the reception area.

Several minutes later, a tall man came over to greet him. "Hi, Heath. I'm James Garza. It's a pleasure to meet you." The man's dark hair was smoothed back. He smiled and extended his hand to shake Heath's.

He followed the man to his office and took a seat.

James seated himself behind a cluttered desk.

Stacks of papers were piled so high, Heath was afraid they'd topple over. On the tall shelf at the rear of the office stood numerous family pictures—his wife and little daughter smiling happily. Seeing them gave

Heath a twinge of envy.

"So." James rubbed his hands together. "You said you are working for the Murrays and staying on their ranch. That must be a busy place with the big wedding coming up."

At the mention of the wedding, Heath flinched. "Yes, there is really a lot to do. Bruce hired me on temporarily, to help get things ready."

James leaned back in his chair. "I don't know Grace or Tyler personally, but this town is buzzing about their wedding. I've played golf a few times with Dr. Ross. He is very proud of his son."

Heath scratched at his beard. The room suddenly seemed to be closing in around him. The air felt heavy and thick, leaving him struggling for breath. James must have sensed his discomfort.

He turned his gaze to the file folder in front of him and cleared his throat. "I contacted the lawyer in Florida handling the estate. They faxed me all the relevant documents. After looking them over, I must say, you've inherited quite a windfall." He whistled as his finger tapped on the sum at the bottom of the sheet.

"That's part of the problem. Seven million is too much money for me to handle at this point in my life. I want to establish an investment account. Someplace where it can sit and grow interest until I've decided what I want to do." The weight of being an instant millionaire sat heavy on his chest.

"That's a smart way to go. I've seen people come into a fortune and treat it like play money." He turned in his chair and took a business card off the bookshelf. "I can give you the name of a financial planner that I trust. She'll set up any type of accounts that you need.

177

She'll also connect you with a CPA."

"Thanks for your help." Another person to make an appointment with. He'd have to deal with the stress of this—sitting through a meeting with a stranger—all over again. Beads of sweat formed on his brow. He wiped them away with the back of his hand.

"Well, okay then. I have some papers for you to sign now." James pulled a small stack of papers off his printer. "Then, once all the paperwork goes through the proper channels, I'll have you return to sign a few more documents, and that should be it."

After scanning through several documents, Heath signed his name at the bottom. When he was done, the two men shook hands.

James led the way to the reception area. "Take care, Heath. I'll be in touch."

Heath made his way out the door. The warm air hit him like a wall, but after being inside the lawyer's office, the heat felt refreshing. James Garza had been nice and helpful. Heath's panic hadn't been the lawyer's fault.

He'd spent years living his life on the fly. No plans. No dreams for the future. For the better part of his adult life, he wasn't even sure he'd live to see the next day, let alone set out a plan for his future.

I don't have to figure out everything right now. He just needed to clear his head. Barely noticing, he passed western wear shops and a hardware store. When he passed the café where he'd seen Grace for the first time, he stopped to peer through the window. She had looked so perfect, sitting in the booth with Molly and Jenny, discussing her wedding plans. At that time, he'd figured a fascination with her was harmless since he'd never see her again. Boy, had he been so very wrong.

Before long, he stood on the Hickory River Bridge. As the strong July wind pushed against the structure, the old wooden bridge creaked and moaned. *Back to the scene of the crime.* The moment he'd jumped in after her, his heart no longer belonged to him. The adage says that possession was nine-tenths of the law—but Grace would never know how much of him she owned.

As he watched the brown water of the river swirl below, he imagined what his life would be like once he left Liberty Ridge and the ranch. What could he see himself doing for the rest of his life? The Army had given him many skills, some of which would be marketable in the workplace. Maybe he could start his own business. He liked building things. Many times in the remote locations where his Special Forces team needed a firebase, they would have to construct the facilities from scratch. He could take a few business classes, learn about licensing and insurance, and start his own construction company.

He'd make that decision another day. Now, he had the power to shape his own destiny. As long as he could stay emotionally unattached from the people around him, he was free to go anywhere.

For the first time in a long time, he felt something other than rage and hate. After John's death, revenge held his mind hostage. He couldn't wait to get back to Afghanistan and kill those responsible. The fire consumed him. When he'd stepped onto the transport plane to head straight into the fight, rage burned deep in his soul.

During one mission, his unit had fallen under attack from a group of Taliban militants. The firefight had lasted hours, with both sides pinned down. Heath had pushed for close air support. He'd argued with his commanding officer, making the case they needed the bombers to end the stalemate before an American soldier lost his life.

Now, as Heath stood on the bridge, he relived that day. He could hear the rumble of the bombers flying above. The shockwave of bomb blasts vibrated through his body.

The bombs had left a large hole where the enemy had taken position, and Heath went along with his unit to survey the area. His stomach lurched at the memory of what they'd found. One of the bombs had hit an occupied hut. The bodies of its victims were strewn across the dirt.

Hot tears stung his eyes as those images flickered through his mind, like a horror picture reel. The worst image was of a young boy, maybe three years old, lying in his mother's arms. Both dead.

After pushing back those memories for so long, they were now crashing over him like tidal waves. He grasped the wooden rail of the bridge for support, and a splinter dug into his palm.

He had wanted revenge, and innocent people had paid the price for the fulfillment of his desire. Heath's chest constricted to the point he could hardly breathe. Dealing with so many emotions at once overwhelmed his body. He closed his eyes and focused on taking long, deep breaths.

"You're not jumping, are you?"

A gentle voice broke his fragile meditation. He opened his eyes and turned to see a petite woman standing next to him.

"I'm not." Although he was grateful for the interruption, he couldn't help but feel annoyed. *Another busy-body.*

"Good, because you got that vibe goin' on here." She stared with an intense gaze.

The woman was pretty, in a girl-next-door kind of way, with big blue eyes and fair skin. Her shorts, athletic top, and lime green shoes hinted she was probably in the middle of a run.

"Colleen Gardner." She held out her hand. "And you are?"

He glanced at her outstretched hand, finally giving it a quick shake. "Heath Carter."

"You work for the Murrays, don't you? Alex told me how you saved Grace when she fell in the river."

He nodded, unsure about this tiny woman who had just appeared. "I'm working there temporarily. The Murrays are a good family." Heath took a step toward the end of the bridge. As he walked, back toward the downtown shops, Colleen's steps echoed behind him.

"You looked like you were in serious trouble just now. I don't mean to be nosy, but are you all right?" She touched his arm.

He involuntarily flinched. Not wanting to be rude, he took a deep breath before answering. "I'm sorry, but it's really none of your business." His chest knotted with tension while he continued walking, with Colleen falling in line beside him.

"Just a second." She stopped at the entrance to a book store. "Please just wait here. I'll be right back." She ran inside.

Heath waited, thoroughly perplexed.

Several seconds later, she reappeared, pen and

paper in hand. She scribbled down a few lines, and then handed it to him.

His gaze snapped up to meet hers. "What is this?"

She stood with a hand resting on her hip. "I'm a Clinical Psychologist. When I approached you on the bridge, my spidey senses tingled. I practiced for several years by the Army base in Killeen and recognize that look from a mile away. Former soldier, right?"

"I don't need a shrink." He extended his hand toward her and flapped the paper.

She raised her hands, refusing to take it. "You may be right. You may not need any help, but please keep my name and phone number just in case you ever want to talk. I've helped many men and women in similar situations. Hope exists. We can find a way to make things better."

His defenses lowered, and he considered what she said. Looking at her, he only saw compassion in her eyes. What if he could find help in this small, blonde, scrappy package? He folded the piece of paper and put it in his pocket.

Without saying another word, she smiled and restarted her run, heading over the bridge.

Heath was left scratching his itchy beard, wondering if this chance meeting could be the answer to his prayers.

Chapter Seventeen

"Sorry, Grace, but that is not happening." Tyler sat next to Grace on the metal bench in her mother's flower garden. A large mesquite tree provided shade from the late afternoon sun.

"You said yourself that you don't spend much time in the office. Your schedule has you traveling most of the week. What is the difference if we live in Dallas or here, in Liberty Ridge?" A hint of desperation marked her voice.

"I'm not moving back to a small town. Plus, I'm making a name for myself at Petro-Holdings. No way am I asking them to work remotely. Not this early in my career." Tyler crossed his arms and raised his chin

"Don't you want our children to grow up with all this space and freedom, not crammed into a city apartment with no yard?" She needed him to understand her point of view.

Tyler stood. "I'm not raising my children in some two-bit town with no opportunities. The only thing these people care about is high school football and feed prices." He paced back and forth and threw his arms in the air. "They even close the shops in town early on Friday night for the high school football game. I spent my whole childhood waiting to get out. No way am I moving back to Liberty Ridge."

The force of Tyler's words struck her like a slap

across the face. She never knew how much he detested their hometown. "How can you say those things? You're talking about our family and our friends."

"Your family, Grace." He pointed a long finger. "My parents barely tolerate it here."

Her hands trembled. For years, she had worked hard to become the type of woman Tyler could love. She'd changed, both inside and out. Now, she was asking something from him, and he wouldn't even consider her request. Grace stood, ready to walk away but then stopped. She turned on her heel to face him. "If we're to be married," she said in a low voice. "You will have to compromise."

"Not about this." He brushed past her and strode away, hands clenched at his sides.

A minute later, she heard the house door slam shut. The tears, which she'd locked away, broke free and spilled down her cheeks. Why were relationships so hard? Shouldn't couples in love work out these problems without turning into a fight? All she had done was suggest they live in Liberty Ridge.

The more time she spent at the ranch, the stronger its pull became. She didn't miss the crowded city streets or constant noise of Dallas. Not once had she felt the urge to go visit for the day. Except for Tyler, everything she loved was right here.

As her dreams crashed around her, they all seemed meaningless. Could she have been wrong to think Tyler was her perfect man? Not that such a person existed.

She'd dated other men in the past, mostly the suit and tie types. Oh, and one rodeo cowboy. She smiled at the memory of their date. His plate-size belt buckle had been too much of a distraction. And when he'd pulled her close for a kiss, the huge piece of metal nearly impaled her.

None had ever lived up to her expectations. She'd raised Tyler so high, no wonder reality dragged him down. Drying her eyes, she strolled along the stone path through the flower garden. Low bunches of ground cover wove their way around rose bushes and tall Texas Star hibiscus. The flowers filled the air with heavenly fragrance.

As she left the garden and approached the house, she saw her dad sitting on the porch, reading the Sunday paper. She climbed the stairs and took the rocking chair next to him.

"What's wrong, butterfly?" He put down the paper.

She let out a long sigh. "I mentioned to Tyler I've been thinking a lot about living in Liberty Ridge after we're married. I really don't want to live in Dallas. He travels so much that I thought he wouldn't mind. Tyler said he'd never move back to this 'hick town.'" She put those last two words in air quotes.

Dad laughed. "I coulda told you that. That boy couldn't wait to see this town in his rearview mirror. He never liked living here and never will."

"I only wanted to talk about the option. He wouldn't even consider it." She increased the pace of her rocking to match the rapid beat of her heart.

"You really want to come home to Liberty Ridge?" Dad raised his bushy eyebrows. "Since you graduated high school, you've been keen on living in the big city."

"I'm honestly not sure what I want." Grace sighed. "But I'd like the option to raise my kids the same way I was raised. Maybe not on a ranch per say, but in a safe place where they can run free."

"Now that's something you and Tyler need to work out." Her dad took her hand and gave it a light squeeze. "You can postpone the wedding if things don't feel right. I'll support your decision, whatever it is."

She replayed her conversation with Tyler. He was probably upstairs packing. He had a flight to Mexico that evening. New doubts bubbled to the surface. Maybe only a case of pre-wedding jitters. Grace wanted to go into the house and smooth things over with Tyler. Before she could get to the front door, a red minivan pulled up, parked, and two little girls tumbled out of the sliding door.

They called out in unison. "Papa. Auntie Grace. We're here!" The girls were halfway to the house when something by the horse paddock caught their attention. They switched direction, like a synchronized school of fish, and took off running. Obviously, they had found something, or someone, more exciting than Auntie Grace and Papa.

A bubble of laughter burst inside her. She couldn't blame them for favoring Heath when she was just as guilty.

****

Horses really aren't that bad. Heath sprayed down a mare with the hose. As the cool water ran over her body, she stomped in obvious appreciation. If he didn't know any better, he would've sworn the horse smiled. He turned to the sound of squeals and giggles and saw Kara and Lizzy running in his direction.

They hopped up on a low rail of the paddock.

"Heath, we're at Nana and Papa's house for a picnic," Kara said.

He remembered Kara always wore a pink ribbon in

her hair.

"Papa said we can ride a horse later," Lizzy piped in. "What are you doing?"

"I'm giving the horse a bath." He walked over to turn off the water, his boots squishing through the mud. "You girls need a bath, too?" Heath pointed the hose at the giggling girls.

"No!" They shook their heads, curls swinging back and forth. "We can't get our clothes wet," Lizzy said. "We brought our swimsuits for later. Papa's got a sprinkler."

"Sounds like fun." He came over to the girls and leaned on the rail. Looking toward the house, he saw Grace sitting on the porch with her dad, Alex, and Jenny. No Tyler in sight. That man was seriously annoying. Every time Heath saw Tyler, he had his nose in his smart phone and a scowl on his face. He couldn't leave work behind, even after being away from his fiancé for two weeks.

Earlier, he had noticed Grace talking with Tyler in the flower garden. Grace looked upset, and Tyler had eventually stormed off. Heath had wanted to punch the guy for being such an idiot where Grace was concerned. Instead, he'd gone back to work, in hopes of cooling his temper.

"Are you coming to the picnic?" Kara asked. "Daddy's making his special chicken. It's so yummy!"

"You bet, munchkins."

The girls broke out into a fresh set of giggles.

Their joy made him smile. "Go over by your mom and dad before you get muddy. I need to finish here then I'll join you."

The girls jumped off the rail. "Promise you'll play

SOLO with us and Auntie Grace. I want to see her lose again." Kara hopped up and down.

Heath laughed at their eagerness. "We'll see." How had he made friends with a pair of six-year-old girls? Whistling an upbeat melody, he led the mare back to her stall.

A little while later, he sat on the patio and the smell of grilled meat made his mouth water. A large canopy had been erected and provided much-appreciated shade. Alex brought out a cooler filled with soda and beer and was now manning the grill. Storm clouds converged in the western sky. The area needed the rain, but hopefully, the clouds would hold off until later.

"Hey." Bruce handed him a beer. "The ladies are in the house getting the food ready. Alex is in charge of the grill. And you and me, we get to supervise." He clinked bottles with Heath.

"I like that." Heath took a drink. No doubt Tyler was inside with the women. That snarky thought brought a smile to his lips.

He and Bruce sat and talked for a while, until the back door opened and Tyler came outside. He went directly over to Alex at the grill.

Bruce tipped his head toward Tyler. "I say you can tell a lot about a man by his hands."

"Pencil pusher," Heath said with a grin.

Bruce let loose a hearty laugh, which got the attention of both Alex and Tyler.

"You're a straight shooter." Bruce took a drink out of his beer bottle. "I like that about you." He pushed to stand and swayed. Taking hold of the arm of his chair, Bruce steadied himself.

"Are you feeling all right?" As he watched Bruce

struggle, Heath's concern grew. More than once, he'd witnessed Bruce unsteady on his feet. Bruce's face, normally a ruddy color, had gone pale, and his hands shook slightly.

After a few deep breaths, Bruce let go of his hold on the chair. "Oh, I'm fine. My body can't take the heat like it used to." He patted Heath on the shoulder and went into the house.

Tyler turned to watch Bruce go inside, and then narrowed his eyes at Heath.

Grace stepped out of the back door carrying a large purple bowl. She set the bowl on the table and took the chair next to Heath. The one her dad had just vacated. "I'm glad you decided to join us. The twins can't stop talking about you. They might start a fan club," Grace said with a chuckle.

"Would you join?"

She looked at him with a soft smile. "You know I'll always be in your corner."

"Grace, can you come here?" Tyler hollered.

"Be right back," she whispered to Heath.

He watched as she walked over to Tyler. Jealousy heated his skin.

Grace's hands rested on her hips while she listened to what Tyler had to say. A frown pulled at her mouth.

"Why is he here?" Tyler asked in a raised voice. "Does he think he's part of the family now?"

"As far as I'm concerned, yes, he is."

Her chin was set at a defiant angle. Heath smiled behind his beer bottle. *What a woman.*

"I expect you'll be polite." She swiped the beer out of his hand and returned to her chair.

She brushed the damp surface of the bottle over her

189

forehead. Water droplets rolled down the side of her face. One came to rest on her upper lip.

His fingers twitched with the need to brush across her desirable lip. *Geez, get a grip, man.* Her jerk of a fiancé was standing only a few feet away. Watching how Grace and Tyler acted toward one another, he wondered if trouble had arrived in paradise. But why should he care? Not like he had a chance with her, whether Tyler was in the picture or not.

****

When the food was ready, the family gathered around the table, prayed, and began chowing down. They looked like a swarm of ants at a picnic. Everyone reaching, grabbing, and shoveling food onto their plates. Grace sat next to Tyler, who now attempted to smooth over things before he left for Mexico. He was being so attentive, Grace wouldn't have been surprised if he offered to cut her meat. Her heart melted a tiny bit from his efforts.

Their wedding was a little over a month away, and her shoulders bore the heavy weight of her indecision. The invitations were sent out, her dress altered and ready for the final fitting, her bridesmaids' and flower girls' dresses were bought and paid for, and the caterer had deposits for their services.

Every day that passed, she felt less sure about spending the rest of her life with him. He had a different vision for their future.

Alex, who sat across from her, turned to Heath. "I heard you met Colleen Gardner the other day. I saw her at the restaurant. She asked how you liked working at the ranch." He tipped his head at Tyler. "Tyler and I went to high school with her. Grace, too, but she was two years behind."

Hearing Colleen was back in town, Grace nearly choked on her corn. "Why is she here?" She narrowed her eyes. "Setting traps for unsuspecting men, no doubt." She didn't even want to think about Colleen going after Heath.

"Colleen opened a practice in Liberty Ridge. If you ask me, she doesn't need to set traps for men. She still looks pretty good…ouch!" Alex said at the same time Jenny's sharp elbow connected with his ribs.

Followed by a look that could have shriveled a tomato off the vine. "Well, Heath should stay away from her." Grace crossed her arms. "Colleen is not a nice person."

"Grace Ann," her mother scolded. "Be nice. Colleen's father told me she graduated from Yale with honors and has worked in Killeen for several years. She is a very well-respected psychologist."

Tyler reached under the table and to hold Grace's hand then gave it a quick squeeze. The comforting gesture only stoked her temper. She wanted to squeeze his hand back twice as hard.

Alex grinned. "Heath, don't listen to Grace. Colleen is a friend. Maybe we can all get together and go out some night."

Heath looked at his plate, pushing food around with his fork.

He studied the mounds of coleslaw and fruit salad like he'd never seen anything so interesting in his life. Was he attracted to Colleen? She was very pretty, if one liked the blue-eyed, perky blonde look. And Colleen did know how to get her way with men. She came across as sugar-sweet but could be as mean as a pit viper. Or at least she had been in high school. The thought of Heath and Colleen together riled her every nerve. "Having Colleen Gardner in the same room with me is not a good idea."

Heath shifted in his seat and turned to Bruce. "I have two tickets for the preseason football game between the San Antonio Rangers and the Timber Lake Warriors. Would you like to go? The game is a week from Friday."

Bruce's face brightened. "I'd like that, a lot. Thanks."

Tyler rested his forearms on the table and leaned in. "You don't strike me as a football fan, Heath."

Resting back, Heath hooked his hands behind his head. "My late friend's widow is now married to the Warriors' linebacker, Reagan Harrison. She sent me two tickets in hopes I could come to the game and see her and the kids. We'll be sitting with Julie and her family in their stadium suite."

If Grace's eyes didn't pop out of her head, they were pretty darn close. "You know Reagan Harrison?"

He shrugged. "Not very well. Julie had some rough years after John died. Reagan's been very good to her."

"I remember reading an article about Reagan eloping last year." Alex nodded. "The media speculated that he'd lose his edge."

Bruce set down his fork. "No chance of that. That man can bulldoze through an offensive line like they're a bunch of little girls." He looked over at his granddaughters. "No offense, sweethearts."

The scowls on Lizzy and Kara's face lifted into smiles.

Tyler pushed back his chair to stand. "I need to

leave to catch my flight. Thanks for your hospitality." He turned to Grace. "Walk me to the car?"

Joslyn stood and gave him a kiss on the cheek. "Travel safe. How much longer do you have to be in Mexico?"

"Only two more weeks." Tyler said goodbye to everyone minus Heath. Once they got to his car, Tyler pulled her into a strong embrace. "I hate leaving you." He nuzzled his face against her neck.

"Then don't leave. Stay here." She knew he wouldn't stay but issued the challenge anyway.

"You know I can't. This trip is important to my career. Doing well there could mean a big promotion." Tyler stepped away. "This is for you, too."

"If you think I care about status and money, then you don't know me." Grace didn't doubt he cared. But she was seeing cracks growing between them. If his loyalty was ever tested, would he choose her or his career?

Tyler pressed his lips to hers.

For Grace, his kiss had lost most of its spark. Instead of producing fire on her lips, her reaction only felt lukewarm.

When he pulled away, he took her hand and turned it palm up. He lightly ran his index finger over its lines.

As if he was reading her future. What did he see? A life filled with social engagements and long nights home alone?

"I love you, Grace. I can't wait to be your husband. We'll get away from here, from whatever's been bothering you, and start our life together."

They kissed one last time before Tyler got in his car and drove away.

When she returned to the table, Heath's gaze followed her like a scientist studying the mysteries of life. The family had finished eating, so she began clearing the plates off the table. She leaned in to take Heath's plate, and he grabbed her hand. Startled, she sharply inhaled. His touch electrified her skin.

"You are perfect," he whispered. "Don't change who you are in order to please anyone." He let go, got up out of his chair, and walked away.

Grace was left holding a stack of dirty plates, realizing her life had just gotten a lot more complicated.

Chapter Eighteen

Heath sat in Colleen Gardner's office, tapping his foot on the tile floor and drumming his fingers. When he'd called yesterday for the appointment, Colleen's secretary had told him since the practice was new, they had plenty of openings. So, after almost canceling more than once, there he sat, ready to ask for help. Which didn't come easy to a man who'd spent his entire adult life in the company of some of the country's toughest soldiers.

While he waited, Heath distracted his anxious mind by looking around the office. The space was bright and cheery, with large windows and comfortable furniture. Several unpacked boxes were stacked behind the large mahogany desk. Besides a few thickly bound books, two large bookshelves sat empty. On the wall opposite the windows hung a large diploma from Yale.

His carotid artery pulsed rapidly in his neck, and his clothes were damp with perspiration. An overwhelming desire to escape the office took hold. He stood, ready to run, when the door unexpectedly swung open. Heath's already rapidly beating heart nearly exploded out of his chest. In walked Colleen, serene as a dove, with cup of coffee in hand.

"Hi, Heath. Sorry to keep you waiting." She reached over to shake his hand. "The painters bought the wrong color, and I had to firmly tell them they were not painting my waiting room crimson red." She laughed and sat in the chair opposite him. "Can I get you something to drink?"

Heath sank back in his chair and shook his head. Around him, the room seemed to shrink and spin. He took a deep breath and focused on Colleen and the sound of her voice.

Her hair was pulled back loosely off of her face. She reached for the black rimmed glasses perched on her head and set them on the bridge of her nose then began reading the contents of the folder in her lap. After a minute, she looked up. "Why are you here?"

He struggled to put his answer into words. "I'm tired of running," he finally said. "I want to learn how to live again." Her blue eyes watched him with an intensity that made him squirm in his seat.

"How long did you serve?"

"I enlisted at eighteen." He drummed his fingers on the arm of the chair. "And separated a year and a half ago, so twelve years."

"Army?"

Was there any other choice? At the recruitment office, he'd selected the Army and never felt anything less than pride at the title of soldier. "Yes, after two years I joined the Rangers. Eventually, I qualified for Special Forces. I was trained as a medic. Toward the end of my enlistment, I served on a Delta Force unit, mostly in Afghanistan."

Colleen's eyebrow arched high on her ivory forehead. "Impressive credentials. What have you been doing since you're separation? What is your life like now?"

His gaze focused on his clenched hands. "I've

196

drifted from job to job. I don't have friends really, except for the guys I served with. The only family I have is an aunt who lives in Florida."

"What about the Murrays? Do you consider them friends?"

Heath nodded. "They've been good to me. Yes, I now consider them friends." He raised his gaze to stare out the window. "I'm exhausted…trying to outrun the world."

"You're also running away from yourself." Colleen pushed her glasses to rest on top of her head. "I've treated many soldiers with PTSD, just like you, but everyone's journey is different. I can't offer you a cure or magic pill, but I can help. The process is not easy, and it takes hard work, but I've witnessed firsthand how therapy can help. If you agree to work with me, then together, we can take those first steps toward reclaiming your future." She reached over and put her petite hand over his.

An hour later, Heath left the office with a small weight lifted off his shoulders. One session hadn't been life-changing, but his acceptance of the problem was a good start.

She insisted he call her Colleen, saying she didn't want her patients to see her as their doctor, but their advocate and guide. He lacked confidence that he would ever feel totally "normal," even so, he was willing to work to see how close he could come. Unfortunately, he was sure no amount of therapy would ever take away the intense guilt he carried every moment.

His thoughts turned to Grace. Colleen was pretty, but as far as he was concerned, Grace's beauty outshone every other woman.

His Harley sat in the parking lot, waiting patiently for his return. As he pressed the start button, the bike's engine roared to life. The deep, throaty rumble reverberated through his body. His spirits lifted at the view of the open road.

He spent the next few hours riding down country roads, enjoying the fresh air and freedom. His mind drifted to the future. When his employment at the ranch was over. Where would he go next? With his inheritance, he didn't worry about money. Maybe he'd stay in Liberty Ridge in order to continue his sessions with Colleen.

By the time he pulled onto the Murrays' drive, darkness had already settled over the ranch. He parked next to the bunkhouse and noticed lights still shining bright in the barn. Country music floated out of the open door. Curiosity got the best of him, so he went to see who was working late. His stomach flipped at the sight of her.

Grace stood in the aisle, brushing her mare, Silver. She wore a baseball cap, and her ponytail poked through the opening in the back. As she ran the brush over the horse's silky hair, she made an enticing picture.

She must have heard him because she lifted her head.

Instead of her trademark smile, her full mouth turned down in a frown. Dark circles framed her brown eyes. "Hi."

Her voice was so quiet Heath could barely hear her over the music. He walked over to grab another brush and went to work on the other side of the horse. "Hi, yourself. Why are you out here so late?"

"I needed a break from my mother and her constant barrage of wedding talk. I'm on a train going full steam, and all I want to do is jump off."

They both worked in silence, the only sound the *whoosh* of brushes rubbing against the horse's hair and the song playing on the radio. Heath walked around and gave Silver a quick rub on the nose. He stood beside Grace and placed a finger under her chin. As he lifted her face, she stilled. "You don't seem very happy." He searched her eyes for an answer to her sad mood. "Why?" His heart stabbed with pain at seeing her upset. He'd move mountains to put a smile on her face.

"I don't know who I am anymore. You told me the other day not to change, but it's too late. If you asked me what I want for my life, I honestly can't answer." She returned to brushing the horse. "I've spent years turning myself into someone I've discovered I don't really like." Stepping back, she set the brush on a wooden tack box.

"You're a confident woman who has spent too much time making other people happy." Heath moved toward her. He had so much he wanted to say—paint a picture of how she looked through his eyes—kind and caring, beautiful on the inside and out.

"Where were you ten years ago?" Shimmering tears glided down her face. "I might have fallen in love with you."

"Then I would be the luckiest man alive." As the radio played a country love song, he took her hand and pulled her close. "Dance with me." His mind scolded him this was a bad idea, even worse than when he'd dated the daughter of Fort Bragg's Garrison

Commander. His heart disagreed and told him Grace was exactly where she needed to be, in his arms.

Her body fit comfortably against his, and she rested her head on his shoulder. Tim McGraw and Faith Hill sang their famous duet about unending love. With Heath's arms wrapped around her waist, Grace fingered the hair at the base of his neck. He'd happily stay in that embrace for the rest of his life. "Do you love him?" His hands tightened their hold.

"I'm not sure I even know what love is anymore." Grace's hips swayed with the music. "Ever since I've moved home, I've felt this shift inside me. This place is reshaping me into the person I used to be. And you know what? I like it." She lifted her head to meet his gaze.

Heath slowed until his feet completely stilled. He became lost in the depths of her dark brown eyes. Right now, he needed to walk away before they made a mistake. Caution rang in his head, but he silenced it. He was under her spell. He wanted her more than he'd ever wanted anything in his entire life.

She took off her baseball cap, tipped her head, and leaned into him, their lips finally touching with a searing heat.

****

Grace jumped off the edge of the cliff, and she was free falling. Hungry for his touch, she offered him an invitation as old as time. Heath's mouth moved over her, and his hand grabbed hold of her ponytail. The soft hairs of his beard tickled against her lips, cheeks, and chin, just like she had imagined.

Inhaling deeply, her nose filled with the masculine scents of sweat and exhaust. Delicious. They increased her hunger for him.

His hands moved down her back, and then gripped the sides of her waist, squeezing with slight pressure. A deep moan sounded from the base of his throat. He parted his lips, gently exploring her mouth with his tongue.

She responded with a new sense of urgency. Grace's heart thumped against her ribcage. She pressed her hands on his broad chest and grabbed a fistful of his shirt. When he pulled away, she sighed.

"I'm sorry." He kissed her forehead. "I should never have kissed you." His voice cracked mid-sentence.

His words stung. "You're sorry for kissing me? Why?"

"Grace," he whispered. "Do you know what you're doing to me? I want to do so much more than just kiss you." He paused, reaching over and twirling a lock of her hair around his finger.

She knew he felt the same magnetic pull between them, which increased her boldness, but he was fighting the attraction.

"I'm not worthy," he said. "You have to understand that I will never be worthy of you."

She took his hand in hers. The heat of his body engulfed her, until she burned so hot with longing. "Don't say that. You're constantly on my mind." Right now, she'd put her heart on the line. "If I call off my wedding, would you give us a chance?"

Heath lowered his gaze. He dropped her hand and stepped away. "Don't hang your hopes and dreams on me. I can promise you only heartache and pain."

The weight of sorrow crushed her chest, and tears

welled in her eyes. "You don't know that." She opened her mouth to plead her case, but when she saw the pain etched in his face, she bit back her words.

"I can't be the kind of man you need." With shoulders slumped, he started for the door.

She followed him, her heart beating rapidly. "Don't push me away." What else could she do to make him stop and listen? "Don't we owe it to each other to explore what's going on between us?"

Picking up her hand, he brushed his lips over her knuckles.

Shivers danced across her now cool skin.

"All I can offer you is my friendship. Nothing more. If you want a man who will give you safety, stability, and a family, then you should marry Tyler. He can care for you like I never could."

"Is that what you want?" Stunned by his rejection and suddenly angry, Grace folded her arms over her body. "For me to be married and out of your life?"

Heath closed his eyes and took a deep breath. He reopened them before turning to walk outside, disappearing into the darkness of the night.

Grace stood frozen and watched him leave. Her first instinct was to follow, but she stopped her impulsiveness. Heath had been clear that although he may be attracted, he had no interest in starting a love affair. How silly to think he'd fallen in love.

Still standing in the aisle, Silver let out a breathy sigh. Grace approached the horse and led her back into her stall. She closed the gate, slid the metal bolt into place, and leaned on the low, wooden wall. "What should I do?" she asked the horse, who munched loudly on her oats.

Silver looked at her and continued to chew.

Her horse acted totally oblivious to the troubles of the human heart. Her first kiss with Tyler had been her Cinderella moment—a culmination of years of her dreams to win his heart. And when he slipped that diamond ring on her finger, the fit was perfect, like a glass slipper.

Her attraction to Heath had come unexpected, leaving her unprepared. Like a summer storm that had a person seeking shelter. Their kiss had ignited a lightning bolt, which rocketed toward earth and struck her heart. Over the past month, a rumble of distant thunder sounded in the distance. She'd seen the warnings. But now the storm was forming above her, refusing to be ignored.

In her younger years, her goals were simple—get away from the ranch and mature into a classy woman who could turn Tyler's head. Everything she had done since high school had been for the purpose of changing who she was. *How pathetic.* Why hadn't she been happy to stay a free-spirited girl? Who had she pleased by changing? And in the end, was she better off after all the effort?

She was done making decisions based on pleasing others. How could she ever be truly happy until she learned to value her own spirit? From now on, she'd listen to her own heart.

Turning off the radio and then the lights, she closed the stable door for the night and went up to her bedroom. She sat in front of her laptop and opened her email. A message from Tyler waited. He'd written that he loved her and was sorry for how he'd acted the last time they were together. Feelings of guilt took root and grew in her core. While Tyler composed words of love, she had been kissing another man.

Did she really want to move to Liberty Ridge, or was she looking for an excuse to call off the wedding? *Too late to think about that now.* She typed Tyler a quick reply, and then shut off her computer. Going over to her dresser, she picked up her engagement picture and studied it. What she needed was an escape, a chance to think, without distractions. She needed to get away from Heath, from her mother, and from anyone else who might influence her decision.

Tomorrow, she and Granny were driving to Oklahoma to visit the Cherokee History Museum. The trip would be the perfect escape.

After she changed into a large T-shirt, she lay in bed and stared at the ceiling. Above her hung a dream catcher, which had been a gift from her dad when she was ten years old. Grace took it off the wall. Her fingers glided across the strings and feathers. He had given it to her after she'd been plagued by a long stretch of nightmares. After Dad had tucked her in, he'd told her the tradition behind the dream catcher, saying it would capture her bad dreams and make them disappear in the morning light. Once the Native American charm had been placed above her bed, she'd only had pleasant dreams.

Now, when she snuggled under the covers, her thoughts drifted to her trip tomorrow to the museum. She wondered what the curator would have to say about her family's Bible. Maybe taking a look into the past would give her direction for her future.

Chapter Nineteen

Heath tossed a two-by-four on the ground and went to sit under the ash tree nearby. Taking a drink of water, he surveyed his efforts. In another hour, the heat would force him to stop working on the gazebo. The weatherman had predicted a storm for this afternoon. That would be a welcome relief because the ranch needed a good, soaking rain. The once-green grass had faded into a lifeless brown. The only color in the yard now came from the rainbow collection of well-watered flowers in Joslyn's garden.

He'd seen Grace leave this morning, carrying a suitcase. She'd given him a wan smile before climbing in her car and driving away. Last night, he'd swallowed the bitter truth—he had no chance of a future with Grace. When he'd told her to marry Tyler, the words had nearly stuck in his throat.

He'd overheard Joslyn say Tyler was home from Mexico earlier than expected. Was Grace on her way to Dallas to see him? Tonight, she'd probably be wrapped in his arms. Frustration over his own inadequacies made him want to punch something—or someone. Tyler's face came to mind.

After taking another drink of water, he picked up the hammer and nailed the last floor board into place. The gazebo was almost done. Only a few final touches and he could start painting. He hoped when everything was said and done, the structure would be a place of joy for Grace. More than anyone else he'd ever met, she deserved her dreams to come true.

"Looks real good." Bruce approached Heath and came to stand beside him. "You've done a fine job in a short bit of time."

"Thanks. I'm enjoying the project." He noticed Grace's father wasn't standing as straight as he had before. Bruce's shoulders hunched forward slightly, and the outer corners of his eyes drooped. "How have you been feeling lately?" Heath's concern grew at the sight of him. "I hope you haven't been working yourself too hard."

"Oh, I'm fine. Thanks for asking." Bruce breathed in deeply, and then exhaled. "Just feelin' a little more tired than usual. Sure glad you're here. Eases the load."

Heath strolled over to the stairs of the gazebo. "Almost time to paint. It'll be ready in plenty of time for the wedding."

"I sure hope you haven't done all this work for nothing." Running a hand over the rail, Bruce shook his head. "If you ask me, my daughter's getting cold feet."

A lump caught in Heath's throat while he kept his expression neutral. "What makes you say that?"

"She has not been happy lately. I can't tell if she just misses Tyler or she's second-guessing her decision to get married." Bruce glanced at him. "You've been spendin' time with Gracie, lately. What do you think?"

That she should run away with me. "She's probably just stressed." He decided not to share his real thoughts with Bruce. *Don't want to expose the fact I'm in love with his engaged daughter.* "Marriage is a huge life decision. I saw Grace leave this morning. Is she visiting

206

Tyler?"

Bruce smiled and patted him on the back.

The strength of Bruce's hand always took him by surprise. Even tired and worn, the large rancher was as sturdy as an ox.

"Grace took a road trip with her great-grandmother. They're heading to Oklahoma to visit the Cherokee History Museum. A real life Thelma and Louise, those two."

Heath laughed at the picture of Grace and an older woman, driving across the country in a top-down convertible. Hope their trip wouldn't end with their car soaring off the edge of the Grand Canyon. "Did she take the Bible?"

"You bet. She seemed pretty excited to show it to the museum curator. Well, I should let you get back to it." Bruce turned to walk away but then stopped. "Oh, and Heath, I see the way you look at my daughter and how she looks at you. Nothin's final until that wedding band's on her finger. You just remember that."

Heath's posture straightened, and he clasped his hands behind his back. "Sir, I care too much about your daughter to interfere. "

"I know you do." Bruce smiled and walked toward the barn.

Heath was left scratching his head. Had Bruce just given Heath his blessing? The man must be delusional from the heat. No father would ever think he was a good candidate for his daughter. While packing up his tools, he kept mulling over Bruce's words. *I know you do.* He'd do whatever necessary to make sure Grace stayed happy and safe, even if that meant saying goodbye.

Around six o'clock, Heath washed and went into town to eat dinner at the Desert Rose. For a weeknight, he was surprised to see the packed restaurant. The hostess found a small table for him, next to a window that overlooked the Hickory River Bridge. He'd become lost in the view when he saw someone out of the corner of his eye standing by his table. He turned his head to see Colleen Gardner.

"Hey, there," Colleen said with a strong southern drawl. She was dressed casually, in khaki shorts and a turquoise ruffled shirt. "Do you mind if I join you? I really hate to eat alone, and I don't see a free table."

He stood and motioned to the empty chair across from him. "Please have a seat. I haven't ordered yet." He watched her sit and set down her purse. "You're not charging me for this, are you?"

She laughed. "I'm officially off duty."

As the hour passed, they ate and shared stories. Colleen told Heath about growing up in Liberty Ridge and her college days at Yale. Heath shared with her his early days in the Army—surviving boot camp as a skinny teenager, his first deployment to Iraq, and his quickie marriage and divorce.

While Heath contemplated dessert, Colleen held out her cup for a coffee refill. "I've heard a lot of activity is happening at the ranch these days," she said. "Must keep you very busy."

"The wedding has made for extra projects. I think Bruce will be glad once it's all over." He glanced back at the dessert menu, hiding his pain at talking about Grace's wedding.

Colleen took a drink of her coffee then rested back in her chair. "I was at Tyler's parents' house for dinner last night and saw Grace and Tyler's engagement picture. They do make a gorgeous couple. I can't believe how much Grace has blossomed."

Heath could only nod. Grace's beauty was the last thing he should think about.

"Tyler and I dated in high school," Colleen said. "I knew how much Grace liked him, and I'm ashamed to say I enjoyed rubbing it in. I hope she won't hold my behavior against me. But to be honest, Tyler was way too self-absorbed to notice her. Or anyone else for that matter."

"Well, he's changed his tune." Heath clenched his teeth.

"It appears so." Colleen watched him across the table, her eyes narrowed. "You've fallen for her."

"What makes you say that?" He needed a distraction for little miss smarty pants. Get her talking about anything else. "I knew a guy in the Army who went to Yale. Or was it went to jail? Well, anyway. Maybe you two know each other."

"Nice trick." Her blue eyes sparkled under arched brows. "Now, back to Grace. I don't need a doctorate to interpret the look on your face when you talk about her. She's a good person with a big heart, plus she's turned out to be a first-class beauty. I can see how easily a man could lose his heart, especially one who's seen so much darkness."

"You're right. I figured I don't have enough problems, so I fall for my employer's daughter, who by the way is engaged," he said in a low voice. The last thing he wanted was for anyone else to overhear his confession.

"I actually think your feelings for her are healthy.

209

You're opening up emotionally. That's good."

"I have no business even thinking about being in a relationship. I would only drag her down." He wrung his hands under the table. "Last night, she reached out to me, and I pushed her away."

Colleen sighed. "I wished you'd give yourself more credit. The fact you're putting her ahead of yourself proves you are an honorable man."

Their waitress came to pick up the empty dinner plates.

"No dessert. I'll take the check," Heath told the waitress and pulled out his wallet. "Dinner's on me."

"Heath." She placed a stilling hand on his arm. Her lips were pressed in a firm line. "Yes, you have work to do, but don't you dare think you don't deserve love and a chance to be happy. I have counseled many soldiers and their spouses. I know that with a strong commitment, those relationships not only survive but thrive. Don't project your fears onto someone else. Let Grace make her own decisions. She may surprise you."

"I can't ask that of her. She's marrying Tyler." Heath set on the table enough cash to cover the bill and a nice tip. He stood to leave. "Someday, I'll tell you about the things I've done. The people who died on my watch. Then you'll know I'm doing the right thing."

She walked with him to the restaurant's front door and followed him outside. Once they were alone, she took hold of his arm and turned him to face her. "I'm sorry if you feel like I'm being pushy, but I can't let you leave thinking your mistakes automatically make you an evil person. You saved Grace's life, don't forget. You deserve to find some happiness, be it with her or with someone else."

Heath heard her words, but he didn't allow them to sink in. What anyone else thought didn't matter. He knew the truth. He didn't deserve love.

****

After several fun-filled hours on the road, Grace pulled into the parking lot of the Cherokee History Museum. The large stucco building was surrounded by well-maintained grounds. Off to the side sat a replica village. Visitors could step back in time and see a reenactment of what Cherokee life was like two hundred years ago.

She parked her car, and then exited to retrieve Granny's walker from the trunk. Grace set the walker next to the car and opened the passenger side door. "Let me help you."

"I'm not a cripple." Without assistance, the elderly woman got out of the car and took a firm hold of her walker.

She was halfway to the building before Grace had finished closing the car door. For a ninety year old, the woman could move.

They walked into a busy lobby.

A tall woman moved past them, followed by a pack of school-age children. She halted in front of a painted map, which took up most of the wall, and spoke to her group. Over by a glass case displaying a gorgeous headdress, a baby fussed in her stroller while her father waved a plush toy before her scrunched-up face. The baby grabbed the offered toy and promptly stuffed it in her mouth, therefore quieting her squawking.

Grace guided Granny over to the information area.

"Welcome to the Cherokee History Museum." The female employee smiled widely from behind a long counter.

"Hi, my name is Grace Murray, and this is my great-grandmother, Evelyn Murray. We have an appointment with Dr. Downing."

"I'll let him know you're here. Please feel free to walk around the exhibits while you wait."

Grace marveled at the intricate basket work. *Wow.* She couldn't imagine the amount of time someone took to weave the beautiful designs. A pair of beaded moccasins captured her attention next. They appeared so delicate and dainty. If she owned a pair, she'd never wear them for fear of ruining the exquisite beadwork.

As she lifted her gaze, she noticed a tall man with salt and pepper hair approach.

"Welcome," he said. "I'm Kenneth Downing, the Director of Genealogy. Please follow me to my office. We can talk more comfortably in there."

Once the three of them were seated, Grace handed him the Bible. "I found this on our family's property in the original dwelling. We're interested in learning more about our family's history. Kamama Burchfield, who is an ancestor on my father's side and my Granny's great-grandmother, was Cherokee."

Dr. Downing put on his reading glasses and opened the Bible. He studied the inscription and jotted a few notes. Then, he closed the book and smiled. "I'll run a query through our records to see if we have any information about either Ezra or Kamama. Please excuse me for a moment." He exited.

Grace took advantage of the time to look around the room. Hanging on the walls were pictures which chronicled Cherokee life, both past and present. She was especially intrigued by a painting of a family standing in front of a log cabin, a painting of a young woman sitting atop a horse, and a black-and-white photograph of a man wearing a large headdress. Another photo of tribal members performing a ceremonial dance looked more recent.

She reached over and held Granny's wrinkled hand. "Thanks for being here." Sure, she could have found the information with an internet search. Honestly though, she had grown bored working on the computer. After she completed the business tasks, she gladly shut off the computer for the day, preferring to be outside and enjoying the ranch. Time spent with Granny was worth a few days away and the cost of gas.

"This trip is quite the adventure." Granny's eyes sparkled. "I'm sorry I don't know more about our family's history. When I was young, I was too busy as a new bride and mother. Then, both my parents were gone, and I had no one to go to for the information."

"Better late than never. I've never heard the story of how you and great-grandpa met."

A smile illuminated the soft, wrinkled skin of her face. "We met during the Depression. Earl was eleven when my pa hired him as a ranch hand. The boy was half-starved and desperate for work. His parents had eight children, you see. They sent out the older ones to work, because they couldn't afford to feed 'em all. Earl lived and worked at the ranch for seven years. During that time, we became best friends. The summer before we officially started courtin', Earl picked wildflowers every morning and left them for me on the front porch. I fell head-over-heels in love and when he asked for my hand, I said yes before he was even finished."

"Your story is very romantic." Grace thought about

the man who now worked on the ranch. The man she'd fallen for.

"We married right before the war." Granny ran her hands over her lap, smoothing out the butter-yellow fabric of her dress. "Both my brothers and Earl left to go fight. I lost one brother in France. Earl and my brother, Bob, made it home. Bob moved to California about a year after the war ended. So that left Earl and I to run things after my parents passed. We had a wonderful life. He used to call me his Cherokee princess." She chuckled.

Grace had few memories of her great-grandfather Murray. He'd died when she was only seven. From the tender look in Granny's eyes, Grace had no doubt they'd had a loving marriage, and Granny missed her husband very much.

Dr. Downing returned to the office, smiling. His hand held a stack of papers. "You will be pleased to learn I found your ancestors in our database." He handed Grace a sheet of paper filled with names and dates. "How much do you know about the Trail of Tears?"

"Only the little I learned in history class." She glanced over to Granny, who nodded.

Dr. Downing got seated behind his desk. "Ezra Burchfield was a private in the US Army. He'd had some medical training. In 1838, he journeyed with a group of Cherokee over what is now known as the Trail of Tears. By that time, the Cherokee no longer had Army escorts, but Ezra volunteered to provide medical care. After he saw the surviving Cherokee to the reservation in Oklahoma, he served for the next two and a half years at an Army fort nearby. The museum has possession of a journal Ezra kept along his journey over the Trail of Tears." He gave Grace a stack of photocopied pages, which contained a large, handwritten script.

"This is amazing." Her breath hitched while her gaze skimmed over the pages.

"Ezra met Kamama during the forced relocation," Dr. Downing continued. "She was probably in her late teens and traveling with her family. We have records of her, her mother, and her sister, all who lived on the reservation. Ezra returned to the reservation to find Kamama after he finished his commitment to the Army."

"Have you read all his journal entries, Dr. Downing?" Grace handed the pages to Granny.

He shook his head. "Unfortunately, we only have a portion of his journal. Some pages sustained water damage and could not be restored. The journal was donated to the museum in 1960 by a descendant of Kamama's sister. What you have are printed copies of the readable pages. You may take them with you. I'm sure you will both find them very informative."

"Can we get the name of the family member who donated the diary?" Grace asked. "I'd like to reach out and introduce myself, if he or she is still alive. Or at the very least, write a note of thanks."

"I can give you the name of the woman who made the donation." Dr. Downing glanced at his computer screen, and then scribbled down a name on a notepad. "If my memory serves me right, she still volunteers here at the museum on occasion."

Granny squinted as she read. A small tear formed at the corner of her eye. "I remember my father telling me the story of the Trail of Tears. People were forced to leave their homes. So many died during the journey. The horror those Cherokee endured."

Grace shuddered. How could a so-called civilized nation have done such a horrible thing to innocent people?

Dr. Downing sat on the corner of his desk. "The history of the Cherokee people is a mixture of bountiful blessings and agonizing sorrow. Today, we carry on the traditions of our ancestors to safeguard the heritage of future generations. I encourage you to spend some time in the museum and the replica village." He escorted them to the brightly lit lobby.

The receptionist brought over a wheelchair.

Grace pushed Granny around the museum for the next several hours. By the time they left, both women were exhausted, both physically and emotionally. They stopped at a small diner off the interstate, and then found a hotel nearby to stay for the night. After checking in and getting Granny situated in the room, Grace went for a walk. The low, flat landscape was bathed in the rosy light of the setting sun. Her mind raced with the information she'd learned that day.

Ezra and Kamama had been caught up in a tragic event. In the pages she'd already read of Ezra's journal, she'd discovered he'd fallen in love with Kamama while on the Trail of Tears. Ezra had done everything in his power to protect her. He'd seen unspeakable amounts of death of both young and old, while providing meager medical care in a hopeless situation.

In the end, their love survived the test, and they found their way back to each other. They married, bought a plot of land on the Texas prairie, and raised their children.

Grace's heart swelled at the strength of that love. The type of love she wanted in her own life. Someone to hold fast to as they walked through life's trials. A love that would stand the test of time. A man who was willing to fight for her, even battle his own inner demons, in order to win her love. And in the process, he'd learn to love himself.

Chapter Twenty

The next morning, Grace drove to Liberty Ridge and dropped off Granny at her apartment before heading home. She couldn't wait to get back and show Ezra's journal pages to Heath. When she pulled into the driveway, she noticed Tyler's car parked in front of the house and saw he stood on the porch, wearing an easy-going smile. *How long can I hide out in my car?* Anticipation of the difficult conversation ahead churned nausea in her gut.

Before she could pull herself together, Tyler opened the door. He pulled her to him, and his lips found hers. The hard urgency behind his kiss was unmistakable.

"I've missed you." His finger traced across her jaw line. "I'm counting down the days until our wedding. I want to wake up every morning and see your lovely face."

She stepped out of his embrace. "I'm glad you're here. We need to talk."

Tyler collected her suitcase from the car's trunk, and she followed him onto the porch.

"Your mom said you were in Oklahoma. Why didn't you tell me?" With a frown, he set down her suitcase next to the door.

"I didn't want to bother you. I know you're busy catching up on things at the office. Granny and I had a good trip." Would he care about her recent discovery? Since the conversation wouldn't involve business or oil, probably not.

"You can tell me all about it over dinner. Let's drive home to Dallas and go to that bistro you like. You can stay for a few days." Tyler wrapped his arms around her waist.

"I've just spent the last five hours driving. I don't feel like spending anymore time in the car, sorry."

Tyler's smile faltered. "What's really going on, Grace?"

"I'd like to take a walk." Her body buzzed with nerves. "Something has been weighing on my mind." As they strolled through the meadow behind the house, Tyler held her hand more firmly than necessary. When they approached the gazebo, she was surprised to see the structure was nearly complete. Heath had done a beautiful job.

Tyler turned and cupped her face in his hands. "I've been doing a lot of soul searching over the past week. I want to tell you I'm sorry for how I acted the last time we were together. I was wrong to dismiss your feelings."

The buzz of cicadas matched the rapid beat of her heart. She struggled over what to say. How could she tell him that while he was off, building his career, she'd gone and fallen in love with another man? How could she express that gently?

He hooked his thumbs in the front pockets of his dress pants. "I am willing to consider living in Liberty Ridge, but first give us a few more years in Dallas to establish my career." His hand brushed her cheek then he tipped her face to meet his gaze.

Skepticism tightened the knot of tension in her gut. "You would do that for me? Live in a small town and buy a house in the country?"

He held her close. "I'm willing to consider it. I finally realized that I don't care where we live, as long as I have you to come home to at night. I love you so much, Grace. You know that, right?"

"I never doubted that." Guilt stabbed her in the chest. She had betrayed his love and trust. "I don't want you to live someplace that will make you miserable."

"Honey, I feel like I'm losing you, and it's all due to my stubbornness. Let's get through this wedding before making any big decisions. I think all the stress is making us both a little crazy."

On their first date, Grace had been so nervous she'd thrown up right before Tyler arrived at her door. He'd looked so handsome in his suit and tie, his blond hair styled to perfection. She'd experienced one of the best nights of her life. And now, she considered walking away from the one person she'd wanted for so many years.

Her heart had broken in two—half staying loyal to Tyler and the other pulled toward Heath. But two nights ago, Heath was clear he did not want her.

What was a girl to do? *Be true to yourself.*

The uncertainty tore her apart. Grace stood on her tiptoes and planted a kiss on Tyler's lips. He clung to her like a drowning man, making her feel a rush of panic instead of the calm reassurance she'd hoped for.

"Not too much longer," Tyler said. "We'll be right here, reciting our vows. Then, we can start our life together.

Frustrated at her own lack of backbone, Grace only

nodded. All the words she planned to say now jumbled in her brain. Dashing someone's dreams was difficult, especially when he stood right before you, declaring undying love. She slipped her hand in his and forced a smile. *What a coward.*

Later, after Tyler had left to drive home, Grace called a crisis intervention. Molly and Jenny agreed to meet her at the Desert Rose. She trusted both to offer straightforward, honest advice—something she desperately needed.

By the time Grace got to the bar, the other two women were already seated, each with a drink in hand. She slid into the booth next to Jenny and ordered a strawberry margarita. The cold, fruity drink was halfway to her lips when she saw Heath enter the bar. She lifted her hand to wave to him, but her smile faded when he walked in the other direction, toward Colleen Gardner.

As Heath sat across from Colleen, he greeted her and smiled.

Holy cow, are they on a date? With his gaze fixed on Colleen, he hadn't even noticed Grace. *I think I'm going to be sick.*

Molly's gaze followed Grace's, and her eyes bugged out. "Is that Colleen Gardner with Heath?"

The scowl on Grace's face deepened.

Jenny leaned into her shoulder. "You still crushing on him?"

"What?" Grace's jaw dropped in shock.

"Oh, please." Jenny's hand gestured through the air while she talked. "After the last time we were at the house, you know, for the picnic, I sensed something in the air between you and Heath. Alex told me I was

221

imagining things."

Grace's face grew warm. "You two have to swear to secrecy…because as far as anyone else knows, I'm marrying Tyler in less than three weeks."

Jenny and Molly nodded then scooted closer.

"I knew it," Jenny whispered. She rubbed her hands together.

"Marrying Tyler would be a mistake." By giving her doubts a voice, Grace felt a suffocating weight lift off her chest. She inhaled deeply, filling her lungs. "For both of us."

"You should marry Tyler." Molly frowned and pointed her finger at Heath. "I understand the appeal of a bad boy, but Heath's type is nothing but trouble."

"Heath is not the same guy you arrested at the bar, Molly. He's changed," Grace pleaded. What could she say to help them understand what made Heath special? "Working at the ranch and spending time with my family has helped. He fought for years to protect our country. Yes, he has problems, but nothing that love and support can't see him through."

"Grace, people who suffer from those issues need more than love." Jenny patted Grace's hand. "He needs professional help."

Grace turned her head toward Heath and Colleen.

Heath broke into a huge grin at something Colleen had said. She then reached over the table and placed her hand over Heath's.

The sight of them enjoying each other's company made her sick to her stomach.

"You are engaged." Molly pointed to Grace's engagement ring. "Have you told Tyler you're second-guessing your decision?"

"I couldn't." Grace hunched her shoulders and slid down farther in the booth seat. "I'm still unsure. I want to live in the country and let our kids grow up with fresh air and freedom. Tyler wants to live in Dallas to be close to his office. The thought of returning to the city gives me hives."

"And what does Heath want?" Jenny asked. "Do you know where he's planning on living in a year? In a month?"

Grace couldn't remember if Heath had ever talked about his plans once he left True Horizon. "He's never said," she admitted. "He lives his life one day at a time. I don't know if he'll ever settle down." Admitting the truth hurt. She honestly didn't know if Heath would be around in another month. Any day, he could hop on his bike and leave, and she'd never hear from him again. "Whatever my decision, my choice has to be best for me. I can't build my life around what makes everyone else happy."

"Time for you to stop pleasing everyone else." Molly set down her drink. "But regardless of what happens with Heath, if you're having doubts about Tyler, you need to tell him."

"It's only fair." Jenny lifted her margarita and took a sip.

At that moment, Heath glanced her way and their gazes locked. After a few seconds, he looked away.

Grace fought the urge to march over there and claim him with a kiss, right in front of Colleen. She was so hopeless. With his long hair and scruffy beard, he was the type of man she normally would reject out of hand. The suit-and-tie type had always attracted her. Her feelings for Heath had little to do with his outward appearance, but instead, the gentle soul he hid underneath. She took another sip of strawberry margarita. The icy sweetness took the edge off the sour taste in her mouth.

Jenny put her arm around Grace and gave her a gentle squeeze. "We love you, Grace. I know you're really torn. Heath seems like a nice guy, and your dad likes him. Not to mention my girls adore him."

Thank goodness for girlfriends. Grace rested her head on her sister-in-law's shoulder.

"I thought you rushed things with Tyler," Jenny continued. "I'm not surprised you're having doubts." Jenny's gaze flickered over at Heath. "When you lie in bed at night and slide into your dreams, which man do you imagine holding you close? That's the man you can't live without."

****

Heath heaved a hay bale off the trailer and onto the barn floor. The repetitive action was a safe outlet for his growing frustration. In that moment, too many uncomfortable emotions slammed him like a tsunami wave, all at once and completely overwhelming. In the years after John's death, he'd only made room for anger and revenge. Sympathy, forgiveness, kindness, and love had all been exiled.

With Colleen's help, he had started opening up emotionally, which left him off balance. He was treading on unstable ground. She'd asked to meet at the bar last night, in order to help him learn how to deal with real world stressors. After some practice, he understood his emotional triggers, how to recognize his body's reaction, and safe coping measures. Although her methods sounded simple at first, the process was the hardest thing he'd ever had to do.

While at the bar, he'd experienced several triggers which normally would have induced a bad reaction. But Colleen had talked him through. What Heath hadn't shared with Colleen was how the sight of Grace, sitting across the room, had made his heart race. When he'd seen her, the rest of the world disappeared, leaving behind a raw desire to possess her body and soul.

Grace was the reason he wanted to become a better person. She was the reason he was putting himself through the emotional wringer. For the first time in a long time, he had a clear mission—leave the past behind and embrace the future.

Unfortunately, time was his enemy. Every day that passed, he knew he had one less to earn Grace's love. A fact beyond his control that frustrated him to no end.

He threw another hay bale toward the ground. Growing hot, he took off his shirt and tossed it off to the side. He continued unloading the trailer until the last bale was on the ground. Then, he drove to the side of the barn, unhooked the trailer, and walked back toward the barn door. Halfway to the barn, he noticed Grace and Bruce on the front porch of the house. Grace stood behind Bruce, who sat on a folding chair. A flash of light reflected off something in her hand. After a moment passed, he realized she was cutting her dad's hair.

Grace looked up and glanced at Heath, standing across the yard. She smiled.

Even at that distance, he still felt the impact. Every smile was a gift, just like the one kiss they'd shared. He remembered the softness of her lips and the way her body fit perfectly against his. Afterwards, he'd been wrong to push her away. Would he have the courage now to speak the truth?

"Heath!" Grace called out. "Come here. I have something to show you."

He walked across the lawn and joined them on the porch.

Bruce stood and brushed off his pants. "How do I look?" He pointed to his freshly trimmed hair.

"Real good, sir. I hope I still have a nice head of hair when I get to be your age." He smoothed down his own hair, which rested on the nape of his neck, tied with a leather strap. His scalp dripped with sweat.

"Who needs a barber when Grace is so talented with a pair of scissors?" Bruce leaned his large frame against the porch rail.

Heath noticed Grace was looking everywhere but at him.

When she finally did look his way, her gaze drifted to his bare chest, and her face instantly reddened.

He laughed to himself, thinking how farm work had left him more muscular that he'd been in years. Nice to know he still had a talent for making a woman blush.

"You're next." She pointed to the metal chair, which had been occupied earlier by Bruce.

Grace's wicked smile jerked him out of his self-admiration.

Snipping the scissors through the air, she stepped toward him. "Time you let that go."

Chapter Twenty-One

The scissors in her hands gave another *snip-snip*.

He stepped backward, out of her reach. "Thanks for the offer, but you know…my hair is, *ahh*…just fine." In no way would he let Grace near him with that glint in her eye and scissors in her hand. He liked his hair, it served a purpose. Then again, maybe he didn't need to hide behind its curtain.

Bruce's deep laughter echoed from inside the house. "You might run, boy, but you're not goin' hide. My girl doesn't give up easy."

Grace stood before him, arms crossed, in full pout mode. Heath slumped into the chair. How did she do that? With just a look, she had him eating out of her hand.

"*Ewww*, you're all sweaty and gross. Go put your head under the outdoor faucet and wet it." She untied the leather strap, and his hair fell to his shoulders. "How did it get this long? Didn't you have to keep it short in the Army?"

"I was part of Special Operations." He grinned with pride. "We had relaxed grooming standards. While we were deployed, most of us had beards and let our hair grow. By the time we got back to the States, we looked like ZZ Top."

"A tribe of wild men…huh?" Her eyebrows arched. "Now go rinse off your head before I get the

227

clippers and give you a military crew-cut."

Laughing, he walked over to the faucet and stuck his head under the icy water. When he came back, he sat and Grace gently ran her fingers through his hair. Her fingertips danced across his scalp, sending tingles of pleasure across his skin. The act was casual, yet so intimate.

"How short can I go?" She stood behind him.

"I trust you." For the first time in a long time, he really meant it. In Grace's hands, he was putty. She could take his battered body and spirit and mold him into whatever she pleased.

Strands of brown hair fell to the floor like autumn leaves. With each one, a piece of his past was set free. As she worked, the breeze reached his scalp, making him feel cooler. When Grace moved to his side, her body brushed his arm. The sensation caused him to visibly tremble.

Grace's smooth hand moved over his beard. "What about this monstrosity? Can I at least trim it?"

"Sure, why not?" By this point, he'd totally resigned himself to her will. If she would ask to dye his hair purple, he'd say yes.

She oscillated around him with a swift, efficient style.

All too soon, she was done.

Her face illuminated in a wide, cheeky smile. "Wait here." Grace disappeared into the house.

While she was gone, he ran his hands through his much-shorter hair. *Feels good.*

Grace came out holding a mirror and a stack of papers. "Take a look." She passed him the hand mirror.

He gazed at his reflection, seeing a man he hadn't

seen in a long time. His brown hair was about three inches in length and wavy. Grace had done a good job. He ran his hand over the small fraction of beard she'd left him and enjoyed the smooth texture. This new look was definitely more suitable for working outdoors in the Texas heat. Heath raised his gaze to see a tear fall from Grace's chin.

"I don't believe it." Grace shook her head and covered her heart with her hands.

"What? You can't believe how good I look?" He wiggled his eyebrows. Finally, she'd admit she found him sinfully handsome and roguishly charming.

"I can't believe you've been hiding big ears under all that hair."

His hands flew up to cover his ears. "Hey, be nice. I'm very sensitive about them. They called me Dumbo in grade school."

Grace pulled down his arms before giving one exposed ear a light tug. "They're actually kinda cute. I like them."

"You did a good job." Heath smiled. "Thank you. I feel like a new man."

"You look like one, too." She took the stack of papers she'd brought out and handed them to him. "These are for you. When Granny and I went to visit the Cherokee History Museum, we found out they were in possession of Ezra Burchfield's journal."

Standing, Heath flipped through the papers. "Amazing."

"The museum has the original, but they gave me scanned images of each readable page. Ezra was a Private in the Army and traveled with a group of Cherokee over the Trail of Tears. That's where he met

Kamama. The story is chronicled in his journal entries."

Heath glanced at the papers while Grace continued to talk.

"I did some research on the Trail of Tears. The Cherokee people had been living peacefully alongside the European settlers until gold was discovered on Cherokee land. Pressure was put on President Jackson, and he signed a law claiming the land for the United States. Kamama's family was living in Tennessee when the Army came and forced them out at gunpoint. Ezra volunteered to be a medical escort."

"Did he say why he volunteered?" Had Ezra been a troubled youth, like Heath, looking for discipline and direction? Or had his reasons been nobler? While he read, words like death, disease, and cold jumped off the page—words which described his past.

"Ezra explains in his journal. I think you'll find that even though there's almost two hundred years of separation, you and Ezra have a lot in common."

The bonds of brotherhood, even distant ones, provided his soldier's heart with a sense of belonging. Heath brushed some fallen pieces of hair off his shoulder. "Thanks. I'll read Ezra's journal as soon as I have a chance. But now, I should get back to work. Thanks again for the haircut. See you around."

Her hand touched his forearm, resting lightly on top of a cluster of old scars, and sighed. "You look very handsome. Colleen will like it."

At the sight of her downturned mouth, he gave a lazy smile. "Why would Colleen have an opinion about my hair?"

She bit her lower lip. "Because...you're dating her."

"Last night was not a date." He didn't want to admit to Grace that he'd sought help. If she understood how dark his soul was stained, would she detest him? But he couldn't let her think he was romantically interested in Colleen. Not when Grace owned his heart.

Man up, cowboy. He raised his gaze to meet her wide, dark chocolate eyes and felt all the air leave his lungs. "I'm seeing Colleen professionally. She's helping me learn to cope with the struggles I've had since leaving the Army." He reached over to tuck a stray piece of hair behind her ear. His finger lingered, yearning to keep contact with the warmth of her skin.

"Oh." She let out a deep breath and twisted the wide bracelet looping her wrist. "I saw you two at the bar last night, and I might have gotten a tiny bit jealous."

"Don't be, sweet Grace. I've found no one on earth I'd rather be with than you."

****

In that instant, her decision firmed. Her heart belonged to Heath. Whether they'd get a happy ending together remained to be seen. But she knew for certain Tyler was not the man she wanted to spend her life with. Later that night, Grace called Tyler. Their conversation was filled with raised voices and a few tears on her end. But she was honest. Marrying him would be a mistake. After weeks of anxiety and uncertainty, she was filled with a wonderful calm. Tyler's chapter in her life was at an end.

For the next three days, she'd listened to her mother's hysterics. Now, Grace sought refuge on the porch. The lowing of the cattle in the field calmed her troubled spirit. They assured her she'd made the right decision. Her heart and soul were at peace.

Still unsure of his intentions, she hadn't told Heath. What if he was preparing to leave the ranch? The night of their first and only kiss, he'd made clear his desire to avoid a relationship. Her new single status might not change anything between them, and that thought scared her into silence.

Her engagement ring now rested next to her engagement picture, which now were both tucked away inside a dresser drawer. As Grace sat outside, she rubbed the bare finger and listened to her mother's voice drift out from the kitchen window. Grace had heard her name several times, followed by the phrases—"please come over soon," and "you have to talk some sense into her."

So, her brother had been asked to help. Mom hoped Alex could convince Grace to go ahead with the wedding. What her mother didn't know was Grace had already talked with Alex, and he, along with Jenny, supported her decision one hundred percent. Follow your heart, they had said—you know the truth better than anyone else.

Grace opened her laptop and spent some time playing with the security features of a new program she'd installed on a client's server. The task wasn't complicated, but it took her mind off her problems. She was in the middle of updating a virus scan when Heath stepped onto the porch. He was dressed in khaki shorts and a casual button-down shirt. Because he looked so different with his hair cut short, she did a double take. When he smiled, Grace caught a glimpse of that devilishly handsome dimple.

Heath walked past her, up to the door, and knocked

twice. "Hard at work?"

"The great thing about being self-employed is I set my own schedule and can work from anywhere. I'd rather be out here than inside, especially right now."

Her mother answered the door. Her narrowed gaze darted from Heath to Grace. "Good morning, Heath. I'm sorry, but Bruce isn't feeling well. He can't come with you to the football game."

Heath's face fell. "Tell him that I hope he's better soon."

"Thanks. I'll tell him." Joslyn stepped inside and closed the door.

But not before giving Grace a look that could have curdled milk. She brushed off the disapproval, adding it to the growing pile. "Are you still going to the game?"

Heath turned to face her, stuck his hands in his pockets, and shrugged. "I don't know."

Closing her laptop, she went to stand next to him. "I like football."

"Oh…yeah," he said. "Everyone likes football around here."

Grace sighed. *Geez, how more obvious do I have to be?* "You know…I could go with you."

He lifted his head to meet her gaze. "You coming would be great, but your mother wouldn't be too happy."

His hazel eyes stopped her heart. "Let me worry about my mom. She doesn't control my life." She did love her mother. Even more so when they weren't living under the same roof. "I can drive." A long car ride with Heath would give them a chance to talk. Maybe she could use the time to get to the bottom of what was going on between them.

"Cool. We should leave soon."

His dimple appeared again. Grace wondered what he'd do if she leaned over and kissed it. How could one little dimple on a handsome face drive her to distraction? "Let me go change." She sprinted up to her room.

An hour later, they were in Grace's car on their way to San Antonio. She turned the radio station to classic rock.

"You're not wearing your engagement ring." He pointed to the bare ring finger on her left hand.

Her breath became shallow, and her heart rate increased. Even though she wanted to look at his face to see his reaction, she didn't take her gaze off the road. "We had a long conversation over the phone several days ago, and I broke off my relationship with Tyler."

"Why isn't he here? If I were Tyler, I would have jumped in the car and come straight to you."

"I told him over the phone. The next day, Tyler had to fly out on a business trip. He was meeting some Congressmen about an environmental bill. I don't think he had a choice." The excuse seemed weak, even to her ears.

"How can you defend him?" Heath spat. "He had a choice, and he chose wrong."

Grace remained quiet and focused on driving. Heath was right about Tyler's priorities. His career came first, which was the main reason she couldn't envision a future with him. She never wanted to play second string to a job.

"I'm sorry." He exhaled. "It's none of my business. I only want to make sure you're all right."

"Thanks for caring, but I'm doing fine. Tyler will

234

be home in two days, and then we'll talk face to face. I won't be dissuaded from my decision."

Heath pressed his lips together and turned to stare out the window.

Grace's self-control cracked and tears blurred her vision. His rejection was her biggest fear.

After a long, quiet car ride, they arrived at the football stadium. As she entered, Heath took hold of her hand. She loved the way his calloused hand felt on hers.

They wandered around for awhile, until Heath asked an usher for help.

The friendly, gray-haired man pointed them toward the ramp leading to the suite level.

She was soon standing in front of the door to Julie Harrison's suite. Grace noticed Heath's nervousness at seeing Julie, his best friend's widow, again. He drummed his fingers against the side of his leg, and his foot tapped on the cement floor.

She remembered the night of the fireworks, when she'd sat with him on the front porch, and Heath told her about the loss of John. Magic had been in the air that evening because he'd opened up. The memory of their almost first kiss brought the curve of a smile to her lips.

Heath opened the door and held it for Grace.

As she entered the suite, a beautiful, red-haired woman jumped off the sofa.

"Heath!" She ran over and pulled him to a hug. "I'm so glad you came." Stepping back, she looked him up and down. "You're looking well. I like the hair."

Heath rested his hand on Grace's lower back. "Julie, this is Grace…a good friend. And Grace, this is Julie Ellis…I mean Harrison. Sorry, old habits."

"It's nice to meet you," Grace said as Julie gave her a quick hug. "Heath was very kind to invite me along."

"I've known Heath a long time so I can vouch he's a sweetheart." Julie gave Heath a nudge in the side with her elbow. "Come over to the balcony. Aiden's out there watching the team warm up."

On the way to the balcony, Julie looked at Grace, and then at Heath. "A good friend, my foot."

Grace's face grew incredibly warm. She kept her gaze on the football field spread out before her. Not on a smiling Heath or a teasing Julie.

A young boy, who looked to be about nine or ten, sat in a chair on the balcony. He watched the action on the field.

On his lap sat the cutest ginger-haired baby girl Grace had ever seen.

The boy turned his head at the sound of their approach. "Uncle Heath." He stood, and Julie took the baby so the boy could run into Heath's outstretched arms. "Mom said you were coming. My dad's playing today." He pointed to the field, and then held up his finger for the baby to grab. "Oh, and you get to meet Hope."

"Grace, this is my son, Aiden." Julie kissed one chubby baby cheek. "And this little bundle of trouble is Hope. She's discovered crawling and has become quite a terror. Nothing is safe." Julie smiled at her children.

A twinge of jealousy tightened in Grace's chest. Would she ever have children of her own to love?

The baby let out a burp, and then giggled. "Just like her dad," Julie said, shaking her head.

Grace only had a short wait for the first kick-off.

As she watched the game, Grace sat next to Aiden, who gave her a play-by-play account. He cheered especially loud when his step-dad, Reagan Harrison, was on the field. Julie seemed distracted with the needs of the baby, so at halftime, Grace offered to take Hope. Besides a momentary crying spell, Hope was a contented baby and had Grace laughing at her antics.

While playing with the baby, she dreamed about her own future child. Did Heath want children? She hoped so. The way her nieces adored him, she knew he would make a wonderful dad.

Chapter Twenty-Two

"I'm happy for you," Julie said to Heath. "Grace seems like a great girl."

"We're only friends. Grace is way too good for the likes of me." He couldn't stay focused on the game. His gaze kept wandering toward Grace, who played peek-a-boo with the baby.

One of Julie's auburn eyebrows arched high. "The way you're staring tells another story. And she can't keep her eyes off of you, either. You're both crazy about one another, just too stubborn to admit it. Don't let her slip away."

Was he strong enough to hold on to such a perfect woman? His breath caught in his constricted throat. Or would Grace eventually see him the way he saw himself—a man with a dark soul?

After the game, Heath and Grace helped Julie pack the kids' things. They agreed to meet at a local restaurant for dinner. On the drive to the restaurant, Grace talked nonstop about baby Hope and Aiden.

Obviously, she had a thing for kids. Seeing Julie and Aiden again had picked away the scab covering painful wounds. Although Heath loved them both, John's widow and son served as a reminder of the loss of his friend. They seemed happy, which helped ease some of his guilt. Julie's new husband, Reagan, provided them with the love and support they needed to heal.

Heath wondered if someday he would experience the same type of saving grace, and then he smiled. Maybe his subconscious was telling him something.

They arrived at a small restaurant and were taken to an intimate table set toward the rear. After a short wait, and more talk of the baby, he looked up to see Julie, Reagan, and the kids joining them.

"Sorry we kept you waiting." Julie huffed and dropped the diaper bag on the ground. "We had to wait for Reagan."

Reagan smiled while he set Hope in the highchair. "Hi." He reached over to shake Grace's hand. "Nice to meet you."

Some people, mostly women, would call the pro-football linebacker handsome. And obviously, Grace fell into that camp. Her face flushed every time she glanced at him. Heath wanted her full attention. "Good game, man." He took hold of Grace's hand under the table. The move was a bit possessive, but he was beyond caring. "Your team looked strong."

"I like what I see out of this year's draft picks." Reagan put his arm around his wife and pulled her close.

"You have the most beautiful children." Grace turned her gaze from Reagan to the baby.

Hope was munching on a baby biscuit. Drool and crumbs covered her tiny chin. Aiden took a napkin and cleaned his sister's face.

"Thanks." Reagan smiled. "They're my pride and joy. How are you, Heath? Julie told me you're living north of Austin and working on a cattle ranch."

"I'm working for Grace's family. They raise Texas

Longhorns. The job's only temporary, though. I'm thinking about going home to Florida to see my aunt in a few weeks."

Grace's face stiffened, and she pulled her hand out of his hold.

Did she not want him to leave? If given the option, he'd stay forever.

The guys talked football, while Grace and Julie shared stories like old friends. Heath's gaze wandered toward Grace. As she watched the baby laugh and play in her highchair, he caught a hint of longing in her eyes. She'd make a good mother, and her future children deserved a good father. Heath doubted he'd provide a child with a safe and secure home. A conclusion that added weight on his despair.

When the time came to leave, Julie pulled Heath to the side. "I worry about you." Julie talked softly. "You look really good, but I know what's lurking underneath the surface. I hope you have found a place that feels like home. Have you been getting any help with your, umm…issues?"

A lump of emotion formed in his throat, and he swallowed hard. "I've actually been seeing someone professionally. I've had only a few sessions, but it's helping."

Julie took his hand and squeezed. "I lost so much time grieving for John. He'd want you to find love and live a happy life."

"I have a hard time imagining a life like yours, surrounded by a loving family. Maybe someday, I'll call you with good news." He doubted he'd make a call like that anytime soon. His journey had only begun, and he knew he'd never fully heal.

"Remember what you told me the day Reagan almost walked out of my life?" The corners of Julie's mouth lifted and she raised one eyebrow.

Heath laughed at the memory of the look of stunned indignation on her face. "I told you not to be stupid."

"Follow your own advice. Okay?" She winked.

With a hitch in his heart, Heath nodded and gave Julie one final hug. She was a part of his past he wanted to hold on to.

He and Grace said their goodbyes and left the restaurant. Dusk had overtaken the daylight, and a steady rain fell from gray clouds. They sprinted to the car.

Grace tossed him the keys. "Would you mind driving home? I'm tired."

Heath opened the passenger side door. "I think I can manage." He sounded more confident than he felt. Or at least he hoped he did. His chest and gut vibrated with nerves.

"Thanks." She climbed into the passenger seat.

As he drove Grace's car out of the parking lot and onto the road, his hands shook. In Afghanistan, driving meant always being on high alert. Anxiety crept inside his body and slithered through his muscles. He was wound up tight, like a rattler ready to strike. His gaze darted back and forth, looking for anything out of place. A bag, parked car, or even a person standing on the sidewalk was suspect. After a few deep breaths, his body and mind quieted. With a mental chant, he reminded himself he was in Texas with Grace.

He merged the car onto the highway. Glancing in the rearview mirror, he saw the city lights of San

Antonio. Out of the corner of his eye, he noticed Grace watching him. "What?" He forced a laugh.

She rested a hand on his shoulder and began kneading his muscles. "You seem very tense. Are you all right?"

Right now, he'd give anything to be a normal guy driving his girlfriend home after a date. No flashbacks, no panic attacks, and no barriers keeping away the woman he wanted more than anything in the world. "I'm fine. I haven't driven a car in a long time. When I was in Afghanistan, driving off base was always a tense situation."

During their last session, Colleen suggested he talk to Grace about his experiences in the military. The truth was big and ugly—a hideous, taunting monster. As much as Heath wanted to share his burden with Grace, he couldn't form the words. His fear and pride prevailed. Heath didn't know how to cross the emotional chasm. Sooner or later, one of them would have to take a chance and jump.

Rain beat against the windshield in a steady rhythm. As they drove north, the downpour intensified. Heath's grip on the steering wheel tightened as he strained to see the road.

"We just passed our turn!" Grace pointed back at the exit.

His heart jumped into his throat. His skin grew ice cold. In the battlefield, people died when soldiers lost their direction. Heath's breathing came out in rapid bursts. *Pull over and turn around.* A simple solution. One his brain couldn't register. In the military, nothing was simple.

"Damn. Why didn't you tell me sooner?" His shout

caused Grace to jump in her seat. As soon as the words left his mouth, he wanted to reclaim them. His panic and anger clouded any rational thought.

"I'm sorry," she said in a hushed voice. "Up ahead is a turnaround. Stop there, and I'll drive the rest of the way home." Grace shifted in her seat.

She's scared of me. His frustration grew. The weight of failure smothered him. He slammed on the brakes, and the car skidded to a stop on the wide gravel shoulder. He needed to escape. *Now*. Once out of the car, he slammed the door. He had to regain control. Everything unraveled inside him. The sight of Grace's eyes wide with fear had punched him in the gut.

Heath ran until his whole body shook with unfettered emotion. Ten feet ahead stood a line of trees. Maybe the trees would absorb him into themselves. He could become lost forever. The echoes of his dying teammates screamed in the wind. Covering his ears with his hands, he attempted to block them out. His effort had no effect because the sound came from the very depths of his soul.

"Heath, wait!" Grace cried.

He turned to see her running toward him, her long, thick hair soaking wet.

When she caught up, she took hold of his arm.

"Go back to the car. You shouldn't be near me," he yelled.

Her dark eyes stared, and she didn't move. "I'm not going anywhere without you," she shouted. "Haven't you gotten that through your thick head, yet? I love you, Heath Carter. I'm not leaving your side."

****

The words tumbled out of her mouth, and she'd

never take them back. Grace loved him. As she witnessed his struggle, she wanted him to know he was no longer alone. He had someone who would love him enough to stick by his side, even during the tough times.

The rain came down in sheets. A crack of thunder sounded in the distance—its rumble rolled over the hills.

Heath tried to wiggle out of her hold, but her grip held firm. She'd fight to keep him close. "Talk to me. Tell me what's going on. Let me in." She brushed wet strands of hair off his face with her free hand. The sparks in his hazel eyes dampened to embers. Tiny water droplets clung to his dark lashes.

"I'm sorry...I never wanted you to see me like this." His shoulders slumped. "I'm dangerous. The US government trained me to be a killer. For twelve years, that's exactly what I was. How could you love someone like me?"

How could she not? She wished he would see his own value. "Your past does not define you. I'm not afraid. I know you'd never hurt me." Grace spoke loud enough to be heard over the drumming rain.

He pulled her into his arms, holding her tight against his damp chest. "I'd rather die than hurt you, which is why I can't be with you."

She trembled against him. "I'm tougher than you think. Don't push me away. Trust me enough to let me in. I promise to listen and not judge."

A flash of lightning brightened the sky, followed by a loud clap of thunder. Grace jumped but didn't move out of Heath's embrace. The threat of the storm was nothing compared to the danger of losing him.

Heath dropped his arms and stepped back. "Get inside the car. You're not safe out here in this storm."

"How many times do I have to tell you that I'm not leaving?" The roar of her voice clashed with a crack of thunder.

Standing before her, Heath visibly shook. With a surprising strength, he reached out to pull her against his body. His mouth descended in a rush of unyielding passion.

He was not gentle, and she didn't want him to be. She wrapped both arms around his neck and grabbed a fistful of his shirt. As she stood in the pouring rain with the wind whipping around them, Heath clung to her. She molded so perfectly into his body.

Her fingers ran through his short, damp hair, and his deep groan sent her over the edge. She wanted a crazy kind of love like this—the kind that had you standing in the middle of the storm, feeling like the only two people on earth. Heath touched an exposed portion of skin on her back. The sensation sent her soaring. She never wanted to come down.

"I love you." His voice thickened. "Grace, I love you." He nuzzled his face against her neck.

The earthy smell of his cologne tickled her nose. "Trust me," she said. "Let me be there for you. I want to be a part of your healing."

"Trusting you has never been a problem. I don't trust myself." Heath wrapped his body around her, protecting her from the rain. "Let's go to the car. We can talk where it's dry."

She ran hand in hand back to her car and climbed inside, caught between laughter and an attempt to catch her breath. Grace turned the key to start the engine and cranked the heat. Heath leaned over to kiss her, holding her face like a precious jewel.

"You need to know the whole story." He touched his cold nose to hers. "Once you hear everything, you may change your mind."

"Doubtful." Lowering her gaze, she saw their hands wound together. She couldn't tell where hers ended and his began.

"Let's go home and dry off. Then, I'll tell you my story, but I'm warning you, it's not PG. I won't blame you if you never want to see me again."

She nodded in understanding and put the car into Drive. After performing a U-turn, she drove back to the missed turn-off and headed home. What if she couldn't handle what he'd soon share? In reality, she was scared she'd fold under the ugly truth. War was something she was fundamentally opposed to, and Heath was a soldier and the man she loved. In her mind, she worked to reconcile the two.

The bright beams of the car headlights cut through the darkness of the ranch and illuminated Heath's bunkhouse. She parked, and then followed him to the front door. Once inside, Heath grabbed her, pressed her back against the door, and proceeded to kiss away her breath. Her lips parted at the onslaught. She lost all sense of time and place.

After Heath pulled away, he walked into his bedroom and returned holding a pair of drawstring shorts and a very large T-shirt. "These are too big, but at least they're dry."

She went into the bathroom, changed out of her wet clothes, and towel dried her hair. When she came out wearing his clothing, she was thankful to be warm.

Heath had also changed and started brewing a pot of coffee. He poured her a mug of the steaming liquid, followed by a dash of creamer.

"Thanks." Her outstretched hands took the warm mug. The aromatic fragrance helped Grace regain her sense of calm.

Heath put down his mug on the table and sat on an empty wooden chair. As he pulled the chair in toward the table, the legs scraped along the plank floor, and the sound reverberated through the otherwise-quiet house. Leaning his elbows on the table, he stared.

She smiled in an attempt to reassure him. If she was nervous, she could only imagine how fearful he was of sharing terrible things from his past.

He cleared his throat. "You already know my Aunt Linda took me in after my mom died. My dad was in prison, and I was on the fast track to prison myself. Aunt Linda gave me the love and support I'd lacked in my life. I was not an easy teenager, but she was tough and fair. During one especially difficult spell, she drove me to the Army recruiting office and made me listen to their pitch. Afterward, I knew the Army was what I was meant to do. I took to the military like a duck to water." He took a sip of coffee and smiled. "First, I was an infantry man, then Airborne, next I became a Ranger. Finally, after five years, I passed the Special Forces qualification and earned my Green Beret."

"It seems the Army saved you...put you on the straight and narrow."

"Without the strict discipline and guidance, I probably would've ended up in jail." He shrugged, and his mouth lifted in a wry smile. "John and I were assigned to the same Special Forces team. We became

247

fast friends. Brothers in every sense of the word. One day, we were called into our commander's office and told we were tapped for Delta Force assessment. After weeks of grueling tests, John and I were both selected for Delta. We weren't just running with the big dogs anymore…we'd joined a pack of Bullmastiffs."

While Heath talked, Grace remained quiet. She was stunned and impressed by his rise up the ranks. He'd worked hard to become elite in his field. So far, he'd only told her how he'd become an exceptional soldier, not a killer.

"Delta Force is called in for the most difficult and secretive assignments. Only a few people know the details for any given mission. I raided lots of buildings and killed lots of bad guys, mostly under the cover of darkness." A muscle twitched on his clenched jaw, and he scowled. "We were the angels of death."

She imagined Heath dressed in full gear, kicking down doors with a rifle in hand. A departure from the normally quiet-mannered man she knew.

He reclined in his chair and wiped a hand down his face. "I was trained to provide medical trauma care in the field. Some soldiers were beyond saving. I watched several of my brothers die in combat. The loss of John was the most difficult to bear, and I still blame myself for his death."

Grace covered his hand with hers. As she gazed into his hazel eyes, which held a bottomless pool of sorrow, her heart ached.

"My life in the Army was a crazy roller-coaster ride of deployments, with short bursts of time at home. If a crisis happened anywhere in the world, my team could be recalled at a moment's notice. I loved every minute of it. But after John died, something inside me changed. I wanted revenge and didn't care who or what got in my way."

"That's understandable." Her words were only partially true. She could never understand what he'd experienced. Grace cleared her throat in hopes of clearing the choking emotion that settled there.

"When Operation Command sent my unit back to Afghanistan, I was out for blood. I hated everything the country represented. My commander had to reprimand me several times." Heath's eyes misted over.

She took a calming breath. "Your best friend was taken from you. You were angry."

He took another drink of coffee, and then exhaled. "During my last month in Afghanistan, my unit was charged with the kill or capture of one of Afghan's most wanted. When we finally located him, he was holed up in a rural compound. After a lengthy gun battle, we came to a stalemate. Two of our guys were shot and had to be medevaced out. I was so desperate to capture the guy, either dead or alive, I pushed for Close Air Support. The bombers would target the hostiles and clear them out."

"You wanted to drop a bomb?" Shock numbed her body. The muscles in his arm twitched, causing his tattoos to ripple like they'd come alive.

"I worked with our TACP, our Tactical Air Control Party, to secure coordinates for the drop. Afterward, we went to secure the scene and survey the damage." He shifted in his chair and dropped his gaze to the table. "I discovered a hut of women and children hidden behind the main structure. We never knew civilians were in the area."

Grace's stomach lurched at the image of innocent women and children, who'd been scared and hurt. "What happened to them, Heath?" Her voice quivered. "What did you do?"

Chapter Twenty-Three

He wouldn't blame Grace if she walked out the door and never spoke to him again. The incident had been three years ago, and he still couldn't forgive himself. Seeing the horrified look on her face, as he told her about the bomb drops he'd helped coordinate nearly sent him fleeing in shame. Fat tears roll down Grace's face as he explained how he'd found the destroyed hut, dead bodies strewn across the ground.

"They all died?" Grace choked. She swiped away tears from her cheeks with the back of her hand.

"Yes. We didn't know they were there. The Taliban put those people there as hostages to use for their own escape, but I was the one who pushed for the bombs." The last confession of a condemned man. "I see those people around me, in the faces of young children. I relive that day over and over in my dreams. My nightmares are violent. Anyone sleeping next to me would be in danger." A warning. Loving him was unsafe.

She scooted back in her chair. "Is your therapy helping with the nightmares and flashbacks?"

"The process is slow. And I'll never be totally free of the effects of war. Colleen is teaching me coping techniques. Plus, I have started an anti-anxiety medication. I spent a long time getting into this deep hole, and I'll need some time to dig myself out." He raised his gaze to the sight of Grace's tear-reddened face. Her pain nearly tore him in two. He'd left a blood stain on pure white snow.

"Your story is a lot to take in." Grace crossed her arms over her chest. "I just don't know what to say."

"I understand." His heart squeezed with panic. Did she see him as an evil monster?

Grace stood.

Heath thought she was heading to the door." His stomach lurched, but he wouldn't stop her. Instead, she walked around the table and curled up on his lap like a small child, resting her head on his chest. For several minutes, all he heard was the beating of their synced hearts.

She sighed. "My feelings haven't changed. What happened was…horrible. But I know you were put into a difficult situation and under extreme stress. You are a good man." Her finger tapped over his heart.

She's not giving up on me. A wave of calm washed over him.

If only he could carry her away, to a world without need for soldiers or war. Only love. "You're better than I deserve. The smartest thing I've ever done was jump into the river after you." His arms tightened around her. "You are the most beautiful woman I'd ever seen, and I never in a million years thought I had any right to love you."

"Good thing I'm a klutz." She kissed the corner of his mouth. "I'll need time to digest everything you shared with me."

He pressed his cheek to the top of her head. Her hair was still damp and smelled like flowers and rain. "I can live with that."

"I should get going."

Her mouth said one thing, but her eyes told him another story. Heath took her face gently in his hands and drew her into a long kiss. Feeling her caress inflamed his desire. He wanted more. Instead he pulled back, taking long, steadying breaths. "I've just told you some pretty awful things. Make sure a relationship with me is what you really want."

Grace passed the back of her hand across the scruff on his face. "Only good dreams tonight," she whispered.

As she ran across the dark yard, to her parents' house, a bright star shot across the sky. What chance did his heart ever stand when even the stars couldn't help but fall for her?

****

The next morning, Grace found her mother in the kitchen, armed with a litany of questions. Cupboards slammed and dishes rattled in punctuation of Joslyn's tirade.

Yes, she had been in Heath's bunkhouse last night. No, she wasn't marrying Tyler. And yes, Heath was the man her heart had chosen.

"I don't believe it." Joslyn spun to face Grace and threw her arms in the air. "You've pined for Tyler Ross since the day you got your first pimple."

She half expected the glassware to shatter from her mother's shrill voice. "Please calm down. You'll wake up Dad." Grace paced in front of the kitchen counter. "Over the years, I made Tyler the perfect man, and I've realized he and I don't see eye to eye on a lot of important things. Marrying him wouldn't be fair to him or to me."

Joslyn arched her eyebrows, creasing her normally smooth-as-ivory forehead. "You want to talk about fair? You're tossing aside Tyler, a man who adores you, for someone who's only home is our bunkhouse."

"Leave Heath out of this." Grace's temper flared. "The reason I broke off the engagement has nothing to do with Heath."

"Really?" Her mother crossed her arms, and her foot tapped-tapped-tapped on the porcelain tile floor. "I think Heath has everything to do with the cancellation of your wedding. You changed the day you fell off the bridge."

Grace sighed in resignation. This repeated conversation had been as productive as a dog chasing its own tail. "I realize you only want what's best for me, but please trust me, I wouldn't be happy with the life Tyler wants. I don't want to live in Dallas and become a neglected oil executive's wife."

"Oh, stop being so overdramatic." Joslyn's face softened, and she opened her arms. "Honey, I love you. I'm worried you're making a hasty decision based on feelings for a man who could potentially ruin your life."

Stepping into her mother's embrace, she groaned. "Why won't you give Heath a chance?" How could her mother not see what a kind and nurturing man Heath was? He spent hours in the fields, caring for their herd of cattle. Or how perfect he and Grace were together?

"Your dad and I gave him a place to live and a job, even after he was thrown in jail. Yes, we know all about the bar fight. We live in a small town, and people talk. Don't ask me to entrust that kind of man with my daughter."

Grace turned toward the window which overlooked

the meadow behind the house. "Just because Tyler has money, comes from the right family, and dresses well doesn't mean he's perfect. He left on a month-long business trip right before our wedding. His career has always taken precedence over me."

"Tyler will be here tomorrow," her mother said. "Promise you'll talk with him and give him a chance to work things out."

"I already agreed to talk with Tyler tomorrow, but right now, I need some space. I'll be at Molly's place." She walked out of the kitchen and headed up the stairs.

"Grace," her mother called. "Please think of your father. Seeing you throw away a secure marriage to run off with the hired hand will break his heart."

Those were the last words she heard before she fled into her room. Twenty minutes later, she was driving to Molly's.

When she arrived, her friend waited at the door.

Grace entered Molly's townhouse and set her bag on the floor. "My mother will be the death of me." Her best friend had been there for many of Grace's disagreements with her mother. She knew better than anyone about Grace's frustrations and heartaches. "Can I move in with you until I find a place in town to rent?"

"You're always welcome here, but I don't think moving here will solve the problem. Tell me what's going on." Molly led her to a cream-colored sofa. Both women sat, legs tucked underneath and faced each other. "Whatever it is, we'll figure it out together."

As she told Molly everything that had happened in the past week, Molly's face stayed neutral.

To her friend's credit, she didn't criticize her decision to jump into a relationship with Heath. Once the heavy stuff was out of the way, they spent the rest of the day binge-watching an entire season of *Zombie Survivor* and eating junk food. For a little while, Grace forgot about her troubled love life.

As the sun set, Molly cracked open a bucket of frozen margarita. By two a.m., Grace was very tipsy and reluctantly called it a night. Crawling into the bed in the guest room, she became infected with a case of the giggles. Maybe her silliness was a release of stress or too much alcohol. She lay under the purple blanket and laughed until tears streamed from her eyes.

Molly opened the door and poked in her head. "What's so funny?"

"I don't know." Grace hiccupped. Clearly, she was overtired. "I was remembering when you threw Heath in jail. He looked a mess, and his beard and face were covered in blood. Now, I'm in love with him. My mother's right." She sat up, and the room tipped to one side. "I've lost my mind." A burst of laughter followed her statement.

Molly sat on the edge of the bed. "That night, I saw a spark between the two of you. Heath was working off a buzz, and you were playing Florence Nightingale. The way he responded to you was special. Tyler screwed up big time by leaving you for so long."

Instantly sobering, Grace's goofy smile turned serious. "I know you don't approve of Heath, but thank you for your support. You're a good friend, Molly Hernandez."

Molly rose to her feet. "Someday, when I find the man of my dreams, you can return the favor." She stood barefoot, wearing pink bunny fleece pants and a Liberty Ridge PD T-shirt.

Last year, Molly had been diagnosed with cervical cancer. Grace was by her side through treatment. Now, Molly contemplated life outside their small town as a Federal Drug Enforcement Agent.

Grace had never loved her friend more than she did at that moment. "I promise." She scooted back underneath the blanket. "Good night."

"Night." Molly closed the door.

Grace turned off the bedside light. In the darkness, she replayed Heath's story from the night before. Her body sickened with raw grief for the innocent women and children who died. The man who'd witnessed such horrible things was the same one whose kiss melted her core. Two sides of the same coin.

Could she sleep next to him and feel safe? Or would violent nightmares and flashbacks cause her unintentional harm? His past would always be a part of who he was. For better or worse, his experiences had formed him into the man he was today. She had to be confident that when the going got rough, and it would, she'd love him enough to stand firmly by his side.

****

The next morning, when Grace finally dragged herself out of bed, she grabbed her cell phone and noticed a text from Tyler.

—On my way. Meet me at the gazebo at 10—

Dread hit her. She was not looking forward to this conversation. She still cared for Tyler but her connection with Heath was soul deep. Maybe Tyler had also realized they'd grown apart. As Grace drove on the long, gravel driveway to her parents' house, she realized the ranch was part of her soul. Most people might not understand why a piece of land meant more to her than anything money could buy.

She parked next to Tyler's sleek car and, out of habit, checked her hair and makeup in the visor mirror. With buzzing nerves, she slowly walked toward Tyler, who waited in the gazebo.

Before Grace was halfway there, her mother opened the screen door. "Grace, I need to see you inside."

Grace waved at Tyler before following her mom into the kitchen. "I don't need any more lectures."

"Sit, please." Joslyn pointed to a kitchen chair.

Her mother's normally smooth complexion now appeared flushed and uneven. Shadows darkened the puffy skin under her eyes. Grace's stomach hummed like a hive of bees. "Mom, what's going on?"

Joslyn lowered her gaze to her folded hands. "Dad's sick. He didn't want you to know until after the wedding."

"I know he wasn't feeling well the other day, but he said it was nothing to worry about.. He's just been busy working the ranch." Her body seized with worry.

"Several weeks ago, he was diagnosed with MS, Multiple Sclerosis. Honey, his symptoms are progressing quickly." Joslyn straightened in her chair. "Soon, he won't have the strength to run the ranch. We plan on selling. I want to travel while he still has the strength."

Shock numbed her to the core. Her mother's words made no sense. Dad was the strongest man she knew. And selling the ranch—how could they give up a place so precious? Grace shot to her feet. "Why didn't you tell me earlier?"

The shimmer of tears shone in Joslyn's eyes. "Dad

didn't want to spoil your special day. He wanted his baby girl happy, not worried about her father."

Grace choked back a sob. "Are you sure the doctors didn't make a mistake?"

"Honey, we've seen a number of specialists." Joslyn held Grace's hand. "You need to understand the full ramifications of calling off your wedding. Dad and I would both feel better knowing you were settled and being taken care of."

The world under Grace's feet tipped on its axis. "Who all knows?"

"Besides, you and me, no one. We haven't even told Alex, yet." Joslyn exhaled a deep sigh. "Please reconsider. Walking you down the aisle while he still can would mean so much to your daddy."

The plea shot straight to her heart. She knew he would support her, no matter what. Dad always understood what made her tick. They were so much alike. "Where is he? I need to talk with him."

"He's out in the south pasture, checking on the heifers." Wiping tears from her eyes, Joslyn sniffed. "He didn't want me to tell you. I only did because I'm afraid you're making a mistake by calling off your wedding."

Frozen with overwhelming grief, Grace couldn't move. The room spun. Despite her emotional state, she needed to make her position clear. "I'm not making a mistake. I don't love Tyler enough to devote the rest of my life to him." She took a deep breath. "I understand your concern, but please trust that I made the best decision for both Tyler and myself."

Joslyn wrapped Grace in a gentle embrace. She brushed her fingers through Grace's long hair. "My wish since the day you were born is that you'd grow into a woman who knew her own mind. Seems like I got my wish."

"I also know my own heart. I want a marriage as wonderful as yours." Grace sighed and rested her head on her mom's shoulder.

"What your dad and I have is special, and you deserve that, too." Joslyn released her hold and stepped back. "I love you, my sweet daughter, and I respect your decision. Now, go outside and talk to Tyler. Then come find me when you're finished. I'd like to hear more about where your head and heart are leading you."

Chapter Twenty-Four

As Grace left the house, she barely felt her legs move underneath her. She walked to the gazebo and up the stairs, still numb with shock.

Tyler took her hand.

He looked like he belonged in a men's fashion ad, wearing a crisp polo shirt and navy shorts. Tan boat-shoes completed the look. Every blond hair on his head was impeccably styled as always. The polar opposite of her hard-working, outdoor-loving father.

He greeted her with a kiss on the cheek. "Hi." Tyler rocked back on his heels.

"Thanks for making the trip down here." She didn't want to do this. Not now. All she wanted was to find her dad, wrap her arms around him, and never let go. Grace grasped a white rail board, careful not to catch her hand on the thorny rose vines wrapped around the wood. The whole gazebo was now covered in red roses. Her mother had transplanted the plants earlier in the week. She thought of all the work both her parents had done to give her a dream wedding.

Frowning, Tyler took hold of her left hand and kissed her bare ring finger. "You took off my engagement ring. When you told me you were having doubts, I thought you only had last-minute jitters."

Grace steeled her emotions. "I can't marry you, Tyler. You want big-city excitement and a high-

261

powered career. I'm happiest here, in the country. I want to run my business and live a simple life. Clearly, our lives are leading us on different paths."

His eyes widened. "When we started dating, you said you loved living in Dallas. What changed?"

"Being here." She moved away. "I'm sorry. The last thing I ever wanted was to hurt you."

He placed a hand on either of Grace's shoulders and turned her to face him. A muscle twitched in his clenched jaw. "I love you." Tyler's blue eyes burned bright. "You are mine, and you will be my wife. I'll do anything necessary to secure my ring on your finger."

"My heart isn't up for negotiation." His touch seared her skin. Outraged, she shrugged out of his hold. "I'm not a business deal. Plus, you shouldn't concede your goals in order to make me happy."

Grace turned to see Heath standing in front of his bunkhouse. Even at the distance of a hundred feet, she recognized his troubled expression. Her mouth twitched in a brief smile.

Tyler's gaze followed Grace's, and he growled. "I see GI Joe is still here."

She placed her hand under his chin and redirected Tyler's attention. "You wouldn't be happy living in Liberty Ridge. Growing up, you couldn't wait to move away. One day, you'd blame me."

"Never." He pulled her into an unyielding embrace. "Marry me, Grace. Don't leave me."

"I love Heath. I can't marry you when my heart is leading me elsewhere." No more dancing around the truth.

Tyler jerked back. "You're crazy. Heath's life is a mess. What could he possibly offer you that I can't?"

"I know his life is unstable right now, but he's changed so much since coming here. He's healing and getting his life back on track." Courage gained from honesty stiffened her spine. "I'm not looking at what he can give me." She pointed to herself. "I can take care of myself. I want to be there for him, and he wants to be a better man for me."

"You have a kind heart, and he's using you." Tyler grabbed her arm. His fingers dug into her flesh, pinching. "When he has angry outbursts, do you feel safe?"

His voice was low and threatening. Had Tyler heard about Heath's bar fight at the Damn Yankee? Probably. And now he used that one mistake to stereotype Heath. As she unsuccessfully pulled away, Grace's arm throbbed. "Let me go."

"Tell me you don't see him as a murdering monster. Tell me he'll be around in another five years…when you have children." His lips curled in a sneer. "Or he won't go off the deep end and leave you, or even worse, lose it and physically hurt you."

"Get your hands off of her."

A deep, menacing voice sounded, causing her to shiver. "Don't, Heath."

Tyler tightened his hold on her arm and spun her around. Her back was firmly pressed against his chest.

Heath stood before her, his eyes narrowed at Tyler in a deadly stare.

"Grace is mine," Tyler growled. "She only feels sorry for you. Crawl into a foxhole, soldier, and die. That's an order."

"I'll tell you one more time…let her go." Heath took a step closer.

"Please, Tyler," she pleaded. Her heart pounded against her ribcage. She raised her shaking hand in a feeble attempt to halt Heath's approach. "Heath, stay back. I'm fine."

"If you really care about her then you'll leave and never return." Tyler stepped backward, pulling along Grace. "I look into your eyes and I don't see a soul. You're empty...a cold-blooded killer."

In seconds, she was out of Tyler's arms and lying on the rough wood of the gazebo floor. She heard a horrible thud before Tyler's limp body crashed down beside her. His nose streamed blood. A scream rose inside her chest and burst through her lips.

Standing, Heath looked down with glazed-over eyes.

Grace pushed past his legs and crawled over to Tyler's motionless form. "Go find my dad," she shouted at Heath. "Go...now!"

Heath turned on his heel and jogged away.

Grace lifted the hem of her shirt and pinched Tyler's nose, stopping the bleeding. What had just happened? Her head spun.

Dad stepped onto the gazebo, carrying a towel and bottle of water. "Grace, I'll take care of Tyler. He'll be fine. Go to Heath."

Grace stood on shaky legs and released Tyler to her dad's capable hands. "Where is he?"

"I'm not sure. He found me outside the barn. He's pretty upset. I'm afraid he'll do something foolish." Bruce put a large hand on Tyler's back and helped him into a sitting position.

She sprinted across the lawn. At the sight of Heath striding toward his Harley, panic took root. "Heath," she yelled.

He straddled the bike, not acknowledging her plea.

"Don't go," she shouted. The roar from the engine drowned out her voice. Breathless, she reached him and grabbed his arm.

He released the clutch and punched the throttle, accelerating down the driveway with a roar.

Foolishly, she ran after him and tripped. Gravel stung her hands and knees. While she watched Heath's retreating back, her heart crumbled.

A large hand rested on her hunched shoulder. "Come on, butterfly. Let's get you cleaned off. He'll come home."

Her dad's deep voice calmed her. As he led her to the horse stable, she saw Tyler sitting on a rocking chair on the front porch with an ice pack pressed to his jaw. Joslyn hovered over him like a protective mother bird.

Inside the stable, Grace sat on a wobbly wooden stool while her dad retrieved the first aid kit. Her knees were raw, with gravel sticking to the bloodied flesh. What a mess. The whole world was angry with her. "I ended my relationship with Tyler. Please tell me I didn't disappoint you." Tears burned Grace's throat and eyes.

Dad opened a metal box decorated with a red cross. He took out a disinfectant wipe and knelt before her. "You did what you felt was best. I'm not mad. In fact, I'm kinda relieved. Never really liked the boy, anyway."

After letting out a shaky breath, she laughed softly. "Daddy, I'm surprised. You mean you're not in love with him as much as Momma?"

"No one is in love with Tyler as much as Momma." Chuckling, Bruce took her hand and turned it palm up. He gently wiped away the dirt and blood.

"This situation is my fault. Heath's gone, Tyler's heartbroken, and you and Mom spent so much money on a cancelled wedding." She sniffled. "Now, I don't know how to fix things with Heath."

"Give Heath a chance to calm down. He probably feels awful for losing his temper with Tyler and wounding you in the process." Her dad peered up to meet her gaze. "His biggest fear is hurting you."

"I wish he was here so I could tell him I understand."

Her dad cleaned off the scrapes on her legs. Two bright red patches decorated her knees. He brought over a stool to sit next to her.

Grace rested her head on his broad shoulder, her throat tightened. "Mom told me about your MS. Why didn't you tell me?"

"I didn't want you to worry. I'll be fine." He patted her thigh. "Your lion of a mother will see to my care."

Grace smiled. Joslyn Murray was a force to be reckoned with, especially when it came to protecting her family. "Of course, I worry about you. You're my pa."

"Thanks, pumpkin. We'll see this through, just like every other challenge we've ever faced…as a family."

"What about the ranch?" The thought of leaving their beloved ranch, her family's home, made her sick with grief. "Will you really sell?"

"I wish we had another choice. A time will come when the MS won't allow me to work the way I need to, even with the help of the ranch hands. And, to be honest, I'm tired and ready for a break." His wide shoulders drooped. "Your mother and I will use the profits to take a trip around the world. The rest will cover my medical care."

"I want what's best for you. But thinking about selling the ranch breaks my heart." Above her, a dove flew into its nest and began to coo.

"I know." Her dad's big hand gently stroked her hair. "I know."

She sat in silence, listening to the horses whinny back and forth. "I love you, Daddy."

"I love you, too, butterfly."

****

For hours, Heath rode the winding country roads. He barely noticed the Texas landscape he usually enjoyed. When he ran out of gas, he walked five miles, rolling his bike to the nearest gas station. By the time night fell, a bitter frost had formed over his heart. He'd been wrong to think he was worthy of Grace. He really was a monster.

The truth was the price of admission. A cost more than he could endure. How could he keep his job with the Murrays, knowing Grace would never be his?

When he returned to the ranch, the time was well past midnight. Grace's car was not parked in its usual spot. She was gone. Tyler's ostentatious car, along with its owner, had left as well. Heath opened the door to his bunkhouse and pictured her sitting at his table. The memory of her lips pressing against his, so soft and sweet, made his body ache. They'd been a perfect fit.

Without her, the bunkhouse felt cold and empty. He picked up the copied sections of Ezra Burchfield's journal and walked to the stable, where Grace's spirit permanently dwelled. He could almost see her in the corner, where they'd watched the horrible zombie movie together. In the aisle, where she'd gotten him up on a horse for the first time. And in the spot where they'd shared their first kiss.

He threw a horse blanket on the ground, sat, and began paging through the papers in his hand. Soon, he was lost in another world.

Ezra wrote about the Indian Removal Act and his role in its enforcement. He had lived with immense guilt over the cruelty he'd witnessed. In an effort to help, he'd asked to be a medical escort for a group of Cherokee heading to Oklahoma.

Heath read through pages filled with descriptions of the trip. How could anyone have survived something so horrible?

After a closer look, some of Ezra's experiences weren't all that different from his own. One particular diary entry caught his attention. While reading the handwritten note, Heath felt his skin prickle at the realization Ezra had carried the same burden of guilt and shame.

November 18, 1838

As I sit by our weak fire tonight and write, I am struck by the hopelessness of our situation. The proud Cherokee people have been reduced to a nation of beggars. Many walk without proper attire. Threadbare blankets and shoes have become great luxuries. I do my part and help the weak and dying. My soul cries out in pain during their passing. So many had no chance of surviving the journey. We have dug too many graves.

I think about my part in this man-made tragedy and shudder. By my bayonet, Cherokee families were pushed outside their homes. I was a tool of a government who used me to carry out its evil purpose. Many nights I lay awake, huddled under my blanket, hiding from the icy winds. I wish my life had taken a different route—following my father into medicine instead of running off to seek glory.

During my time with the Cherokee, my respect for them grows every day. They are proud and self-sufficient. Earlier, I wrote about a beautiful girl. Her name is Kamama, which I learned means butterfly. She is only seventeen, but by taking responsibility for her mother and sister, is very mature. I have fallen deeply in love with her. Her hair is like black silk, and her eyes are so dark that when I look into them, I feel like I am drowning in a deep pool.

Kamama's father died shortly after we set off. His death was merciful, as he was ill even before the march. I will do whatever is in my power to make sure she reaches her new home, along with her mother and sister. Kamama's little sister, Leotie, often rides atop my horse and sings, while Kamama and I walk side by side. She teaches me Cherokee, and I am helping her improve her English.

I find myself thinking about Kamama often, especially at night when we are separated. I worry. Is she cold? Has she found a comfortable place to rest? If it was proper, I would never leave her side.

When the time is right, I will propose marriage. First, I will finish my obligation to the Army and save my meager pay so we can buy a piece of land and start a family. My deepest fear is Kamama will always see me as the enemy. She, along with every Cherokee, has every right to hate me.

A day will dawn when the generations to come will judge our actions and deem each involved innocent or guilty. I want them to know that I, a lowly foot soldier, only followed orders forced on me by my betters. I ask for forgiveness for my part in the death of so many innocents.

The time is getting late, and the air is ice cold. Another night, praying I keep from freezing and wishing I see Kamama in my dreams.

Ezra Burchfield
Private, US Army

Chapter Twenty-Five

Heath sat reading the diary most of the night. He recognized a thread, which spanned almost two hundred years, connecting himself to Ezra. Guilt, regret, and love were all elements of a soldier's life in every generation—no matter the mission. Every soldier with a conscience always carried the cost of war.

He could never erase the mistakes of the past. John was dead, and so were those Afghan women and children. No one knows the true number of the other innocent people who were caught in the crossfire. The Taliban were notorious for using villagers as shields for their own cowardly purposes.

Just as Ezra had worried if Kamama would accept him, Heath wondered the same thing about Grace. On the last page was an entry from the day Ezra asked for Kamama's hand in marriage. He wrote how he'd gotten sick with nerves, thinking the beautiful woman loathed him. She surprised him by saying yes. Heath smiled as he read Ezra's joy in knowing he'd spend the rest of his life with the woman he loved.

Early morning sun filtered through the windows of the barn. He raised his head to the sound of footsteps and saw Bruce coming toward him. His large frame had shrunk as of late.

"Grace went over to Molly's house last night. Something about eating gallons of ice cream and

271

watching chick flicks. I didn't ask for more details." Bruce laughed as he lowered himself onto a hay bale.

"I'm sorry for hurting your daughter. I don't know what happened. Tyler wouldn't let go, and I just snapped." Heath ran his hand through his too-short hair. Bruce was the closest thing he'd ever had to a father. He hated knowing he'd disappointed him.

"Grace is a strong girl. She knows you didn't mean to hurt either her or Tyler. My daughter has always forged her own path, but along the way she lost her identity. You appreciate Gracie for the wonderful person she is on the inside and accept her without condition. That, son, is a precious gift." Bruce wiped a tear from his eye. "She wants you to know she still loves you."

I am the luckiest man in the world. His chest expanded with emotion. "Tyler was right about one thing…I can't promise her a secure future like he can."

Bruce crossed his arms. "Loving someone and wanting to build your life with them can be scary. And you've spent so much time avoiding that very thing. I know you don't want to hurt her or disappoint her, but don't go using your fear as an excuse to run away."

"How could she still want me?" He still didn't understand why Grace chose him over Tyler.

Bruce leaned forward, resting his arms on his legs. "I'm gonna give you a bit of advice. You'll never accept love until you learn to love yourself. Take some time. Grace will wait. You can put money on it."

Heath nodded. "I need to leave the ranch. I know you have the cattle auction coming up—"

Bruce raised his hand. "The Montgomery boy has been asking me about a job. He's from a ranch family and can take over the position starting tomorrow."

"Thank you," Heath choked out. Leaving the ranch and the Murray family, a family he considered himself apart of, would be tough.

"Before you go, I should tell you that we're putting up the ranch for sale. I've been diagnosed with early stage MS. Joslyn wants to see the world with me while I still can. Grace, of course, took the news pretty hard."

His words jabbed a blow to Heath's gut. He glanced over at Bruce's large, calloused hands, which still seemed indestructible. Maybe the doctors were mistaken. "I'm so sorry."

"Don't feel sorry for me, young man." He chuckled. "I got plenty of life left in this ol' body. The sale of the ranch has me losing sleep. But we have no choice. At some point, I won't be able to work and good medical care isn't cheap." Bruce sniffed. "I broke Grace's heart when I told her the property won't stay in the family."

Taking Bruce's arm, he helped him stand. What would the sale of her beloved ranch do to Grace? Her family's land was her identity. True Horizon stood as testament to a dream realized by a former soldier and his Cherokee bride.

An idea floated into Heath's head, and he almost laughed out loud with delight. The solution was so simple. "Bruce, I owe you a lot. You took me in when I was on the path to destruction. I want to repay you for your kindness."

"You don't owe me anything, son. You've earned your keep."

Heath patted Bruce on his broad back. "I owe you more than you'll ever know, sir. Remember the inheritance I told you about. Well, let me make a suggestion."

****

As Grace entered the Sunrise Café, her mind slipped back to the day she'd seen Heath for the first time. She could picture him, slumped over the counter, shoveling food into his half-starved frame. Back then, he'd seemed so lost. But he'd saved her life, and his act changed the direction of both their futures. If she could go backward in time, would she do anything differently? She knew in her heart and soul she would fall into the river all over again. Grace slid onto a worn stool by the counter.

Mabel handed her a menu. "Hello, sweethcart. How you doin'?" She poured coffee into a white cup.

Grace smiled at the woman's strong Texas drawl, who as far back as she could remember, had served coffee and good advice from behind this very counter. "Oh…I'm doing all right. I'm sure you heard my wedding's been canceled."

"Not much I don't hear." Mabel returned the coffee pot to the warmer before taking out her order pad from her apron front pocket. Then, she withdrew a pen from the center of the gray bun topping her head. "If you ask my humble opinion, you did the right thing. You belong here, in Liberty Ridge. In your soul, you're a small-town country girl."

"I took a long time to figure out Liberty Ridge is where I want to stay." Grace laughed. "Can I get a spinach omelet, please?"

"Two eggs or three?"

"Two."

"Comin' right up, darlin'." Mabel went to the pass-through to give Grace's order to the cook before turning her attention to three old-timers who had taken seats down the counter.

As she sat and waited for her meal, she wondered what Heath was doing. Two days ago, he'd moved off the ranch, only leaving behind a short note. He'd asked for her forgiveness and said he needed some time away to work on himself. He ended the note by declaring his love and asking for her patience.

His empty bunkhouse had left her disheartened. She'd turned on him when he needed her the most. He'd sensed her fear, which had driven him away. Would he really come back, or was he gone forever?

"Hi, Grace."

A quiet voice interrupted her musing. Grace turned to see a petite blonde standing next to her. Her defenses automatically rose, and her appetite plummeted. "Hi, Colleen."

"Mind if I join you?" Colleen's eyebrows arched over wide, baby-blue eyes.

Grace sighed. Surely, acting nice to Colleen wouldn't kill her. "Okay. How about we grab a booth?" She pointed to a small, corner booth.

After they were seated, Colleen picked up a menu. "I don't know why I bother looking at the menu since I always order the same thing."

A grin tugged on Grace's mouth, and she let the expression bloom into a real smile. Both she and Colleen were now adults. Time she started acting like one. "I know what you mean. I order the spinach omelet every time."

Colleen set the menu on the table and leaned forward. "Grace, you know I've been seeing Heath on a regular basis. Because I'm his doctor, I can't talk about his sessions, but I do care about him as a friend."

Guess she shouldn't have let down her guard so soon. "A friend?" Grace leaned back and crossed her arms over her chest. No way would she sit here and listen to how friendly Colleen wanted to get with Heath.

Color spread over Colleen's cheeks. "He's a good-looking man, but I'm his doctor. And he's obviously very much in love with you."

Now, warmth spread through her body. "Have you seen him recently? I mean, in the last few days?"

"He stopped by my office yesterday. He's deeply committed to his recovery and wants to earn your trust."

Grace lined up the fork, knife, and spoon set before her on the table. "I was frightened when Heath attacked Tyler." Her guilt over her reaction weighed heavy on her heart. "He was so different than the gentle man I love."

"Don't be too hard on yourself." Her expression softened, and she leaned forward. "No one this side of sainthood can be in a relationship with someone suffering from PTSD and not feel some kind of fear or doubt. You're only human, and what Heath is going through can be very destructive if left untreated."

"I should stick by his side, especially when he needs my support. Instead, I sent him running away." She pulled out a napkin from the silver holder and dabbed at her eyes, and then blew her nose.

"You've given him something priceless—motivation. He will return, Grace, and when he does, he will need your honesty." She nodded. "Let him know if something he does or says hurts you. Help him build his self-awareness, which in turn will slowly develop trust between you."

Hot tears stung her eyes again, and she tried hard to contain them.

Colleen reached across the table and took hold of her hand. "In the past, we've had our problems, but I'd really like to be your friend. Alex told me about your dad and the ranch. You have a lot to deal with."

"A woman can always use a good girlfriend." She liked the mature version of Colleen, who seemed to care about others instead of ripping them down. Grace's smile overpowered her tears. "Dad's illness came as quite a shock. And selling the ranch, well, it's only a piece of land. I'll learn to deal with the loss if the money will help my dad. Maybe someday, I'll buy a small farm of my own."

"I'm glad you're staying in town." Colleen sniffled. "You always seemed so happy at True Horizon."

Mabel came over to take Colleen's order. "Nice to see you two ladies finally gettin' along."

Both Grace and Colleen laughed. Ten years ago, Grace would've rather eaten with pigs than sit at the same table as Colleen.

"You play cards?" Colleen asked after Mabel left. "I'm inviting a few people over for a weekly poker game."

"Sounds like fun. My card game has been reduced to playing SOLO with my nieces." She laughed, again. A good feeling after the emotional turmoil of the past few days. Grace set her elbows on the table and rested her chin on her folded hands. "I've got to warn you, though, I'm obnoxiously competitive."

Chapter Twenty-Six

Grace stood by the fence of the south cattle pasture, the early autumn breeze blowing warm on her face. Tens of dozens of Longhorns dotted the rolling hills and filled the air with their lowing. She thought back to the day Dad told her they'd found a buyer for the ranch. She was heartbroken when she learned an investment group made the winning offer.

At first, Grace bristled at the thought of bankers operating their ranch. But once Dad explained the investors made the deal on the condition a member of the family stay on to manage, she'd cooled off. She could live at the house and manage the ranch while her parents would have enough money for travel and Dad's medical care. The best of both worlds.

Grace's parents left for their big trip a little over a month ago. Yesterday, she received a short email, assuring her they were all right. Attached was a picture of her mom and dad sitting on top of a truck. A herd of elephants stood behind them.

Even though she missed them terribly, Grace was happy for her parents. Over the past month, she worked with the investment fund manager to make upgrades to the ranch. She'd overseen the start of a major barn remodel and replaced large chunks of old fencing. The only thing missing in her life was Heath.

Grace meandered back to the house. Alex and

Jenny were working in Mom's flower beds. They'd come over for the day, mostly to give the girls a chance to run around and play with the animals.

Passing by the stables, she heard the sounds of the horses call to her. Time spent exploring the ranch on horseback would lift her sullen mood. "I'm taking out Silver for some fresh air," Grace called out to Jenny, who knelt in a flower bed with a handful of dried-up weeds.

Jenny glanced up and waved. "It's a beautiful day. Enjoy."

Grace went to the stable and saddled her favorite horse. Silver nuzzled Grace's neck. The horse got a kiss on the nose in return. "Come on, girl. Let's go for a ride." As she led the horse through the gate and into the pasture, she took a deep breath of pure country air. The weather was perfect. The sun shone bright in a cobalt blue sky. Small, white puffy clouds floated leisurely above her. After years of searching—searching for her place in this world—home was where she'd always belonged.

Despite the warm temperature, she'd put on a flannel shirt. Heath had left it behind in the bunkhouse, along with his dog tags. In bed at night, she'd wear the shirt and imagine him by her side.

The ranch wasn't the same without him. She missed the sound of his laughter and the way his hazel eyes sparkled with mischief.

Silver trotted to a small hill and halted at the top.

Grace surveyed the rolling pastures and shallow creeks. She could see her family's house in the distance. As much as she loved the ranch, True Horizon would never truly feel like home without the other half of her heart.

****

Downtown Liberty Ridge lay quiet as Heath rode his motorcycle along Main Street. He traveled over the Hickory River Bridge, and then turned right and headed out of town. A nervous flutter settled in his stomach throughout the fifteen-minute ride to True Horizon Ranch. After more than a month apart, would Grace slam the door in his face? He wouldn't blame her if she'd given up on him.

From what Bruce said in his last email, Grace was happy managing the ranch's daily operations. She had no idea he was behind the investment group.

For the past three weeks, he'd lived in Austin. The quirky town was a good fit for a man in transition. He drove to Liberty Ridge twice weekly for his appointments with Colleen. Her approach to therapy made him a believer. She was tough when she needed to be but also gentle and understanding. He learned and practiced coping techniques during every session. With Colleen's help, he discovered a strength and determination that he'd thought he'd lost.

His progress was nothing short of a miracle. For the first time, he allowed himself to believe he could have a wife and children some day. His scars would always be there, but his wounds were healing. They'd lost most of their sting.

The long, gravel driveway stretched out before him. He passed under the metal arch reading *True Horizon Ranch*. A refreshing lightness filled his chest. He was home. The white farmhouse's rambling form beckoned him forward. He parked his bike and made his way up the front porch steps. After standing before the front door for several minutes, he gathered the nerve to knock. He heard no sound from the other side. Guess no one was home. Just as he was turning to leave, the door opened.

"Hey, man." Alex opened the creaky screen door. "Good to see you. Come on in."

Heath stood transfixed on his spot on the porch. "Umm…hey. Is Grace around? I need to talk to her."

A huge smile spread across Alex's face. "About time." He grasped Heath's hand in a firm handshake. "She went out riding. Should I saddle a horse for you?"

The thought of getting on a horse made his skin prick cold with sweat. His urgency to see Grace drove away all other fears. "Sure. Guess I'm willing to risk my life in order to get to her."

Thirty minutes later, Heath sat uncomfortably astride a massive, black horse. He could've sworn Alex had chosen the largest, meanest-looking horse. *Must be payback for breaking his sister's heart*. He clung to the reins and, after a brief test of wills, steered the horse onto the trail.

Bruno, the beast underneath him, snorted.

If he had to guess, Grace would be at the little meadow with the pond where they'd shared a picnic. Under the cover of tree branches, he shivered, most likely from anticipation. Gravel crunched underneath the horse's hooves and the sounds of bird songs filled the air. His urge to throw up grew with each step toward the meadow. For so long, he'd dreamed of the moment he'd see Grace again. Reality might tragically disappointing. As he fought to regain control, he reminded himself that he'd stormed into armed buildings and faced down suicide bombers. At what point had he turned into such a coward?

Suddenly, the field came into view. He noticed Silver first, then Grace, sitting in their spot by the pond. She wore his old flannel shirt, which had kept him warm on many nights in Afghanistan. Looks like his shirt had found its way into the light as well. He dismounted and walked toward her, his footsteps crunching over the grass.

Grace lifted her head and shielded her eyes from the sun.

Something looking like relief flashed in her brown eyes. He sat beside her, totally unsure of what to say.

"Hey, there." In her hand was a long piece of sawgrass, which she spun around her finger.

"Hey." He met her gaze and smiled. Warmth spread from his heart, through his chest, and filled his body. His love moved inside him like a hurricane waiting to be unleashed, but he held the force in check. "I want a chance to make things right. I've made so many mistakes."

"We've both made mistakes," she said.

He hushed her by putting a finger to her lips. "I want you with me every day. I want a chance to show you I can be the kind of man you deserve. I've come a long way. Please say you'll still have me." He leaned in and stopped, just short of kissing her. The warmth of her breath flowed over his skin.

Without warning, she stood and walked away.

****

Grace halted and spun. "You ran away, Heath...you left me with just a note. Why?" Her heart pounded wildly, emotions swirled and collided.

Heath jumped to his feet.

282

After not seeing him for so long, she drank in the sight of him. His hair was still short but lighter from time spent under the sun. The beard on his face had been reduced to light stubble along his strong jaw line. She longed for him to smile, so she could see his devilish dimple.

Heath's posture was military erect, and his feet spread wide. "The night I left, your dad and I had a long talk. I realized I needed to straighten out my own life before I ever had a chance to make you happy. I had faith you loved me enough to wait."

"So much has happened since you left. My parents sold the ranch. I've stayed on to manage and made a commitment to build my life here." She reached out to him, taking his hand and placing it over her heart. "I did wait for you, every minute of every day."

His arms wrapped around her, and his lips began a delicious kiss.

Grace lost herself in the sensation of his body. Her other half had returned.

"I'm not done with therapy." He touched his forehead to hers. "I'll probably always need it, to some degree. Call me a work in progress. But I'm in a good place. Better than I have been in years. I can imagine you and me rocking on the front porch. We'll snuggle and watch the sunset."

As she imagined the scene, her heart soared. "I promise to stand by you." She brushed her finger over a scar running along his chin. No memory can feel as good as touching the real man. "You've been through a trial by fire and have come out the other side stronger. I'm so proud of you."

They went to get their horses to head home. "Why

do you have Bruno?" Grace laughed. Had he grown out of his fear of horses? Or did he have a death wish?

"Bruno is your brother's idea of a cruel joke." From inside his saddle pouch, he pulled out a small box. "I have something special for you." He smiled as the box disappeared behind his back. "Before I give it to you, I need to make a confession."

What did he have tucked inside that little box? Better be something good if he had to make a confession before handing her the gift. She narrowed her eyes. "Oh boy, now what? Did you join the rodeo?"

"Nothing that bad." He hesitated. "I bought the ranch from your dad. So technically, I'm your boss."

"What?" she croaked. Her eyes widened. "An investment group bought it."

He shrugged. "A very small group, just me, myself, and I. Well, and the fund manager, who you already know."

"So you're rich?" Shock jolted through her. How could her parents have kept such a big secret?

"Not as rich as before I bought the ranch. You've spent my money left and right, but I'm still doing all right. When your dad told me about his plan to sell, I finally understood what I wanted to do with the inheritance."

"No wonder everything I've wanted has been approved." Her loud laughter startled the horses. She placed a calming hand on Silver's rump. "Am I allowed to kiss my boss?" Grace tipped her chin to meet his gaze.

"Most definitely." He kissed a trail down her neck and nipped her collarbone. "True Horizon is yours. I'll sign over everything to you right now. But only if you agree to hire me on as your ranch hand." His gaze lowered to her mouth. "Your very own sexy ranch hand."

She definitely liked the sound of that. "The ranch should stay yours for now. Maybe, someday, it can be ours."

He held out his arms. In one outstretched hand was the jewelry box. "Today is the start of something new. I want to date you, Gracie. I want to wine and dine you, and someday, marry you."

Grace carefully opened the lid of the box. Inside was a gold filigree butterfly attached to a delicate chain. The body of the butterfly was set with a baguette-cut diamond, and its delicate wings were laced in an intricate design. Tears of joy filled her eyes. Her heart fluttered like a real butterfly.

"I had the necklace made for you," he whispered into her ear.

His warm breath made her shiver. She lifted her hair so he could place the necklace around her neck. "Thank you. The butterfly is exquisitely beautiful." Her fingertip traced the wings.

"Not as beautiful as you."

"We've both made transformations during our lives," she said. "The journey hasn't been easy, but the hardest parts usually make the greatest rewards." She noticed the sun hanging low in the sky. "We should get home before dark."

"Okay, but I'm not getting back on that horse. He hates me." He scowled at Bruno.

The horse snorted and shook his large head.

Bruno appeared to agree with Heath's assessment. She patted his shoulder. "My strong warrior is afraid of a horse."

"I don't think Bruno is a horse. My guess is he's someone's science experiment gone wrong."

Grace held Bruno's reins with one hand and gave Silver's to Heath. She'd never been so happy and so incredibly content. They walked along the path, hand in hand, and stopped when they reached the end.

Looking across the cattle pasture, Heath pulled her close for another kiss, as the sun set over the western horizon.

Epilogue

Lightning flashed through Grace's bedroom window. One-one thousand, two-one thousand, and then a crack of thunder rattled the house. Sheets of rain pelted the windows.

"I can't believe it's storming on my wedding day." Grace turned to the full-length mirror. She wore an ivory strapless gown which was overlaid in lace. A wide ivory satin sash encircled her waist. Excitement bubbled like her stomach was filled with champagne.

Her mom secured a bobby pin in Grace's up-styled hair. "We can't control the weather. Dad and Alex moved everything inside the stable."

Instead of an outdoor ceremony held in the gazebo Heath had built, she'd be married inside a horse stable. Granted, the building was larger and more up-to-date than earlier in the year. She and Heath had added an arena, along with extra stalls. Today, their renovations would serve double duty. Grace spun to see her mother's eyes misting with tears. "How do I look, Mom?"

"Absolutely stunning. Heath is the luckiest man alive."

"Let's get Daddy and head over. I don't want to be late for my own wedding."

Joslyn lifted Grace's train so she could safely walk down the stairs. Her dad stood at the bottom, wearing a smile as wide as a Texas mile.

As she took hold of his hand, flashes of lightning lit the sky.

"Thanks for pulling up the truck to the porch." She kissed him on the cheek.

"A carriage fit for a princess." He opened the door for her to step through onto the covered porch.

After a short drive to the stable, Bruce pulled into the wide aisle. He exited the truck and opened the passenger door.

Grace gingerly stepped out of the truck, holding Dad's large hand for support. She gasped at the breathtaking transformation. Rows of white chairs ran along the main aisle, and white tulle wrapped with twinkle lights swagged across each horse stall. The horses stuck their heads over the gates to watch the activity. She breathed in deep the scents of animals, hay, and flowers.

At the other end of the aisle stood an arched trellis covered in red roses. And standing straight and tall in the center was the love of her life. Heath wore a light gray suit and red tie. Across the distance, her gaze locked with his. He was so handsome, she practically fainted. She tightened her hold on her bouquet of wildflowers while nervous anticipation danced across her skin.

Her mother gave her a kiss before Alex walked her down the aisle to her seat.

Grace glanced around at her family and friends. Granny sat in front in her yellow dress. She turned in her chair and waved.

Lizzy and Kara skipped ahead and tossed rose petals, which soon covered the straw on the wood plank floor.

Dad gently placed his hand under the crook of her arm. "You ready, butterfly?"

Her dad had lost some weight since his diagnosis, but he was still larger than life. "Yes." She wiped away a tear from her eye. Her nervous jitters were now replaced by an absolute peace. "I love you."

He gave her a kiss on the cheek before walking her slowly down the aisle, finally handing her over to Heath. "Take care of my little girl." Bruce shook hands with Heath.

"Always." Heath turned his full attention to Grace and grasped both her hands. Then, he glanced down at her feet and smiled. "Nice boots."

She loved his smile as much as she loved the resulting dimple. The tips of tan cowboy boots stuck out from underneath her dress. "Remember, darling, you're marrying a country girl." Smiling, she turned with him to face the pastor.

Heath leaned in and whispered in her ear, "You're finally here. I can't take my eyes off of you."

Love swelled in her heart. "You won't have to." She squeezed his hand. "I'll be standing by your side…always."

A word about the author...

Laurie Winter is a true warrior of the heart. Inspired by her dreams, she creates authentic characters who overcome the odds and find true love. She keeps her life balanced with regular yoga practice and running. When not pounding the pavement or the keyboard, she's enjoying time with her family, who are scattered between Wisconsin and Michigan. Laurie has three kids and one fantastic husband, all who inspire her to chase her dreams.

http://lauriewinter.com

~~

**Other Titles by This Author
and available from The Wild Rose Press, Inc.**
"Warriors of the Heart Series"
Home Field

Thank you for purchasing
this publication of The Wild Rose Press, Inc.

If you enjoyed the story, we would appreciate your
letting others know by leaving a review.

For other wonderful stories,
please visit our on-line bookstore at
www.thewildrosepress.com.

For questions or more information
contact us at
info@thewildrosepress.com.

The Wild Rose Press, Inc.
www.thewildrosepress.com

Stay current with The Wild Rose Press, Inc.

Like us on Facebook

https://www.facebook.com/TheWildRosePress

And Follow us on Twitter
https://twitter.com/WildRosePress

www.ingramcontent.com/pod-product-compliance
Lightning Source LLC
Chambersburg PA
CBHW050656290626
47170CB00015B/774